SNOWBOUND

Visit us at www.boldstrokesbooks.com

SNOWBOUND

by

Cari Hunter

2011

ISBN 10: 1-60282-581-5
ISBN 13: 978-1-60282-581-9

THIS TRADE PAPERBACK ORIGINAL IS PUBLISHED BY
BOLD STROKES BOOKS, INC.
P.O. BOX 249
VALLEY FALLS, NY 12185

FIRST EDITION: DECEMBER 2011

CREDITS
EDITOR: CINDY CRESAP
PRODUCTION DESIGN: SUSAN RAMUNDO
COVER DESIGN BY SHERI (GRAPHICARTIST2020@HOTMAIL.COM)

Acknowledgments

A big thank you to Cindy for guiding a newbie through the editing process. Jay for showing an interest and knowing how to keep a secret. Chris for fielding obscure questions about police procedures that were often random, and often in the middle of the night. Helen and Phil for keeping various versions safe, and for not peeking. Matt for guided tours and surname consultancy. Everyone at BSB for the warm welcome and support. And Cat for everything else.

Dedication

For Cat, who waited so patiently for her story.

Prologue

The gunshot had been deafening in the small room. The gun dropped to the floor between them as they stood, inches apart, both too shocked to continue their struggle for the weapon. Sam blinked. Her ears were ringing and she felt slightly off-balance for a reason she couldn't fathom. She heard Steve swear once, then his fist connected with her face and she fell. Unable to brace herself, she hit the floor, the wind knocked from her in an instant. She gasped for breath on the cold stone, twine still taut around her wrist when she raised a hand to her cheek. There was blood on her fingers, hot and fresh, and she realised the air was thick with it, sweet and cloying with that metallic edge that always made her sick to her stomach.

Steve seemed angry about something. He was cursing, his hands tearing through his hair as he looked down at her and his brother. He reached low, grabbed her hand—the one with all the blood on it—and pulled her onto her front. That brief movement was enough to send agony flaring through her right thigh, ripping into her and robbing her of the breath she had fought so hard for. She started up a litany of curses of her own, more colourful, more creative than his had been, as he kept her in place with a knee in the small of her back and bound her hands once more. She could feel the blood now, oozing onto her trousers. Two wounds: one to the front of her leg—the pain sharp as she lay on it—and a larger one to the back, air chilling the ragged flesh the bullet had exposed. Steve tied off his knot, and the pressure on her back vanished as he left her to go over to Eric.

Adrenaline fading fast, Sam lay shivering, the pain in her leg starting at the core of the wound and screaming outward, her blood sticky as it pooled beneath her. Shock brought detachment with it, and she wondered if the bullet had hit an artery or shattered her femur and how long it took, on average, to bleed to death. She bit her lip to stop herself crying, at least while Steve was still in the room. He was dragging Eric toward the door, berating him for being too heavy, for not helping, for causing this in the first place with his stupidity.

Then they were gone, the door slamming completely, spitefully, shut and plunging the room into darkness. Sam sensed the cold seeping into her and closed her eyes, feeling exhausted and bizarrely matter-of-fact. That was that. She couldn't do anymore; the realisation was strangely liberating and peaceful. Her head was swimming, she could distantly hear herself gulping for air, and she gave up the struggle to stay awake. Her only source of comfort as grey drifted across her vision was the fact that Mac wouldn't be the one to find her body.

CHAPTER ONE

32 hours earlier

"Officer Lucas, I think this one may be beyond our help."

It was the look on Cally's face that gave the game away, the sly quirk at the corner of her mouth, not to mention the fact that the front window of the house was a seething mess of flies and that a stench of decomposing flesh had greeted the officers at the garden gate.

Police Officer Samantha Lucas concentrated on taking shallow breaths, attempting to speak without opening her mouth. "You sure about that, Cal? I hear you can do some pretty miraculous things these days. I've seen it on the TV."

The paramedic snorted and stepped to one side as her ashen colleague hurried down the garden path with their defibrillator. "Yeah, all that *'Fight! Come on! I love you, dammit! Don't give up!'* crap? Followed by a cough, a splutter, and a miraculous recovery with no broken ribs and no brain damage?" Cally took Sam by the arm, pulled her to one side, and spoke confidentially into her ear. "I hate to be the one to break it to you, Sam, but it just doesn't work like that in this ugly, violent world."

Cally handed over her paperwork and a rhythm strip from the defib displaying the requisite flatline. Sam shook her head.

"Oh, Cal, you didn't make him put the leads on a decomp, did you?"

Cally's grin was answer enough, her brown eyes sparkling as she shrugged. "He's been out on the road for four weeks and insisted on following the protocol to the letter. *'The Diagnosis of Death form states that an asystolic rhythm strip must be obtained.'* I didn't tell him he'd read the wrong side of the form. I told him to knock himself out and he damn well nearly did when the smell hit him. And now"—she cocked her head in the direction of the ambulance—"that would be him throwing up."

Sam folded the paperwork in half, feeling a familiar pang as she watched Cally shiver in the cold air, oblivious to her attention. "I better get in there before Mac has my arse," she said more decisively than she felt. The smell really was appalling.

Cally nodded. "I'll see you around, darling. Say hi to the big guy." Then the ever familiar, "Be careful out there."

"You too. Go get that poor mate of yours a cup of tea."

Grinning, Cally started to walk down the path then paused and looked back over her shoulder. "Oh, just for you, Sam, she died in front of her gas fire. But, hey, at least the house is warm…"

Sam briefly contemplated how professional it would be for a police officer to launch a snowball at a paramedic in the front garden of a recently deceased lady, decided against the idea, and surreptitiously flipped her the bird instead. Cally blew her a kiss before climbing into the ambulance and starting the engine.

Shaking her head and steeling herself, Sam pushed the front door open. "Mac, where you at?"

"Follow your nose." Mackenzie's flat, Mancunian accent came from somewhere off to her left.

Sam did as he advised, picking her way across three weeks' worth of junk mail and a hallway narrowed by the owner's predilection for saving her weekly issue of *Take a Break Magazine*, seemingly every issue for the past twenty years. She found Mackenzie in the living room, where the smell reached eye-watering intensity and the heat was enough to make her wish she had opted out of her aunt's round-robin thermal underwear Christmas extravaganza. The living room was alive with bluebottles, crowding on the greasy windows, as desperate for escape as Mackenzie looked. His dark hair was sticking to his forehead with sweat and he'd hung his jacket over the kitchen door. The figure on the chair seemed to creep into the corner of Sam's vision despite her best efforts.

"Christ," she said softly, trying not to breathe.

"Yeah. Poor old sod." Mackenzie was leafing through the heap of bills and doctor appointments the woman would neither pay nor keep. "Doris Fielding, born nineteen eighteen, which makes her"— he counted on his fingers—"ninety-three years old."

Doris Fielding had died in her favourite chair, the one with the blocks under its legs and the booster cushion so she could get up without too much effort. Her tray table was within easy reach; a mug of tea sat half-drunk, green and furred, alongside something on a saucer that might once have been a sandwich. Her emergency pendant hung untouched from one of the table handles. Doris was barely recognisable as anything that had once been human, let alone the slender lady who smiled out from the mantelpiece photographs. Blackened and bloated, her body had been slow-roasted by the gas fire, juices soaking into the fabric of the armchair, providing a feast for the bluebottle larvae that had taken up residence. No one had seen her for almost three weeks.

"Where's the warden?" Sam asked, wondering, not for the first time, how vulnerable elderly people managed to slip under the welfare radar so often.

"Next door, drinking tea and no doubt wondering how much shampoo it'll take to get this stink out of her new perm."

Sam smiled. "Everything secure, boss?" A cursory glance about the downstairs had already told her there was nothing suspicious about Doris's demise. The woman had been taking a hefty amount of medication, and there was a discharge sheet from the local hospital dated two weeks prior to her estimated date of death.

"Yep. No sign of forced entry. Nothing at all to get giddy about. I already put out a call for next of kin, but the warden didn't seem to think there was anyone local, hence…" Mackenzie gestured at the body and the more mundane mess in the living room. Keepsakes and cheap ornaments sat forlorn and undusted, and a bed in the corner alongside a filthy commode suggested Doris had occupied only the downstairs floor of the house for the last years of her life.

"You been upstairs?"

Mackenzie shook his head and made a *be my guest* gesture as he continued to sort through old telephone numbers and pension books.

Upstairs, the smell was more bearable. Taking a quick peek into two bedrooms and a bathroom, Sam concluded she was probably the first person to have ventured so far in over a decade. Framed photographs on the dressing table spoke of a husband and possibly two sons, but a carefully preserved local newspaper clipping announced the death of her husband and bore no mention of any surviving relatives but the grieving widow. Outside in the street, curious neighbours had suddenly decided that now would be a good time to wash their cars or prune their hedges despite the snow, and the ones who couldn't be bothered with discretion were just standing, gesturing at the house and gossiping.

"Shame they weren't that interested when the poor woman was still alive," Mackenzie said, having crept up behind her—no mean feat for a man who measured six foot two and was wearing steel toe-capped boots.

"Yeah, so much for Neighbourhood Watch." Sam shivered. Away from the stifling heat of the living room, the upstairs rooms were frigid. "We good to go?"

Mackenzie was fastening his jacket, which Sam took as a good sign. "Undertaker's just pulled up and the coroner's been informed, so we are indeed good to go." He pulled his gloves on. "You hungry? I'm hungry." He was making his way downstairs. "I'm not sure I really should be hungry after that." He gave the living room one last glance as he passed. "But I am."

Sam shook her head with a smile, relieved to be back outside, dirty snow squelching underfoot and a grim sky promising more by nightfall. She took a deep, deep breath. The air smelled of exhaust fumes and an overfull bin, and still it tasted sweet. "You buying? 'Cause we could go to Fanny's. She had hot turkey and stuffing day before yesterday."

Mackenzie threw her the keys to their patrol car. "Sounds good. Lead the way."

"Did you see Cal? She says hi," Sam said casually, starting the engine.

"Briefly. She mainly stood to one side and let her mate make a prick of himself. She cut her hair again?"

Sam shrugged, easing out of the double-parked street. "I didn't notice." Sam had noticed. Cally had had new auburn highlights as well. She'd also lost a few pounds.

Mackenzie nodded sagely and Sam knew he hadn't been at all fooled by her attempt at nonchalance. "Well, it's been a while, so why would you notice?"

"Yup, two years now." Casual, so casual. Two years, three months, and eight days, to be precise. And one of these days Sam would get around to moving past her.

Sam looked up at Mackenzie as they stopped at a red light. "Mac, can I have a chocolate bar?"

"Oh, Sam, I'll even let you have a king-sized."

❖

If she squinted very hard, Dr. Kate Myles could just about make out the shape of Kinder Scout in the distance. The highest of the Dark Peaks, its craggy edge towered above the valley, but for days now its outline had been softened by thick snow. It was late, and from the doorway Kate could see a few house lights, shadows occasionally flitting behind the curtains, but most of the village slept. She yawned, her breath frosting in the frigid air. Cradling her mug of tea in stiff fingers, she listened to the gentle rustle of snow falling on snow. She hated night shifts, but this was so peaceful and so beautiful, it made this particular shift worthwhile.

"He's bloody well gone and pulled it out again!"

Kate turned with a grin, knowing full well what the irate nurse was referring to.

"Mr. Rogers, I presume?"

"It's not funny, Kate. Every time I have to put it back in, he just sits there with this huge grin and makes weird noises with his false teeth." Laura sounded and looked genuinely flustered. Her blond hair had escaped the braid it had started the night shift in, and her cheeks were pink with frustration.

Kate took pity on her friend. "You want me to do it?" She took the catheter packet and swapped it for her empty mug. "You get rid of that and I'll insert this. My damn hands are so cold, he'll be lucky if he's got anything to stick it in once I get a hold."

Laura laughed. "That'll teach the randy little bugger. Oh, before I forget, Thora's had her neb, and Percy was sober enough to play grab arse the last time I looked in on him."

Kate nodded. "He can go in the morning. I just didn't want him out overnight in this." She took one last look at the hills before shutting the fire escape door. "Get your head down for a bit. I know you're picking Charlie up at eleven. I think I might be able to hold down the fort."

"Thanks, Kate." Never one to look a gift horse in the proverbial, Laura headed for the staff room.

Kate checked the size of the catheter and grabbed a pair of latex gloves. The brutal weather and absolute dearth of interesting cases had enabled her to catch up on her medical journals for much of the shift, which had made for a pleasant change. Thora, Ernie Rogers, and Percy were the sum total of Birchenlow Cottage Hospital's current patient load. The tiny district hospital had a thirty-bed capacity, with a casualty department well attended by the clumsier members of the farming community and an operating theatre for desperate emergencies that couldn't wait for Helimed. The staffing level at the hospital was proportional to its size, but thirty beds available in the National Health Service inevitably meant thirty beds occupied most of the year round. Double or split shifts were not uncommon for the doctors, nurses, and orderlies, whose commitment was largely a result of being a part of the community the hospital cared for.

It was a more than equitable arrangement for Kate, whose training had seen her rotate through several major city hospitals, learning the skills and gaining the experience she had hoped would eventually take her back home to Birchenlow. She had been working there for five years now, and aside from the occasional temporary placement to enhance and refresh her skills, she hoped to stay put. It wasn't everyone's cup of tea, but her patients still managed to conjure up a surprising variety of illnesses and quite spectacular traumas, particularly those involving agricultural machinery or the region's country roads. The remote nature of the area meant she was often paged to attend the more severe accidents, and even when she was not officially on call her mobile phone number was common knowledge amongst the staff. Her dedication rarely went unrecognised by the locals. Her fridge and freezer were usually bulging with fresh produce, and she never had to search for handymen or women when something went wrong with her eighteenth century cottage, whose maintenance had been an ongoing labour of love for the past four years.

She tapped twice on Mr. Rogers's door and pushed it open when she heard a very eager, "Come on in, love."

Mr. Rogers was sitting bolt upright in bed, the sheets smoothed down, and his hands resting at his sides. Kate could have sworn he'd combed what was left of his hair. His false teeth gleamed in a welcoming smile, which fell as soon as he saw her.

"Oh." His disappointment was palpable. Kate wondered briefly whether to be offended that she didn't seem to be the dream girl of an eighty-four-year-old with an enlarged prostate but decided it was probably for the best.

"Mr. Rogers, I hear you've been having a spot of trouble with your plumbing again."

"Aye, Doctor. It's the darnedest thing, but it keeps on falling out."

She made a noncommittal noise, snapping her gloves into place and trying not to smile as he cringed. "Right, well," she said, pulling his covers back. "If it keeps *falling out,* I suppose we'd better try a slightly larger size. Now this may smart a little..."

As she whipped down Mr. Rogers's pyjamas and took a firm hold of him to sterilise his groin, his shriek was so loud it made her jump.

"Jesus Christ, woman!" he yelled. "Where've you had your hands? The bloody freezer?"

❖

Sam's alarm screeched like an air raid siren, snapping her out of the middle of an entertaining dream she immediately forgot. Resisting the urge to launch the clock across the room, she fumbled with the *Off* button and flicked on her bedside lamp before she could give in to the temptation of falling back to sleep. Four fifty-five a.m. No sane human being should be getting up at four fifty-five a.m.

The strange white light peeking underneath her curtains told her more snow had fallen overnight. It had been years since England had had a sustained period of heavy snowfall, and the country was gradually grinding to a halt. Trains that ran late if the wrong type of leaves fell in autumn had been cancelled altogether; airports struggled to de-ice runways, grounding flights; and only the city centre roads were being efficiently cleared. Most people were enjoying an unscheduled holiday, staying in bed or taking their children sledging. Samantha Lucas, being the conscientious type, was in the shower at five a.m. trying to figure out which end of the bottle the shampoo came out of.

Working in the city meant a forty-minute commute in the best of weather, but the journey was worth it just to escape the grim terraced streets, rubbish-strewn back alleyways, and petty crime of Manchester's urban sprawl, to live where she could see trees, sky, and the outline of the Peak District on the horizon.

Mackenzie had tried to drag her out for a drink last night at the monthly 999 Bash in one of the city's clubs. Six years ago when she joined the police force, Sam would have tagged along, not wanting to stand out as someone who turned her nose up or kept herself on the sidelines. Having found her feet and realised she fit in just fine regardless, she had started to be more selective, opting out of the larger gatherings, preferring instead to go home, have a bath, and sit on the sofa with her cat and the television remote. She could live without the hangover or the regret of a flirt taken one step too far and the gossip that would inevitably follow. There was certainly no shortage of eligible girls in the emergency services, but living vicariously through everyone else's mistakes was somehow far more entertaining. Not to mention that seeing Cally twice in one day would have been more than she could bear.

"Hello, baby boy." Sam's cat Mitten met her on the landing, weaving between her legs before attempting to send her flying downstairs by stopping precisely where she needed to step. The little terraced cottage was cold, frost clouding both sides of the windows, and she briefly considered putting the central heating on through the day just for Mitten, before deciding that his fur coat and her old fleece jumper would have to suffice, regardless of the mournful look he was currently giving her. She suspected he missed Cally, who had heated the house like a furnace, fed him scraps from her plate, and then ditched them both for a nurse in casualty.

Sensing her darkening mood, Mitten pushed himself onto Sam's knee as she laced her boots, butting his head under her chin and purring.

"Well, I miss her more, Mitts," she said firmly, unwilling to let the damn cat muscle in on her misery. "I just don't think we were exciting enough for her." She kissed the top of his head then threw a handful of biscuits into his dish, leaving him munching and ignoring her as she headed out into the snow.

Her car was half-buried on the path, snow still falling thickly and silently. She wondered how many of her colleagues would use this as an excellent excuse to nurse their hangovers and call in for emergency leave. She checked her mobile phone to see if Mackenzie had sent her a text and was relieved to find no messages logged. They had worked together for four years and Sam always hated it when he was away on holiday or sick. It was like working without her stab vest on; she just didn't feel as safe.

By the time she had cleared her car windows and dug out the driveway, she was covered in snow and had lost sensation in most of her fingers. The car slid as she pulled out onto the road, and she turned the radio on to allay the feeling that she was the only person alive in the world.

"Good morning! And if you're listening to this, I hope you're tucked under your duvet because this is certainly not a day to be going into work!"

Sam muttered a stream of her favourite swear words, switched the heat up another notch, and opted for a CD instead.

❖

A plaintive mewling greeted Kate as she unlocked the back door of her cottage.

"Oh, Lotty, please don't tell me you went out in this."

The fact that the tiny tabby cat sported a thick layer of snow and looked thoroughly miserable confirmed Kate's suspicions: her cat was indeed an idiot. Kate dropped her bag onto the step and leaned down to brush the snow from Lotty's back before scooping the cat into her arms. "You have a cat flap, you know. It works both ways. You don't have to wait to be invited back in."

Lotty purred, oblivious as ever to Kate's instructions but liking the gentle tone of her voice that promised food and a warm spot on her quilt. Shaking her head, Kate stomped the snow from her boots and set Lotty on the kitchen floor where she proceeded to wrap herself around Kate's legs, yowling with feigned but fairly convincing starvation. Operating on autopilot, Kate added wood to the stove, fed the cat, and too tired to eat anything herself, stumbled upstairs.

The twenty-minute journey from the hospital had taken over an hour, and on more than one occasion she had considered ditching her geriatric Land Rover and walking the rest of the way. Even at seven in the morning, she had passed no other traffic. Schools had been closed for the past three days, and the village was on the verge of being completely isolated by the amount of snow that had fallen.

She shivered against the chill of her bathroom and the bone-aching cold that always seemed to permeate every inch of her at the end of a winter night shift. The body was simply not designed to function effectively at night, and by the end of a twelve-hour shift, she was barely sentient enough to brush her teeth and button the top of her pyjamas. She added bed socks to her ensemble, then a sweater, and finally, for good measure, a hot water bottle. After lowering a blackout blind against the glare of the snow, she eased herself into bed. A combination of the hot water bottle and her body's meagre heat thawed the mattress by a few degrees, and she uncurled gradually from a foetal position. She felt the bed dip as Lotty settled by her feet and then the gentle sway and nudge as the cat began to wash herself. Kate smiled, grateful for the company.

The wind made the cottage creak and groan around her, but she had never been spooked by the odd noises the old building made. She switched off her lamp and with a huge sigh of relief, closed her eyes. Sleep came instantly.

❖

The small car had hit a patch of black ice, spun out of control, and slid to an ungainly resting place in the middle of a hedge. The owner, a tearful and endlessly apologetic forty-something career woman, was shaken but unhurt in the back of the police car— soothing words and a blanket the only treatment required. Her car's condition was slightly more serious, the front end having borne the brunt of the impact and rendered the car unfit to drive. Her husband was walking around to escort her back home. She had managed to travel less than a quarter of a mile from her house before her close encounter with the hedge. Standing at the side of the wreck, snow building up on his jacket lapels, Mackenzie was not impressed.

"I could've stayed in bed, could've taken Jack out snowballing, could've just called in stranded like every other bugger, but oh no, I make the effort and here we are again. For the third bloody time."

He stomped his feet, trying and failing to restore circulation to them. Beside him, Sam patted his arm in sympathy and tried not to let her teeth chatter too loudly as she asked Comms to chase down an ETA for the recovery truck.

The number of police officers turning in for their shift had been drastically depleted by the snow, even the most enthusiastic and conscientious having had to admit defeat and promise to turn in as soon as they were able. Sam and Mackenzie had been assigned to a four-wheel drive usually reserved for the traffic sector and told to respond to whatever came their way. This had mostly involved minor traffic collisions as people endeavoured to travel against their better judgement and their lack of experience of the conditions. The local government's predilection for cost-cutting when it came to gritting roads only exacerbated the problem, and it was taking longer and longer for the wrecked vehicles to be collected from each accident.

Sam trudged over to the police car, opened the back door, and tried to resist the urge to clamber inside and insist the woman share her blanket. The woman had stopped crying, leaving dark trails of mascara down her cheeks and a nose Rudolph would have been proud of.

"Mrs. Garner?"

The woman looked up at Sam and sniffled in acknowledgement.

"We should have your car recovered in about ten minutes. It'll be taken to the nearest lot. I'll write the phone number on the back of this." Sam watched Mrs. Garner carefully, pretty sure that most of what she was saying was barely scratching the surface of the woman's comprehension. She was no doubt preoccupied with the cost of the repairs to her car and whether she would be liable for the damage to the hedge. Sam was in the middle of explaining that she needed to take her insurance details and licence to her nearest police station, when the passenger door was flung open by a ruddy-cheeked middle-aged man who knelt in the snow and pulled Mrs. Garner into a crushing embrace. The man had obviously left the house too stressed to realise that trainers, his pyjama bottoms, and a dressing gown were not perhaps the best attire for the current climate.

"Oh, Babs! The hedge. It's a wonder you weren't killed!"

Sam decided not to spoil his apparent love of melodrama by pointing out such practicalities as the low speed of impact, so low that the air bags hadn't even deployed, and the fact that his wife was sitting in front of him, fully conscious, without a scratch on her.

"Are they taking you to the hospital, darling? I really think you should be checked out by a doctor." He was looking deeply into her eyes as if that alone would suddenly reveal the serious injury his scenario seemed to be craving.

Sam decided to be the voice of reason. "Sir, Mrs. Garner has decided not to go to the hospital and she doesn't seem to be injured. Would you like us to give you a lift home? You're only around the corner, aren't you?"

Looking past his wife, Mr. Garner seemed to notice Sam's presence for the first time.

"I'm fine, Edward," Mrs. Garner spoke with surprising firmness. "I just want to go home." She smiled at Sam. "A lift would be wonderful, thank you."

"Right then. As soon as your car's sorted, we'll get you back." Sam shut the car door, turning into the icy wind as the orange lights of the recovery truck rounded the corner.

"Perfect timing," Mackenzie announced. "And a tea, no sugar." He picked a mug up from the garden wall and handed it to Sam, who cradled the drink as if it were the Holy Grail.

"Where? How? Mmm." She slurped a mouthful before the snow falling in the mug could chill it.

"The hedge owner took pity on us. Probably the most excitement the old boy's had for a few years." Mackenzie waved and gave a thumbs-up as the elderly gentleman peeked around his curtains, watching the mechanic hitch the car up onto a breakdown truck.

"Speaking of excitement…" She kicked idly at the snow as the car was slowly towed away. "Are you as bored as I am?"

Mackenzie grinned at her, reached over, and brushed snow from her shoulder. "Officer Lucas, I don't know how you can stand here and say that!" His ability to keep a straight face was admirable. "When we're out here, freezing, battling to keep the good people of…" He looked around and shrugged. "Um, where the hell are we again?"

Laughing, Sam shook her head. "I'm not actually sure, but we certainly ain't in Kansas anymore."

They had been pulled farther and farther away from their regular working area all morning and were now so far from the city that the air smelled cleaner and the foothills of the Pennines were occasionally visible through the sullen clouds.

"We get sent any higher, I'm going to get a nosebleed," Mackenzie said, ever the city boy at heart. He always found it disconcerting patrolling unfamiliar territory and took every opportunity to remind Sam that too much fresh air gave him asthma.

❖

Mr. and Mrs. Garner lived in a standard semi-detached house with a postage stamp-sized lawn and parking space for three cars. Sam held the passenger door open for them and watched as they slipped and skidded their way up the drive. She acknowledged a brief wave from the woman before they disappeared inside.

"Another life saved." Mackenzie grinned as Sam turned the heater up fully and huddled in the front seat. "What are the odds we get back to the station for lunch?" He leafed through the street map trying to figure out a way back to their own area.

Sam peered out the window. "I think if we set off now we may make it in time for supper," she said, resigning herself to yet another late finish. She was trying to remember whether she had pulled a lasagne out of her freezer or whether supper would be egg on toast again when the car radio crackled into life.

"Any units free to respond to a silent alarm activation in Birchenlow village? Any units, please call in."

Sam felt her pulse speed up as Mackenzie reached for the mike.

"Alpha Mike One One, we are approximately two miles from the location given. ETA eight to ten minutes given the conditions, over."

"Roger that, Alpha Mike One One, I'm sending exact location and route details now. Proceed with caution. Be advised the closest backup unit is thirty minutes away at least. Update from scene ASAP. Received? Over."

Sam confirmed that the details had been received and they were mobile to the incident as Mackenzie flipped on the blues and attempted to make reasonable progress without wrecking the car.

"It's a jewellery shop, just off the High Street," Sam said, butterflies dancing in her stomach.

Mackenzie hit the sirens as he slowed for a major junction, a grin splitting his face.

"Look at it this way, Sam: it's got to be more fun than a car in a hedge."

CHAPTER TWO

The High Street was practically deserted, shop shutters closed and only a handful of people braving the elements, hurrying to get home as the heavy clouds forced an unnatural dusk to fall.

"There, on the corner. Kingston's," Sam said, trying and failing to spot anything unusual about the small independent jeweller's shop as Mackenzie drove slowly by. He had entered the village inconspicuously, extinguishing the lights and sirens before their approach. Sam shrugged as Mackenzie turned the car around to head back to the shop. "Maybe it was a false alarm."

Mackenzie nodded. "Probably. We'll park, go have a little look-see." He pulled up behind a large SUV, the tinted windows and personalised registration plate loudly announcing the wealth of its owner, an owner who would certainly not have driven his pride and joy in the current climate with a smashed passenger window.

"Mac?" The hairs were standing up on the back of Sam's neck.

"I see it. Shit." He reached for the radio. "Alpha Mike One One. Can you run a plate, urgent."

Sam didn't hear the rest of his transmission as she quietly opened her door and, casting a wary glance at the shop front, made her way to the SUV. Training her torch through the broken window, she saw the telltale damage to the steering column indicating the vehicle had been stolen. The junk food cartons and cups littering the floor suggested two perpetrators. She tapped her radio to convey the information to Mac and then dropped to her knees instinctively as a huge bang sounded in the shop, closely followed by a second.

"Jesus, Mac, I think we got shots fired."

Shouts and screams and a high-pitched wail: "Oh my God, oh my God!" Then the shop door was wrenched open and two figures all in black—black balaclavas, black gloves, black holdall, black shotguns, and black pistols—ran out straight toward the SUV, straight toward Sam who automatically raised her hands, nowhere for her to hide. She vaguely heard Mackenzie shouting over her earpiece, heard his door opening as he abandoned common sense to try to reach her. Then another explosion, the windscreen of the police car vaporised, and Sam, deafened by the blast, never heard the blow from the handgun that knocked her to the ground. The men's lips were moving beneath their masks, and from a weird, detached place she wondered at how very pink they were against the monochrome surrounding her. She felt a hand on her collar, hauling her to her feet, and she stumbled, failing to find purchase in the snow and annoying her captor enough to earn a second blow from his weapon, which made no sense to Sam because it certainly didn't help her stand up.

The fabric of the SUV's backseat was rough under her cheek as she was unceremoniously bundled inside. Doors slammed, making her head spin, and she choked down vomit and the coppery taste of blood where her lip had split. Someone got in the back with her, pushing something hard and freezing cold against her neck. He wrenched her earpiece away and pulled the wire linking it to her radio so hard that it snapped.

"Don't move." A normal man's voice, not like a monster at all.

The SUV was moving, wheels spinning in the snow and crunching on shattered glass as they passed the ruined police car. In the shop, someone still shouted repeatedly but with more purpose now, calling for help. Her face pressed hard against the seat and her head throbbing dully, Sam tried not to think that help was thirty minutes away, that Mackenzie had been in a car so casually blown to pieces, that she was so scared but couldn't move because there was a gun bruising the back of her neck. She held herself rigid, eyes tightly closed, while inside she shook and screamed.

❖

By Sam's estimate, approximately ten minutes had passed before the driver of the SUV began to panic. "Steve, where are we gonna go?" His voice was shrill with fear. "Half the fucking roads are closed."

Steve. That would be the man in the backseat with her, the man whose sour sweat she was breathing in, the one who wasn't panicking, whose hand holding the gun to her neck was steady and unrelenting.

"Just drive, Eric." He almost sounded bored. "Put some distance between us and the shop. They won't be able to get a chopper up in this, so chill the fuck out."

"Okay, okay, no choppers, that's good." Eric chanted the words breathlessly, but his control of the vehicle was less erratic than before. He took a deep breath, let it out slowly. "What do we do with her?"

Sam swallowed dryly. All the air in the car seemed to disappear as she waited for her fate to be declared.

"I dunno yet, little bro. We'll have to hole up somewhere, so she might be useful."

It took a massive effort for Sam to contain the sudden hysterical laughter bubbling up inside her. They didn't have a plan. They had probably seen a lot of American television shows where idiot criminals made outrageous demands for ransoms and transport to Caribbean islands. Those episodes never ended well for anybody, least of all the hostage. *Hostage.* The word swirled around her mind as she tried to recollect any relevant training she might have had for surviving this particular scenario. The advice would probably have centred on not putting yourself in the situation in the first place, which really didn't help much.

Second-guessing her actions was making her head ache, and she squeezed her eyes shut as Steve ordered Eric to turn left off the main road onto what felt like a country lane. Eric swore as he tried to keep the SUV steady, but he didn't argue. It didn't take a genius to conclude that the elder brother was the one in charge.

"Keep going about six miles down here, then there should be a right turn," Steve said, rustling a map above Sam's head. Maybe he did have a plan after all. She smiled grimly to herself. Their parents must be so proud.

❖

Sam was finding it difficult to judge exactly how long or how far they had managed to travel. The edge of the map tickled her cheek and she realised Steve had relaxed his hold against her neck. He was using both hands to unfold the map, a large map that now seemed to be covering her upper body. As quietly as she could, she edged one hand under her torso, inching it toward her belt and the CS gas canister that hung on it.

Above her, Steve seemed distracted as he considered then rejected various options for their destination. Sam's hand brushed the buckle where her handcuffs should have been fastened. It was loose; the cuffs must have fallen when she had struggled. Her baton was also missing, but she could feel the gas canister digging painfully into her thigh. She shifted slightly, holding her breath as she heard the map rustle, but Steve was paying no attention to her. She cupped the leather strap in her hand, wriggled her fingers around the press stud fastening, and gently worked it free, muffling the noise with her palm as it finally came loose. The canister was easy to manipulate from its holder, and once she had a firm hold she allowed herself to relax slightly, resting her cheek against the car seat and trying to stop her heart from racing.

Still beneath the map, with the gun pointed away from her and darkness falling outside, she knew she was not going to get a better opportunity. Without giving herself time to consider the consequences and persuade herself it was a bad idea, she threw herself upward, hitting out with her fist toward Steve then firing a spray of gas straight into his face.

CS gas hurts. It burns, makes breathing incredibly painful, and temporarily renders the victim blind. Once it had had the desired effect on Steve, Sam sprayed a second burst at Eric as he turned to see exactly what had caused his brother's roar of rage. He let out a yell and automatically used both hands to claw at his face, sending the SUV spinning out of control. Sam scrambled as far away from Steve as she could and tried to make herself as small as possible. The side door was within her reach and she gripped onto it to brace herself for impact. She didn't have to wait long. The SUV hit a grass verge buried under the snow and slid across to the opposite side of the road. It gained momentum on the ice before a collision with a stone wall flipped it onto its side. It spun once in a complete three-sixty and then came to a graceful stop.

Thrown into a footwell, Sam lay stunned for a few seconds before she was able to force the door open. The two men were already beginning to stir as she crawled out onto the side of the SUV, and she looked around frantically for somewhere, anywhere she could run to for help. Pitch black surrounded her, no lights in the distance, no signposts or conveniently placed telephone boxes. There was only the snow rolling over fields, hedges, and hills, making her breath frost as she panted in fear, setting her body shivering.

She staggered sideways as soon as she hit the ground, the sudden movement and a sharp pain in her left wrist making her dizzy. With few options open to her, she set off at a run in the direction they had driven from. Her mobile phone was still in her pocket and hope flickered for the seconds it took her to pull it out and find the *No Signal* message stark on its display. Behind her, she could hear Steve shouting at his brother. She risked a glance back to see smoke billowing from the car's engine and the orange glow of flames beginning to lick at the spilled fuel.

She kept running, trying desperately to think of a plan that didn't involve hiding in a field and freezing to death overnight. She could hear the footsteps as one of the men gave chase. The cold air was blowing away the crippling effects of the CS gas and restoring his senses as quickly as it was numbing Sam's. She was tiring, tears blurring her vision, and she slipped when her path veered into the ice of the SUV's tyre tracks. She put her hands out to break her fall and groaned at the pain that flared up in her injured wrist. If it hadn't been broken before, it was now. She could feel the shattered bones as they ground against each other. The sensation was so awful it made her nauseous.

That was how Steve found her: on all fours, retching helplessly in the snow, perspiration frozen in her hair. When he pushed her forward onto the ground, she tried to kick out at his ankles, more in defiance than with any real hope of success, but he sidestepped her easily and took hold of her wrists. He bound her hands tightly behind her, indifferent to her rough sobs of pain. When he had finished, he pulled her upright.

Determined not to show her despair, Sam met her tormentor's eyes, noting the dark streak of blood from a head wound that hadn't been enough to debilitate him. He pushed her ahead of him, back toward the SUV which now burned brightly. Eric was standing a short distance away, a silhouette calmly waiting with the holdall at his feet and a shotgun slung casually over his shoulder. Sam blinked at the surreal image, so perfectly framed it could have been a Hollywood publicity shot. She wanted to scream at the absurdity of it all, that this wasn't the Wild West, that people couldn't just run around with guns, kidnapping police officers, that it was freezing cold in the middle of nowhere and their only vehicle was a bonfire. Instead, she swallowed hard.

"What now?" she asked, the first time she had spoken to him.

There was no hesitation in his answer, no indication that the predicament Sam had caused had troubled him in the slightest. For some reason, it terrified Sam more than his anger would have.

"We walk."

❖

When she heard the ringing, Kate's immediate reaction was to wonder why she had set her alarm clock when she barely managed six hours sleep after a night shift at the best of times. As she burrowed her way out from under her quilt and finally poked her head into the chill air of her bedroom, she realised the ringing was her phone and that only the direst of emergencies would compel someone to wake her up when she had been on duty all night. Staggering against a head rush and bed socks bunched around her heels, she grabbed the receiver.

"Hello?" Her pulse raced in her chest.

"Oh, Kate! Sweetheart, you'll never believe what Stephanie is making your poor brother do now!"

Kate blinked, licked her dry lips, and sat on the edge of her bed. "Mum," she stated. Not a question; there was no mistaking Margaret Myles's voice.

"Well, of course, dear. I said I'd phone when we'd been to the appointment with the planners."

"The planners," Kate repeated, stupefied.

"The wedding planners! Kate, I really do think you should begin to take an interest in this. It's only eighteen months away now."

Kate couldn't choke down her laugh; her mother actually sounded hurt. "Mum, can I ask you what time it is?" Kate stared at her bedside clock, clearly indicating *14:00*.

"Two o'clock. Stephanie wants orange napkins. Orange! It's going to clash with the terracotta on the bridesmaids—"

Kate cut her off mid-flow. "Mum, what time do you think I got to bed last night?"

That finally made her mother pause. Kate could practically hear the cogs clicking into place as she checked Kate's shifts where she had marked them on the calendar.

"Oh. Oh dear."

"Mum, I give you my shifts for a reason." Kate curled her legs back under the quilt. "And yet we have to do this at least once a month." She could picture her mother's look of contrition, the one that traditionally ran as a precursor to the defensive excuse-making or the pass-the-blame-to-the-daughter tactic.

"Well, Kate, I really can't keep up with you if you're so far away, and why you want to live up there in the middle of nowhere is beyond me. You can't even be a bridesmaid for your own brother."

So we were going with Option B. Kate sighed and stroked Lotty, who had shifted to rest her chin on Kate's legs. It had always been her dad who had loved the Peak District and he had passed that love on to her. After his death, Kate had been the only one not to follow her mother as she had returned to her own roots in London, a fact that—even seven years later—never failed to irritate her mother.

"Mum, I'm sure six bridesmaids are more than enough for Steph and David. I'm sure she'll come to her senses about the orange, and I really need to get dressed now, if you don't mind, because I'm freezing." Kate's goose pimples had goose pimples.

"Freezing?"

"Yes, Mum. Don't you watch the news? We're pretty much snowed in up here."

"Oh yes, there was some talk of that during the weather report. You know we have an inch of snow down here! The Tube is barely running, the motorways are like car parks, and Mrs. Evans next door slipped and broke a rib."

Kate obviously wasn't going to win this one, not when her situation was compared to the cataclysmic signs of impending apocalypse that traditionally accompanied snow in the nation's capital city.

"Mum, I love you. I'm going to go and have a shower. Tell David to hang in there."

Her mother relented, and with a promise to call again soon for "a proper catch-up," Kate was left in peace.

Kate hurried into the bathroom and turned the thermostat up on her central heating, relieved that installing a new boiler had been toward the top of her priority list when she had started the renovation of her cottage. Fixing the leak in her kitchen, decorating the spare room, and figuring out exactly what the strange smell in her garage was could all wait. Cold toes, on the other hand, most certainly could not. She suspected Lotty agreed with her wholeheartedly.

The water may have been warm, but her bathroom wasn't and Kate didn't stay in the shower for long. In an effort to stave off hypothermia, she jogged on the spot in front of her wardrobe and decided she might just have to wear every piece of woolly clothing she owned. Practicality won out in the end and she stopped at two sweaters and a complete set of thermals. Cleaning her teeth as they chattered was quite a challenge, and she was spitting out toothpaste and specks of blood into the sink when her phone began to ring again. She patted her lips dry as she crossed the landing, determined to insist that her mother call her back after she'd managed to have breakfast and a lot of caffeine.

"Hello?" she said, trying to hide her frustration and waiting for her mother to launch into yet another debate regarding colour choices and overpriced photographers.

"Kate, it's Tom Delaney." Tom was one of two consultants at the hospital, and his voice was serious in a way that gave Kate shivers entirely unrelated to the cold. "I know you were on all night, but there's been an incident. A robbery in the village. We have four casualties, two critical. They're on their way in now. We're short staffed because of the snow. I wouldn't ask otherwise, but—"

"I'm on my way, Tom." She was already looking for her keys.

"Don't set off. We have a police four-wheel drive coming over for you." Tom laughed, but there was no humour there. "I don't think your bone shaker is up to the roads right now and we need you here safe. He should be with you in about ten minutes." The reception was breaking up, the phone lines straining under the snow and ice.

"Do you need me to bring anything?" She rolled her eyes at her own stupid question. This wasn't a party she was getting a surprise invitation to.

"Just yourself." There was a tremor in Tom's voice that Kate couldn't put down to bad reception. "Two men hit Kingston's Jeweller's. Michael Kingston was shot. One of the injured is a police officer. His partner's missing."

"Jesus," Kate whispered. "I'll be there as soon as I can."

As Tom hung up, Kate stood still and stared out her window. The hills stared back, frozen white and beautifully framed by the thick grey sky. Nothing moved, and for a second she held her breath, expecting something out there to reflect the chaos churning in her stomach, but the heavens didn't tear themselves apart, there were no claps of thunder or streaks of lightning, only Lotty mewling behind her. As she turned to pick the cat up, there was a sharp knock at the door.

❖

Kate relaxed her grip on her seat as the police cruiser came to a stop outside the hospital's main entrance. It had taken all the officer's concentration to keep the vehicle on the road and travelling at a reasonable speed, so Kate had not pressed him for details, aside from the sparse information he had given her before they had set off. Two of the casualties had been working in the shop and had sustained bullet wounds, a third was a customer with minor injuries, and the last was the police officer who had answered a silent alarm call. Due to the weather, it had been impossible to activate one ambulance, let alone four, and in desperation the owner of the village grocery store had swept the glass out of the wrecked police vehicle, marshalled three of his customers to help carry the casualties into it, and driven them to the hospital.

Eddie Capper was standing at the bottom of the hospital steps. His hand shook as he tried to light a cigarette and he dropped the lighter into the snow. Kate stooped, picked it up, and held the flame steady for him.

"You okay, Cap?" The village grocer obviously wasn't okay. His overalls were soaked in blood, gore splashed up his arms. He was breathing too fast to inhale effectively.

"Yeah. Yeah, I think so, Doc. Shit." He was staring at the vehicle he had abandoned by the access ramp. He seemed to notice for the first time the trail of crimson blotches stark against the snow, marking out the frantic effort it had taken to haul the victims out and onto the waiting stretchers.

"Shit," he repeated, then turned to one side and vomited.

"Can you stay with him?" Kate asked the police officer, who was also staring at the blood. "Get him back inside, sit him down, and get him some tea. If he looks like he's going to pass out, have him lie down or stick his head between his legs." She put a hand on Cap's shoulder. "Cap, I've got to get inside. Don't try and finish that cig. You just puked on it."

The hospital Kate walked into was barely recognisable as the peaceful sanctuary she had left just hours ago. She hesitated in the doorway, momentarily taken aback by the noise and the sickly smell of blood and other bodily fluids. Off to one side, a young man sat in a plastic chair, crying openly, a dark bruise across his cheek. Villagers who lived within walking distance had turned out in force, and one made her way over to him, offered him a hot drink, and then wrapped her arms around him as he wept. The door of the euphemistically named Relatives' Room was shut, curtains drawn and someone sobbing uncontrollably inside. Kate made her way to the changing room, threw on a set of scrubs, and headed for the resuscitation bay.

The curtains were drawn around both beds. She could hear Tom's voice behind the first and stepped inside.

"I can't hear you breathing on your right side, Emma. Your lung has collapsed. That's why it's so hard for you to get your breath. I need to put a tube into your chest to give it room to expand again."

The patient was a young woman who Kate knew worked part-time at the jeweller's. Her face was grey with pain and blood loss, and she was snatching her breath in gasps.

"Tom, what do you need me to do?"

Kate saw the relief pass across Tom's face as he noticed her for the first time. "God, I could kiss you."

"Maybe later, huh?" Kate winked at Emma, who managed a smile. "How are you doing, sweetheart?"

"I'm okay." Emma's answer was muffled beneath an oxygen mask and it was a barefaced lie, but Kate squeezed the girl's hand as Tom gave her a rundown on Emma's condition.

"Bullet wound, upper right chest. It's a through and through, but it's nicked the pleura somewhere. X-ray shows a pneumothorax, but I'm betting there's blood in there as well."

Kate glanced at the monitors Emma had been hooked up to. Her oxygen saturation was poor at seventy-four percent and her blood pressure was beginning a slow decline as her body reached the limit of what it could compensate for.

"IV access, type and cross, Gelofusine, ECG. You do the chest drain now, then an exploratory repair in theatre?"

Tom nodded. "I had Anthony in here, but Simon needed an extra pair of hands next door with Mr. Kingston." Kate picked up on the undertone and didn't press the matter of the jeweller's condition. "But," he said brightly, "Emma and I have been getting on just fine."

Kate collected the equipment necessary for the cannulation and fluids. "Emma, how's the pain?"

"Bad." She sounded exhausted.

"Mmhm." Kate tightened a tourniquet around Emma's upper arm and was surprised when a decent sized vein appeared. "Sharp scratch here, Emma." The cannula slid into place without difficulty, allowing her to draw off blood samples before she connected the IV plasma substitute. "I'll start her with five of morphine, given her BP." She was muttering more to herself than anyone, but Tom nodded as he drew up a local anaesthetic.

"Emma, this is going to feel a bit like a bee sting in your chest." Tom injected the site for the drain in several places, giving it a few seconds to work before he took up a scalpel and made the incision between her ribs. As he burrowed his finger into the space he had made, Kate held Emma's hand tightly. A rush of blood and air into the drain told her that Tom had sited the tube. Emma slowly relaxed back into her pillows, the colour returning to her cheeks as her breathing became easier.

"Good, Emma, you did really well there." Tom quickly placed the stitches that would hold the drain securely in place and then nodded to Kate, who helped to lean Emma forward so that Tom could listen to her chest and assess air entry.

"Bilateral chest sounds, that's a definite improvement. O-two sats are ninety-four percent. Excellent."

"Blood pressure is up to one hundred with the fluid." Kate gently guided Emma back. "That feel better?"

Tears were beginning to glisten in Emma's eyes as she nodded, and Kate realised for the first time that she was probably no more than sixteen years old.

"Is my mum coming?"

"I'm sure she's been contacted, and I'm sure she'll be here as soon as she can manage. The snow's still pretty bad," Kate said as she placed electrodes for a heart trace. "Hold as still as you can for me a minute." The trace appeared with no abnormalities. She signed and dated the paper.

"Just rest now, Emma. I'm going to have a quick word with Dr. Delaney."

Kate left the curtains open slightly so Emma was not completely alone. She found Tom at the desk, scribbling notes on a chart.

"You know, if you take your gloves off before you do that, you don't smear as much blood on your paperwork."

Tom blinked, only just noticing that he had obliterated pretty much everything he had written. "Crap." He flicked his gloves into the bin and reached for a fresh chart.

"ECG's normal. She's stable for now. BP was one ten, sats ninety-seven percent," Kate reported.

"Michael Kingston is going to be the priority for theatre. He took a bullet central chest. Simon was worried about a tamponade. I'm going to scrub in with him as soon as Kingston's stable enough to move."

"And the police officer?"

"He's okay. I left Laura with him in cubicle three. Mainly superficial lacs to face and arms. Laura was getting pretty handy with a pair of tweezers when I came in here. He has a lot of embedded glass so she's working off his X-rays."

Kate winced. "Ouch. I'll go and see how she's getting on—"

The shriek of a monitor made them jump. Kate turned immediately to check on Emma but realised the activity was coming from the neighbouring bed. She grabbed a new pair of gloves and pulled the curtain aside.

"Simon, where do you need me?"

The surgeon didn't pause to look up. "Airway. He's arrested. I've almost got this done."

Simon Jones had a needle deep within his patient's chest, drawing off the blood that had collected around the heart and had just stopped it beating.

Kate kicked a footstool to the side of the bed. "Anthony, get up on that. CPR as soon as Simon tells you to." The nurse nodded and stuck defibrillator pads on Michael's chest in readiness. Kate tilted his jaw in her hand, inserted a plastic airway to hold his tongue in place, and took a firm grip on the bag and mask as she breathed for him. She watched the rise and fall of his chest and knew it was useless without a functioning heart to pump the oxygen around.

"Go, go!" The needle was out. Anthony immediately began chest compressions, a firm, steady rhythm to take over the work of the heart while it recovered from the procedure.

"Let me check the rhythm. Hold compressions," Simon called out as he watched the monitor.

"V-fib. Charge to two hundred." The defibrillator sounded a shrill tone that became more insistent as it approached its selected energy level. "Stand clear."

Kate lifted the mask away and waited as the shock made Michael's body lurch on the bed then settle back.

"Got a pulse with that?"

The monitor showed a normal sinus rhythm. Kate reached for the carotid pulse as Simon felt for a femoral. They smiled at the same time.

"Good and strong here, Simon." The next time she fed a breath through the bag she felt Michael resist slightly. "Respiratory effort. About twelve a minute." She kept the bag in place, complementing the breaths Michael was taking as he gradually gained strength.

"We need to get him to theatre, find the bleed before he fills up and tamponades again." Simon preferred to be known as a pragmatist rather than a pessimist. Kate nodded, watching Michael closely for further signs of recovery.

"Tom's going to scrub in with you. He's always been better at slicing and dicing than I have," she said with a wry smile. She much preferred to keep her patients awake and talking whenever possible. "I can keep an eye on Emma and check up on the police officer Laura's with."

Tom's voice carried across to them from behind the curtain. "Ready when you are."

❖

The first thing Kate did when Michael had been taken to surgery was to arrange for her second patient to be moved next door to her first. Emma's mother had arrived, and Kate was explaining the extent of Emma's injury when there was a bang in the neighbouring bay, followed by muttered swearing and a slightly louder apology. Kate recognised Laura's voice and poked her head around the curtains to see her steering a bed away from the cabinet she had crashed it into.

"Bloody stupid thing, worse than a bloody shopping trolley. Sorry, Mac, we only have one porter in today."

The man in the bed smiled. "S'okay, love. You've never seen my driving have you?"

Kate turned back to Emma and her mother. "I need to start you on these antibiotics, Emma." She hooked the small bag up to Emma's IV line. "We'll clean your wound out properly in theatre. How's the pain?"

Emma nodded. "I'm okay, Dr. Myles."

"Good girl. I'm just going to go and make sure Laura's not breaking her neck out there. Give me a shout if you need anything. I'll leave the curtain open so I can keep an eye on you."

Her brow furrowed in concentration, Laura had resumed picking glass from Mackenzie's face with a pair of tweezers. What was left of his uniform immediately identified him as a police officer, but it was the expression in his eyes that identified him as the police officer whose partner was missing.

Kate walked over to the bed. "Hey," she said softly, not wanting to startle Laura as she wrestled with a sliver of glass close to his eye. "Kate, hey. Hell of a wake-up call, huh?"

"Yeah, I definitely preferred the phone call from my mother. Do you need anything?"

Laura shook her head. "The X-rays have been cleared. I'm just using them for guidance. All the wounds are superficial. Officer Mackenzie is refusing any pain relief because he wants to return to duty when he's stitched up." She tugged on a shard and winced when Mackenzie grunted. "And he's an idiot," she added quietly.

"Let me know if you change your mind," Kate told him as she raised an eyebrow at one of his X-rays. The amount of glass she could see explained why Mackenzie's jaw was clenched stiff, his face clammy. "You can always have something that won't knock you out, Officer." She tried and failed to count the number of lacerations in his face and neck. She knew from her cursory briefing on the journey in that his windshield had been blown out by a shotgun blast. The wounds to his hands and forearms implied that his quick reaction was the only reason he still had his eyesight.

"Thanks. I might take you up on that when the local wears off." His voice was strained. He held out a bloody hand. Kate smiled and shook his thumb, the only part that wasn't bleeding.

"Mackenzie. Andrew Mackenzie. 'Mac' unless I'm really in trouble."

"Dr. Kate Myles. Wish it were under better circumstances. You're not hiding any other injuries, Mac?"

"No, just what you can see. I was still in the car. Sam…" He swallowed dryly. "Sam had gone to check their truck out. I tried to get to her, but…" Mackenzie's voice trailed off. Kate could see the smears of blood on the sheets where he gripped them.

"I'm sure they'll find her." She suspected empty platitudes were not what Mackenzie wanted to hear, so she focused on the practical. "Have your family been informed?"

Mackenzie nodded and then moaned as the motion made a wound beneath his chin open more deeply. "Got one under here, I think." He pointed and obediently lifted his chin as Laura cupped it gently and worked the tweezers into the wound.

"My wife's with my son in Manchester," he said, more to distract himself from Laura's digging than anything. "She knows

I'm all right, but I told her to stay put. Not that the weather's giving her much of a choice."

Kate had started to clean the cuts on his left hand and arm.

"How old's your son?"

"Seven. He, um, he doesn't know about Sam. I told Joanne to keep him away from the news reports. He thinks the world of her."

"They haven't found the car or anything?"

Mackenzie shook his head before remembering that was a bad idea. "Ouch. Shit. No. They got a good head start. We can't get a helicopter up in this, and once they got out of the village no one was around to see what direction they went in."

Unable to offer any comfort, Kate kept silent. She knew as well as he did that the odds were not on his partner's side. The men who had taken her had shot two people already and had not hesitated to shoot at a police officer. Mackenzie seemed to read her thoughts.

"I know they've probably killed her already."

There was nothing Kate could say to that. Her head bowed, she continued methodically cleaning and bandaging his wrist.

❖

Sam was familiar with the routine by now. She stumbled and fell to her knees in the snow. Unable to balance or steady herself with her hands, she would wait for the hand on her collar to drag her back to her feet. There would usually be swearing, or a sharp blow to the back of her head, rattling her teeth. She would stand up, take a breath, bow her head to lessen the wind on her face, and set off walking again. They seemed to have been doing this for hours now, but in reality she knew less time had passed. She suspected the cold was playing tricks with her, and on more than one occasion, she had blundered into Steve's back, not realising he had stopped walking. She couldn't feel much of anything. Her uniform was sodden, ice chips had formed in her hair, and she had stopped shivering in the last half hour. Some distant section of her brain told her she was hypothermic, but the rest of it was past caring and the only rational thought that was currently cheering her up was the fact that she was so numb her broken arm had stopped throbbing.

"Yes! That'll do. See here on the map?"

They had stopped again. Steve sounded animated, pointing to his map with a torch as Eric nodded and grinned. Sam stood behind them, grateful for the respite. When they set off again, it was with a renewed sense of purpose, and finally, squinting, she could make out a dark shape in the distance that seemed to be their destination. There were no lights on in the building, no smoke from the chimney to suggest it was occupied, and she breathed a cautious sigh of relief that they weren't about to take a family hostage. As they grew closer it became apparent that the building was some kind of half-refuge, half-barn. It seemed structurally intact and entirely deserted.

Breaking in was easy. A swift kick to the front door shattered the padlock that was the only sign of security. The farmer had obviously never foreseen that his building would be used to shelter two criminals and a half-frozen police officer.

It took a minute for Sam to become accustomed to the dark after the glare of the snow. The living section was tiny, comprising a paraffin stove, a small table with one chair, a metal framed bed, and a fireplace. She waited quietly as Steve and Eric dumped their bag and weapons on the bed and ransacked the only cupboard to find a tin of coffee, sugar, one mug, and a box of matches.

"We can light a fire, Steve, get warm." Eric was practically hopping up and down in his excitement.

"Right, genius, great idea. You see any firewood anywhere?"

"Well, no, but what about outside?" Eric said, crestfallen.

"There's three foot of fucking snow outside!"

Sam backed away from Steve as he gestured angrily with his gun, and found herself against a door connecting to the barn. "They might have stored it in here," she said, shivering now she was out of the wind.

"You want to find a shovel and go dig up a woodpile?" Steve was still yelling at Eric, who was studying his shoes like a scolded schoolchild.

"The firewood," Sam tried again. "They might have put some in the barn."

Steve heard her that time, pulled her out of the way, and yanked open the door. He stepped inside and shone the torch around. She could smell animal musk and straw. Seconds later he let out a whoop and returned with an armful of wood and old newspapers.

"You're good for something then, eh, sweetheart?" Steve dropped the wood by the fireplace, returned to Sam, and took hold of her arm. "In there," he said with finality, pushing her through into the barn. She stumbled as he shoved her to the floor. "You don't move, you don't speak, and I might leave the door open a crack."

He was as good as his word, allowing a tiny chink of light through to where she huddled with her knees drawn up and her chin resting on top of them. Minutes later, as the fire crackled into life, she curled up onto her side, pretending that the warmth was reaching her as she closed her eyes.

CHAPTER THREE

S am wasn't sure whether she had slept or not. When she opened her eyes she had no idea how much time had passed. For some reason, it was important to her that she kept track of a timeline; it gave her something to hang on to in what, she had to admit, was an increasingly unreal situation. She was marginally warmer, but although the glow from the fire was brighter, only a meagre amount of heat was reaching her. She struggled to sit up, biting her lip when she accidentally put pressure on her left arm.

"Well, that's just great," she whispered to herself, as she realised the tiny increase in temperature had only succeeded in making everything hurt again. Her head, however, despite throbbing relentlessly, was clearer now. She cast a glance around, squinting in the gloom to distinguish the rough outline of hay bales, water barrels, and a wheelbarrow, none of which would be of any use to her. Disheartened, she leaned her head against the wall and was surprised when the wall clanked and swayed. It was hard work to push herself around when only her legs were any use to her, but encouraged by the sound of metal against the stone, she persevered. It took her a long moment afterward to catch her breath. When she finally lifted her head she stared at what she had disturbed, barely able to believe her luck. A shovel, rake, and digging fork hung in front of her, suspended from an improvised rack.

Headache forgotten, Sam blinked as her heart thudded against her breastbone. She could hear the two men muttering to each other.

Remembering the shots that had been fired in the shop, and the indifferent violence that had shattered Mackenzie's windshield, she knew they would not hesitate to kill her if she became too much of an inconvenience. She was vaguely surprised that moment hadn't come the minute she had reached for her CS gas but decided not to dwell upon her relatively good fortune. She was the only person who could identify the brothers, and she was more than aware that once he had the time to think everything through, Steve would realise that. She reached her conclusion without much deliberation; sitting bound in the dark and waiting for her fate to be decided on a whim didn't really appeal. Her obvious choice, in that case, was the shovel.

Standing up was agony. Her muscles seemed to have responded to the forced march in sub-zero temperatures by seizing up and refusing to cooperate. Having stretched and bent her legs and somehow managed not to overbalance and end up flailing around on her back like an upended beetle, she was able to regain some semblance of control, although her feet stubbornly remained like blocks of ice, leaden in her boots.

She found a clear spot at the side of the rack and leaned on the wall. With her shoulders flush against the stone to support her, she began to push herself steadily upward. A cold sweat appeared at her hairline as the continuous jarring of her broken arm made her feel light-headed. She concentrated on slowing her breathing, determined not to pass out, and was finally able to straighten up beside the tools. The shovel hung in the middle of the rack. She took two steps to her left, gripped its handle in her good hand, and lifted it free of the nail it had been hanging on. The metal of the blade clanked against the fork and she closed her eyes, not daring to breathe while she waited to see if the men had heard her. The door didn't move and she could still hear them talking to each other with no indication that they were giving her a second thought.

She propped the shovel up against the wall and worked her way back down to sit at the side of it. With her back to the blade, she stretched the rope binding her wrists as far as it would go, biting back a whimper as she felt the broken bones shift and grate. Her eyes fixed on the slat of light coming in through the door, she began to rub the rope methodically back and forth over the metal and hoped to remain forgotten for just a little while longer.

❖

It always looked so easy on the television. Heroes and heroines had been breaking free of restraints for years without so much as mussing their hair up or smudging their lip gloss. By Sam's reckoning, she had been working the rope for almost an hour and she had only just started to feel the strands snapping. Her injured arm was a mess of muscle cramps and spasms, hanging uselessly as she used her right arm to drag it along. The rope was slick with blood as it bit deeply into her skin, but she gritted her teeth and ignored everything except for the steady snapping and loosening and the door that still hadn't moved.

Her shoulders burned as her wrists finally fell free, and she brought her arms forward. Tears of exhaustion mingled with the sweat on her cheeks as she tried to find a comfortable position to rest in. The second part of her plan remained a little vague; she really hadn't taken the time to brainstorm. She was untied, and she had a shovel, and one arm she hoped would be functional once the circulation returned to it. Her opposition comprised two men with guns, and three feet of snow.

She sighed, not liking her odds at all. If she wanted to be optimistic, there was always the possibility that the farm whose shelter they were using was relatively close by and daylight would make navigation easier. She considered two options: try to incapacitate both men and make a break for it, or try to incapacitate both men and sit by the fire until someone came to find her. The only thing in her favour was the element of surprise. That, and a bloody-minded determination to get home to feed her cat.

❖

"Thanks, Laura." Mackenzie took the cup of coffee gingerly in his bandaged hand.

Laura set a mug of tea beside Kate, who was finishing the notes on her patients' charts.

"You're an angel. Anyone ever tell you that?"

Laura grinned. "Mr. Rogers, on a daily basis."

Kate sipped her drink, wishing she had a bar of chocolate to go with it for the perfect caffeine and sugar rush solution to surviving shift work. Everything finally seemed to be under control. Michael Kingston was still in surgery, but updates suggested his condition had been stabilised. Mackenzie was stitched, bandaged, and on the verge of signing himself out, and in the next bed Emma was fast asleep, her mother dozing beside her. The rest of the hospital was remarkably quiet, with more volunteers than patients, and they were managing to keep things running as close to normal as possible.

She checked her watch. 19:00. She had already worked an hour of her night shift and hadn't even had breakfast yet. As she was debating whether to ask a volunteer to rustle up a piece of toast for her, the door of the resus bay swung open and a police officer stepped inside, the stripes on his epaulettes identifying him as a senior officer. He nodded at Kate.

"Is it okay if I have a quick word with Officer Mackenzie, Doctor?"

"Of course."

Mackenzie had already put his cup down, his face pensive.

There was no preamble.

"We found the car."

❖

Sam bent and flexed her arm and her fingers again. She had good control now, the last of the pins and needles banished by her repetitive exercises. She practised her grip on the shovel, experimenting with different hand positions to give her the maximum amount of force.

The men were quiet. She suspected one of them was sleeping, which was crucial, as she knew she wouldn't be able to take both of them on at once. Although she had worried briefly about killing them, she knew that realistically in her current condition she would be lucky even to knock them unconscious. She refused to worry about failure and its consequences. Failure simply wasn't one of her options.

❖

The sergeant had wished Mackenzie well and excused himself to return to his post. Kate watched as Mackenzie struggled to button the clean shirt one of his colleagues had brought in for him.

The news had been mixed. What was left of the car had been discovered after a vigilant farmer had reported a fire. The SUV had burnt itself out, but preliminary forensics had reported no obvious human remains, and evidence suggested that the car's occupants had set out on foot. Search parties were now being briefed and Mackenzie intended to be in one of them.

Kate made no attempt to reason with him. She took hold of his hands and moved them away from the shirt, then fastened the buttons herself.

"Thanks." Mackenzie did well to hide the tremor in his voice.

"You took the painkillers, didn't you, Mac? I don't have to check under your tongue or anything?"

He shook his head with a smile. "I swallowed them down. They're helping a bit."

"Good." She reached for a piece of tape and stuck down an errant piece of bandage. "I don't need to tell you: no lifting, no driving with those hands. And as soon as all this is over, you get a sick note until the stitches are out and the physiotherapist is happy."

Mackenzie nodded. "Yep, no problem. I'm just going to walk with the search. I need to be out there and the sarge said it's okay."

"The *sarge* is understaffed and doesn't have thirty stitches in his hands," she said with a sense of futility.

"I can walk and I can keep a lookout. I can manage, Doc."

Kate sighed. "Be sure to come back when they all pop open, won't you?"

Mackenzie grinned at her. "I can manage, Doc," he said again with more conviction.

"Okay then, off you go."

He remained perched on the edge of the bed.

"What?" Kate wondered what she was missing.

"Um, Doc?" He looked incredibly sheepish. "Can you fasten my boots for me?"

❖

Sam heard the footsteps before the door opened. She was already crouching low against the wall, away from where she had calculated that the light would fall. She tightened her grip around the shovel. Butterflies churned her guts and adrenaline was making her palms sweaty and her mouth dry. The door began to move and Eric's bulk appeared in the frame, a cup held in his hand. He stopped just over the threshold as if not entirely sure where his brother had left her.

She waited until he was away from the light but not so long that he became suspicious and alerted Steve. Two more steps and she moved. The shovel made a dull thud as it hit his head. He was tall, but she had adjusted for that, reaching upward with her swing to hit him as hard as she could on the side of his head. The effect was instantaneous and surprisingly quiet. His knees buckled and he fell onto them, enabling Sam to deliver a second blow that took him to the floor. The only noise came from the cup of coffee dropping from his hand and the gurgling he was now making in an effort to breathe against an occluded airway.

"Shit." She was shaking as she heaved Eric onto his side into a rough recovery position, tilting his chin to prevent his tongue choking him. She felt for the pulse at the side of his neck and found it easily. It beat full and strong beneath her fingers. There was already a lump raised on his head, but there was no blood and she worked to steady her own breathing as she tried to remember what she was supposed to do now.

"Eric, where the fuck are you?"

Steve's shout made her jump. She had no time to think as he swung the door open again, a gun in his hand. He paused at the sight of his brother but Sam didn't give him the opportunity to work out what had happened before she swung at him.

The angle was all wrong. Despite his shock, Steve was able to deflect the blow easily, catching the shovel with his hand and tugging it to knock her off balance. She stumbled, trying to stay on her feet before letting go and making him stagger as she reached for his gun instead. Digging her nails as hard as she could into his hand, she was encouraged by his grunt of pain, but she felt his grip on the weapon shift and tighten. Her strength was all but gone. She hadn't planned on fighting both men in quick succession, and she absently considered how unfair everything was as he used his free hand to grip her around her throat. He was so close to her she could smell the coffee on his breath and the splash of cheap aftershave he had put on that morning.

Unable to stop him with only one hand, Sam kicked instead, aiming up with her knee toward his groin. She barely made any contact with the soft flesh there as Steve released his hold around her neck and flung her aside. She panted hoarsely before reaching for the gun again, but her touch on the metal made Steve's hand jerk impulsively. She vaguely registered the kick of the weapon, the heat from the muzzle as the gunshot echoed in the barn and everything stopped for a second.

The gun dropped to the floor between them as they stood, inches apart, both too shocked to continue their struggle for the weapon. Sam blinked. Her ears were ringing and she felt slightly off-balance for a reason she couldn't fathom. She heard Steve swear once, then his fist connected with her face and she fell. Unable to brace herself, she hit the floor, the wind knocked from her in an instant. She gasped for breath on the cold stone, twine still taut around her wrist when she raised a hand to her cheek. There was blood on her fingers, hot and fresh, and she realised that the air was thick with it, sweet and cloying with that metallic edge that always made her sick to her stomach.

Steve seemed angry about something. He was cursing, his hands tearing through his hair as he looked down at her and his brother. He reached low, grabbed her hand—the one with all the blood on it—and pulled her onto her front. That brief movement was enough to send agony flaring through her right thigh, ripping into her and robbing her of the breath she had fought so hard for. She started up a litany of curses of her own, more colourful, more creative than his had been, as he kept her in place with a knee in the small of her back and bound her hands once more. She could feel the blood now, oozing onto her trousers. Two wounds: one to the front of her leg—the pain sharp as she lay on it—and a larger one to the back, air chilling the ragged flesh the bullet had exposed. Steve tied off his knot and the pressure on her back vanished as he left her to go over to Eric.

Adrenaline fading fast, Sam lay shivering, the pain in her leg starting at the core of the wound and screaming outward, her blood sticky as it pooled beneath her. Shock brought detachment with it, and she wondered if the bullet had hit an artery or shattered her femur and how long it took, on average, to bleed to death. She bit her lip to stop herself crying, at least while Steve was still in the room. He was dragging Eric toward the door, berating him for being too heavy, for not helping, for causing this in the first place with his stupidity.

Then they were gone, the door slamming completely, spitefully shut, and plunging the room into darkness. Sam sensed the cold seeping into her and closed her eyes, feeling exhausted and bizarrely matter-of-fact. That was that. She couldn't do any more; the realisation was strangely liberating and peaceful. Her head was swimming, she could distantly hear herself gulping for air, and she gave up the struggle to stay awake. Her only source of comfort as grey drifted across her vision was the fact that Mac wouldn't be the one to find her body.

❖

"Emma, they're going to be taking you to theatre in a few minutes." Kate recorded a final set of baseline observations as

Emma opened one eye in acknowledgement before falling back to sleep.

"Aren't pre-meds great?" Laura whispered and Kate smiled easily at her.

Michael Kingston was being settled into an ITU bed, critical but stable at present. Emma was about to have her wound repaired, and the fact that she had shown no signs of deterioration suggested the surgery would be straightforward. Five minutes ago, Mackenzie had sent Kate a text telling her that he was standing with three local guides in the middle of a field. He had snow up to his knees but none of his stitches were leaking, and she had finally felt the tension across her neck and shoulders ease slightly. The appearance of a volunteer with tea and sandwiches was consequently greeted with a quiet cheer and a warm hug.

"Maggie, you are brilliant," Kate said, trying not to fall on her plate of food before she had escorted her patient into theatre. Laura had no such qualms, devouring a sandwich so quickly Kate wondered whether she had chewed and swallowed it, or whether it had just been absorbed by her mucous membranes.

"That's a rare talent, Laura."

Laura waggled her eyebrows in response as Simon appeared at the doors and waved at Kate.

"You eat your sandwich. I can play porter," Laura said, unlocking the brakes on the bed and manoeuvring it toward the door. She gestured at her own plate on the way past. "Eat mine, though, and you'll be having the last bed in ITU."

Kate heard Emma giggle as the bed was wheeled out of resus. She picked the tray of food up and made her way to the staff room, where she sank into a chair with a sigh of relief and kicked off her shoes. Her feet up on the low coffee table, mug in hand, and sandwich finished, Kate had her eyes closed when the staff room door opened.

"Your tea's still warm and I haven't touched your sandwich," she announced.

An unfamiliar male voice answered, making her sit up with a start. It was one of the police officers who had remained at the hospital to interview witnesses.

"I'm looking for one of the doctors. We have a situation."

❖

"Absolutely not." Tom stopped pacing and turned to face Kate, who was perched calmly on the arm of a chair. His scrubs had specks of Michael Kingston's blood on them. He had been in the process of changing in preparation for taking over the care of his patient in ITU when Kate and the police officer had come for him. The officer stood by the staff room door, having been ordered by his superiors to wait for an answer.

"Tom, it's our only option. Kingston is your patient now with Simon already back in theatre." Kate looked up at him, holding her hands clasped in her lap to stop them from shaking and betraying her. "I don't have kids, Tom. And I don't have anyone at home watching the clock until I get in safely."

"That's not the point and you know it! They can wait. They can bloody wait till their own medics get here!" Tom said, his voice high and desperate.

Kate shook her head. "If that was possible, you know they wouldn't have asked us. You heard the tape. He said one hour. I can't sit here and let her die."

The 999 tape had been brutal in its simplicity and used to excellent effect by a police force not above resorting to emotional blackmail to protect one of its own. The man had managed to sound remarkably composed as he stated his location, identified himself as one of those responsible for the robbery, and demanded a doctor to treat his injured brother. Without going into detail, he had stated that his brother had sustained a head injury, didn't remember what had happened and had started to vomit. When the operator had asked for corroboration of his claims, the man had paused, the line falling quiet, as the operator—terrified she had lost the connection—tried to call him back to the phone. Seconds later, his voice had been distant.

"Say your name. Tell them your name!"

Another pause followed by a barely audible, "Sam Lucas." Then slightly clearer as if she had gathered up all her energy for one last effort. "My name is Samantha Lucas. Collar number 18749."

He had left her then, sounds of him walking away and closing a door. Then his trump card. "She got shot and she's bleeding everywhere. You send a doctor to my brother and they can help her too. Get someone here in one hour or I'm going to put *Samantha* out of her misery."

Kate looked at the floor. "I don't need your permission, Tom. This is my decision." She didn't need his permission, but she was begging for his blessing, needed him to tell her that it would be all right, that it was the right thing to do, and that nothing would happen to her. She caught his eye as she raised her head and he sighed heavily.

"God." Tom walked over to her. He held her by her shoulders and looked directly at her. "Are you sure?"

"Yes, I'm sure." She didn't flinch under his scrutiny and he wrapped his arms around her, resting his chin on her head.

"You have family here, you idiot." A quick kiss to the top of her head. "The trauma bag is packed in resus. We only have the metal oxygen cylinders so it'll weigh a ton. I'll try and find a lightweight. I'd take a few blankets, plenty of fluids…"

Kate knew all this, but she let Tom tell her anyway. Then she stood and nodded at the police officer.

"Let's go."

CHAPTER FOUR

They had given Kate a Kevlar vest to wear and tried to prepare her as best they could: do as the man told her, don't be combative, don't make sudden movements or try to negotiate. She was to let the police specialists take care of that just as soon as they arrived. In the meantime, she was to treat the casualties and keep her head down. Any questions? She hadn't had any. She had stared out the window at the glistening grass verges and icy hedgerows and tried to pretend that her palms weren't sweating as she was driven to the rendezvous point.

The impromptu command centre was half a mile away from the shelter. The police had agreed to a perimeter with the man on the phone, but beyond their established boundary, Kate was on her own. As they grew closer, she could see red and blue lights flashing, guiding their approach. Two battered Land Rovers were parked beside a police van, loaned to the operation by the local guides who had brought their search teams back in now that they had nothing left to find.

The car came to a careful stop. Kate startled when her door was opened from the outside, but it was Mackenzie who smiled in at her and she smiled back, relieved to recognise a face amongst the uniforms and noise.

"Hey, Doc." Mackenzie held out his hand to help her from the backseat and grinned when she gave him her bags instead and then clambered out unassisted.

"How're you feeling, Mac?" she asked. She pulled on a pair of thermal gloves as snow began to fall steadily again.

"I'm okay. I think I blew a stitch or two." He indicated a bandage stained lightly with blood. "But I'll live." He held Kate's gaze. "I'm glad you came."

She nodded. "I'm scared to death," she whispered, her voice cracking at the admission.

Mackenzie put an arm around her shoulders and pulled her close. "Me too, for what it's worth." Then his voice brightened. "But you have all of Manchester's and a few of Derbyshire's finest watching your back, so what could possibly go wrong?"

Kate looked where Mackenzie gestured and counted nine uniformed officers, most of them so young she wondered whether their mothers knew they were out so late. None of them was armed and there was no helicopter hovering reassuringly overhead. The command centre comprised a fishing shelter housing a ramshackle table, a large map of the area, and a man struggling to use a mobile phone that had only tenuous reception. Kate didn't know whether to laugh or cry, managed a laugh that was bordering on hysterical, and buried her face in Mackenzie's jacket.

"Take me to your leader," she said. "Before I change my mind."

❖

Kate concentrated on placing one foot in front of the other. She kept her head low, watching her boots sinking into the snow and her breath clouding thickly. Her bag was heavy on her back and a second pack carried in her arms was making them ache. She focused on the discomfort, the drag across her shoulders, and how numb her face and hands were. Anything to stop herself thinking about what she was actually doing; that she had volunteered to walk toward two armed men whose trail of wounded she had spent most of the day trying to save. She didn't want to think about how the two injured people might already be beyond help, which would leave her as the only hostage, or how she probably should have told her mother what she was doing before her mother accidentally found out via a random news report.

Shifting the bag in her arms, Kate raised her head, sighted the flickering light in the window of the shelter, and adjusted her direction slightly, maintaining a steady pace as the light drew closer and closer.

❖

The door opened a crack as Kate approached. For a brief moment, she saw a man's outline, then nothing as he shone a torch directly into her face.

"Bring your bags over but stay outside." His accent was local and Kate wondered for the first time whether she actually knew the men. She followed his instructions, placing the bags at the door then taking a step back as they were dragged inside and the door closed again. She waited, listening to the rustle of packages and equipment as the bags were searched. When the door reopened, she raised her hands slowly in an effort to look as harmless as possible.

"Keep your hands there and come inside."

Kate glanced over her shoulder toward the red and blue lights dancing in the distance, but there was no encouraging nod from Mackenzie, just broken glimpses of human shapes through the falling snow. Taking a deep breath, she stepped inside.

Vomit, coffee, and sweat. In the absence of vision, Kate's sense of smell overcompensated, and she took shallow breaths as her eyes adjusted to the gloom. The man was tall, with dirt and congealed blood on a face she was relieved not to recognise. He studied her carefully and then gestured to her to turn around.

"Put your hands against the wall."

Remembering her briefing, she did as she was told, placing her hands on the stone wall. He patted her down for concealed weapons, clearly unaware that there were no armed police in the vicinity, let alone armed doctors.

"You're a doctor?"

"Yes," she said as he ran his hand under her jacket and across the back pockets of her trousers. "I work at the district hospital. My ID badge is in my coat pocket. There's a radio in there. The police said it would have better reception than a mobile phone." He dug his hand into her pocket and pulled the badge and radio out.

"Dr. Kate Myles." He shone the torch onto her photograph.

She nodded. He had stopped touching her.

"Well, Dr. Kate Myles, my brother's over there."

She turned around slowly, her hands still raised. A quick glance showed all there was to see: a second, larger man sleeping on a bed, a fire in the fireplace, a table, and a chair. There was no one else in the room, and her heart sank as she realised the police officer could have died and the man standing staring at her wouldn't have told a soul; he would have continued the charade to ensure that his brother got his doctor. She made a decision she hoped she would not regret.

"Where's the police officer?" Her voice sounded surer than she felt. "I'll help your brother, but I need to know she's okay first." Kate knew she was taking a gamble as she watched his hand tense around his gun.

"She's next door." He was grinding his teeth.

She looked to her right and noticed the dividing door for the first time.

"Is she still alive?" She closed her eyes as she waited for an answer.

"Yeah, yeah. See to Eric. He got his head hit." He took her arm and she stumbled as he pulled her roughly in Eric's direction. *Do as the man tells you.* It replayed in her head like a mantra as she picked up her bags and walked over to the bed.

"What happened to him?" Kate could see a large swelling on the side of Eric's head and a second less vivid area of bruising overlapping it.

"That bitch hit him with a shovel." He pointed the gun toward the closed door and Kate successfully fought to keep from looking impressed. Eric was taller and wider than his brother, and it must have taken a good deal of effort to knock him down. She crouched beside him and automatically began an examination. He was maintaining his own airway without difficulty and the pulse at his wrist was steady and regular.

"Was he knocked unconscious?" she asked, shining a penlight into his eyes and watching his pupils constrict equally.

"Yeah, a few minutes. Then he was sick and asking me the same stuff over and over." He was watching Kate as he maintained his place by the window.

"Mmhm." She put her stethoscope in her ears, wrapped a blood pressure cuff around Eric's arm, and took a reading. "That's good," she commented mostly to herself, relieved that the signs were pointing to a concussion rather than an intracranial haemorrhage. "When was he last sick?"

"I don't know! I don't know! I wasn't keeping a fucking chart!"

"Okay, okay." She raised her hands in supplication. "I'm sorry... sorry, um, what's your name?" She was desperate for something to humanise him, some way to make a connection, to make him see that she wasn't a threat.

The man hesitated, trying to work out what game she might be playing. Having taken a long look at her, he seemed to dismiss the idea of subterfuge with a thin smile.

"Steve."

"Okay, Steve." Such a banal pair of names: Steve and Eric. "Has he been sick since you called the police?"

"No."

Eric was stirring. He opened his eyes and yawned hugely. Kate saw the confusion pass across his face and he sat up in the bed, searching for Steve and relaxing again when he found his brother.

"You okay, bro?" The rage had gone from Steve's voice in an instant.

"Yeah. I have a headache, but I feel better."

"Found a doctor for you."

Kate smiled at Eric, watching him closely for any signs of impaired motor functions, but he moved exactly as she would have expected a large man with an even larger headache to move. "Is it all right if I take a spot of blood from you, Eric? Just to check your blood sugar?"

Eric nodded. "Our mum's diabetic," he told her casually.

She smiled again and tried not to think how incongruous it was to be discussing family medical anecdotes with two armed men in a barn in a snowstorm. "Sharp scratch here, Eric," she said sweetly before jabbing the needle hard into his finger. Eric yelped in surprise, but she kept hold of his hand, squeezing the blood onto a test strip and watching the glucometer as it calculated.

"Six point eight. Perfect."

Eric had his wounded finger stuck in his mouth. Kate knelt by her bag, tidying her equipment away. She rummaged until she found a small bottle of paracetamol. "Here, Eric. Take two of these with some water."

Steve stalked over to Kate, grabbed the bottle from her hand, and studied the label carefully. "Paracetamol? That's it?" His voice was low and hard.

She stood, intensely aware Steve's behaviour was so unpredictable he might not believe a word of what she was about to tell him.

"Steve, I think Eric has a concussion. The blows to his head shook his brain around, but there are no indications at this point that they caused any bleeding in the brain or permanent damage." She gently reached out and took the paracetamol bottle back. "He needs these painkillers, some rest, and me to keep an eye on him while we're all stuck here. I'll keep checking on him every half hour or so."

"What about him forgetting everything? That's not caused by brain damage?"

She shook her head. "That can be normal with a concussion. Some mild amnesia and confusion is nothing to be concerned about." She opened the bottle, shook two pills out, and watched as Eric washed them down with water.

"You'd tell me anything!" Steve snapped and Kate shrank back as he gestured wildly with the gun. "You just want to see to the woman. You don't give a shit about Eric!"

She tried to keep her voice steady. "Of course I want to check on the police officer. You were the one who told us she was 'bleeding everywhere.' But I'm not stupid enough to risk my life by not treating your brother properly." She took a deep breath. Getting annoyed with the man wielding the gun was not in her best interests. "Steve, I know none of this has turned out as you planned it, but the two people you shot in the jeweller's got to the hospital and they're okay. You and Eric haven't killed anyone, but I need to see to Samantha to make sure it stays that way."

Steve was quiet, but Kate saw what she thought was relief pass fleetingly across his face. Eric had settled back down in the bed and was snoring softly.

Walking back over to his place at the window, Steve shrugged and pointed to the dividing door. "You know where she is."

❖

Kate didn't give Steve an opportunity to change his mind. She grabbed her bags and opened the door. Freezing air hit her as soon as she stepped over the threshold and she shuddered. The barn was silent and pitch-black. There was a torch in the end pocket of her bag but she hesitated before she took it out. She could smell blood now and had a sudden terror of what the light would reveal.

At first all she saw were hay bales and a well-used wheelbarrow, then, finally, the dark stain showing her which direction to shine the light in.

"Shit." Kate stared, stunned for an instant. Sam lay on her side in a thick pool of blood, her hands tied behind her back. Her face, beyond pale, was the waxy yellow of a pre-terminal patient. Livid bruises mottled her forehead and jaw. Kate felt sick, blinked back tears, and tried desperately to detach herself from what she was seeing. They had bound Sam, shot her, closed the door, and left her to die in the dark.

From the step, Kate couldn't tell if Sam was alive, but when the light played over her face, Sam's hand twitched as if she would have shielded her eyes if she hadn't needed all her energy just to take one breath after another.

"Samantha?"

Kate hurried over to her, dropping her bags as she knelt by her side. There was no pulse palpable at Sam's wrist when Kate felt for it. The ropes around Sam's wrists had cut deeply into her flesh, and Kate struggled with the knots, cursing her numb fingers as they fumbled. The bloody strands finally came loose and she threw them to the floor.

"Oh, God." Sam's left wrist was broken. It was badly swollen, and Kate could feel the crepitus as the fractured ends jarred against each other. She did not want to consider the pain the men had caused by tying her wrists behind her. Instead, she rolled Sam gently onto her back, bringing her injured arm to rest across her stomach. One thing at a time, Kate told herself. She could only deal with one thing at a time. She pulled on a clean pair of latex gloves, then rolled Sam's shirtsleeve up and pushed on the inside of her elbow. When that yielded nothing, she pressed her fingers firmly on Sam's neck, against her carotid artery. She willed her fingers to stop trembling as she finally located the faint throb of a heartbeat. The presence of a carotid pulse allowed her to estimate Sam's blood pressure at 50-60 systolic, which meant Kate was kneeling in approximately fifty percent of Sam's blood volume. Sam's pulse was too fast to count and every breath was a shallow gasp taking a terrible effort.

"It's okay, Samantha. My name's Kate. I'm a doctor and I'm just going to have a quick look at you." Kate was pulling equipment from the bags, trying to organise her thoughts and her priorities as her mind screamed that her patient was bleeding to death and there was probably nothing she could do to change that. ACBC. Airway, C-spine, Breathing and Circulation. Focusing on the basics lessened the screaming slightly. Sam was managing to maintain her own airway and, despite the car crash, Kate discounted cervical spine injuries on the basis that Sam had walked several miles from the accident to the barn. The fact that she had managed to whack Eric twice with a shovel was also in her favour. It was far from an exact science, but Kate decided there were more definite problems for her to worry about.

"And it's not like you're going to be doing somersaults at the moment anyway," she muttered as she pulled out the oxygen cylinder and attached a trauma mask to it. The cylinder wouldn't last forever, but it would help while Sam was so shocked.

Kate placed the mask over Sam's nose and mouth then tucked the elastic around the back of her head. "Sorry, sorry," she said in a whisper as the elastic caught in Sam's hair, but there was no reaction from her.

Taking the torch up again, Kate trained it slowly over Sam, working her way from head to toe, using her free hand to search for any signs of concealed injury or bleeding. There were numerous minor scrapes and contusions, probably from Sam being handled roughly, but the only glistening of fresh blood was coming from her right thigh. Satisfied that was the only source of haemorrhage, Kate scrambled to her bag and grabbed scissors and a handful of dressings. Holding the fabric of Sam's trousers taut, she cut steadily through the material from the ankle to the point where the bullet had penetrated the middle of the thigh. She eased the fabric away, wincing as she saw the puckered flesh around the entry wound, the surrounding tissue an angry red that was speckled with the black tattooing of a point-blank shot. Running her gloved hand around the back of Sam's leg, she encountered a mess of torn muscle and skin. She could feel blood, warm and slick within the gaping wound, and when she pulled her hand back it was covered with the bright red of an arterial bleed.

It was nothing she hadn't already suspected, and there was no obvious deformity to suggest a fracture of the femur. Opting to leave Sam's trousers in place at the back of her leg so as not to disturb any areas that had already formed clots, she cleaned the entry wound with saline and sterile wipes, then wrapped pressure dressings around both wounds and pulled them as tightly as she dared. She shone the torch around the barn, searching for something she could use to elevate Sam's leg. A broken crate was the best candidate, so she pulled it over. She lifted Sam's lower leg to prop it on the wooden panels and supported the underside of her thigh with a rolled up blanket. Pushing away a gnawing feeling of futility, she decided that a garden cane balanced in a bucket would suffice as an IV stand. "I feel like I'm in the A-Team," she murmured as she padded the cane with straw and paper and positioned the bucket toward Sam's head. She tightened her tourniquet around Sam's upper arm, then hooked a bag of Gelofusine on the end of the cane and primed a giving set before returning to Sam's arm in the hope that a decent-sized vein would be declaring itself loudly.

"Crap." A combination of hypothermia and low blood pressure was conspiring to make her job very difficult indeed. "Samantha, I'm going to apologise in advance for this." Kate swabbed Sam's inner elbow, took her cannula, and aimed for where the vein should have been, digging in deeply with the needle and hoping for the flashback of blood in the hub of the cannula that would indicate success.

It took three attempts, and Kate's hands were shaking with desperation when blood appeared and she was able to guide the cannula into place before securing it firmly. She wasted no time attaching the fluids and running them wide open, not concerned at this point about anything other than raising Sam's blood pressure. She could worry about breaking open clots when Sam was stabilised.

She worked methodically to clean and dress the wounds on Sam's wrists, doing her best to pick out the embedded threads of twine, and wiping the lacerations with a swab soaked in saline. She jumped sky high when Sam moaned softly beneath the oxygen mask.

"Shh, shh, it's okay. I'm all done." Kate ripped off her bloodied gloves and took Sam's hand, squeezing the limp fingers. "Samantha, can you open your eyes for me?" There was no response. Feeling slightly heartened anyway, Kate pulled on fresh gloves and considered her next task. "I'm going to put your wrist in a sling, Samantha. That way it'll give you some support and you won't cause yourself any more damage when you wake up and forget that it's fractured. Here we go…"

Kate had fallen into maintaining a quiet commentary for Sam, although she wasn't sure who the real beneficiary was. At the hospital she was used to working with a team, friends and colleagues whose techniques and working practices she was familiar with and whose support she could always count on during difficult cases. Tom had a tendency to whistle tunelessly and would defend himself by announcing that fifty percent of his patients were too deaf to realise. Laura had a filthy laugh you could hear from three wards away. There was always noise—voices and chatter and machines, doors opening and closing. It was the noise Kate missed, the sense of organised chaos that should have been surrounding Sam, an experienced team to take care of her injuries and the complications they were causing her. Instead Sam had one doctor with limited resources trying to work in a squalid barn with a flickering torch.

Kate sighed and glanced at the IV line. The bag was almost empty. She pulled out another one, snapped it open, and replaced the first, piggybacking a smaller bag of antibiotics along the same line. She took blankets from the second rucksack and tucked them around Sam. The arm with the IV line was closer to Kate. She drew it out from beneath the blankets and rubbed it between her own to try to make it warmer. When that failed, she held the hand gently, curled her legs beneath her and, for the first time that day, allowed herself to rest.

❖

Kate reached over and turned the dial on the oxygen tank down slightly. The gauge indicated only a quarter of the tank remained. She had been listening to Steve shouting over the radio for the past twenty minutes, his tread heavy on the rough floor as his demands were repeatedly stonewalled. Although she was unable to hear the finer details of the negotiations, Kate knew from his tone that the crisis was unlikely to be resolved quickly.

Trying not to think about the violence implicit in Steve's voice, she rested her fingers on Sam's wrist and almost cheered with relief at the thready pulse she found there. Over the past hour, Sam's breathing seemed to have become easier. Her face was now a ghastly pale, which was a marked improvement on her initial deathbed yellow. Kate smiled wryly that such dubious success would take on such significance, but under these circumstances she would take any encouragement she could get.

Pressing her hand to the back of Sam's leg, however, she could feel the stickiness of fresh blood, and her mild euphoria evaporated immediately. She reduced the flow rate on the IV, trying to find a balance between maintaining a blood pressure compatible with Sam's survival and keeping it at a level that would not cause excessive haemorrhage. After a moment of uneasy contemplation, she reluctantly pulled one of the blankets covering Sam away. The freezing temperature had undoubtedly saved Sam's life, slowing her body's systems to the point where the blood loss had been similarly slowed. While the haemorrhage had been severe, it had occurred over a far longer period of time than was normal.

Tears of exhaustion stung Kate's eyes as she wrapped a third dressing on top of two already stained and soaked. She didn't know how much longer she could do this. The enormity of the responsibility was making her breath catch in her throat and her stomach churn, she was freezing, bone-tired, and more scared than she could ever remember being. She tied off the bandage, closed her eyes, and tried to steady her breathing.

"Oh shit."

Kate's eyes flew open and she swiped at them with the back of her hand, her fatigue instantly forgotten. "Samantha?"

"Mmhm?" It was barely a mumble, but it was definitely coherent, and in the dim torchlight Kate saw Sam's eyes flicker open for the first time.

"That's it, Samantha, open your eyes for me. Good girl." Kate smiled hugely as Sam blinked and then looked toward her, focusing on her face.

Kate shook her head, barely believing her luck. She carefully pulled the oxygen mask down and switched the tank off. "Hi there."

Sam licked dry lips, her throat working hard to swallow. "Hi." She stared at Kate and then her head lolled to one side. She straightened it and returned Kate's gaze with a groan. "Still...still in the barn?"

Kate nodded. "Yes. Sorry. Steve demanded a doctor for Eric after you smacked him. The other half of the bargain was letting me look after you as well."

"Kate?" Sam was struggling to keep her eyes open.

"Yes. How did you? Bloody hell! You could hear me back then?"

"Heard you swear at my veins." Sam gave a hoarse laugh that quickly became a cough, leaving her breathless. She reached out her hand, blindly searching for Kate's, who took it and squeezed it gently.

"You shouldn't be in here," Sam said with more force than Kate would have thought possible.

Kate ran her thumb over the back of Sam's hand. "Well, I didn't have any plans and there was nothing on TV," she said lightly. "Besides, Mac said he'd kick my arse if I let anything happen to you."

"Mac? Is he okay?" Sam was trying to push herself up.

"Hey, hey, lie back." Kate guided her back to the floor, meeting no resistance as Sam's shoulders shook with quiet sobs. "He's fine. He's got plenty of stitches, but right now he's half a mile down the track hanging on to a radio and refusing to follow any of my advice."

Sam nodded. "That sounds about right," she mumbled, her eyes heavy. "He always was an idiot."

"Here, lift your head a little." Kate returned the oxygen mask. "That's it. You just rest now."

"Good idea," Sam whispered, and then she remembered something that seemed vitally important. "Kate? Kate?"

"What? What's wrong?"

"My mum…"

"I'm sure Mac's contacted her," Kate said quickly.

"No, no. My mum. She's the only one ever calls me Samantha."

Kate laughed. "Oh, okay. So it's Sam then?"

"Yeah, just Sam."

"Okay then, *just Sam*. Sleep. I'll be right here if you need me." Kate felt Sam's fingers curl loosely around her own and she returned the soft pressure as she watched Sam's eyes close.

❖

"It's not that fucking difficult! Charter a fucking jet and get us a chopper to the airport."

Steve's voice carried easily through the closed door. Kate could just about hear the reasoned response of the man on the other end of the radio, patiently explaining why he couldn't just arrange an armed escort to Manchester Airport and allow a jet to fly Steve and Eric out of the country. He offered hot drinks and sandwiches instead, which immediately sent Steve into another fit of rage.

Kate edged herself closer to Sam and watched the door for movement as she waited for him to calm down. Something banged once, then again with more force, but when Steve eventually spoke it was to agree that an officer could bring the provisions to a halfway point. There was a long pause as a question was lost beneath a crackle of static. Kate cringed at Steve's answer.

"How the fuck should I know? I'm not a doctor!"

The negotiator's reply put the outburst into context. "Would it be possible to speak to Dr. Myles? Perhaps she would be able to tell us if she needs anything?"

Kate's head snapped up at that. Seconds later, the door opened and Steve stood silhouetted in the light. She squinted against the brightness.

"They want to talk to you, *Doctor*." There was a sneer of emphasis on the last word. Kate had reassessed Eric no more than half an hour ago, once again finding him stable and comfortable, but she suspected Steve remained unconvinced of her professional competence despite Eric's only complaint being one of hunger.

Kate pushed herself to her feet, glancing at Sam, who hadn't reacted to the light or the voices. She had barely stirred since Kate had told her to sleep, and Kate had been trying to convince herself that this was a good thing, that Sam was resting, not deteriorating.

"Sam, I'll be right back," Kate said with more confidence than she felt. She walked past Steve, who pushed her into the centre of the room. She gritted her teeth and didn't react to the physical reminder of exactly who was in charge. He had treated her in a similar fashion each time she had checked Eric—a shove forward, a jerk of her arm, as if the fact he was standing in front of her with a gun wasn't enough for him.

"Here." He threw the handset at Kate, who reacted quickly enough to catch it before it shattered on the stone. Turning away so he wouldn't see her flush of anger, she pressed the button on the side of the set.

"Hello?" Kate realised she didn't have the slightest idea about proper radio protocol. "Can anyone hear me? Mac, are you there?"

There was a pause, just crackles and feedback, and then Kate remembered to take her thumb from the button to allow the other side to reply.

"Hey, Doc…Kate. Good to hear you." The reception was poor, but Kate could hear Mackenzie's grin as he spoke, and she smiled, relieved they were all out there, that she wasn't as abandoned as she had been feeling.

"Hi, Mac. Steve said you wanted a word." She could feel Steve's glare boring into her back and knew the conversation would have to be succinct.

"We're sending some provisions out. Wondered if you needed any medical supplies?" The inference lingered in the static; if she needed supplies that would mean Sam was still alive.

"I need a bit of everything, Mac," she said, suddenly very weary as she considered what she needed and what was impossible to obtain. "Fluids, dressings, more O-two. The cylinder ran out an hour ago. The brother's okay, but Sam was shot in the thigh. Mac, I think an artery was nicked." She paused, imagining Mackenzie's face as he found out that Sam was alive in one breath and miles from the help she urgently needed in the next. "She'll need blood. If I can, I'll get a sample out to you for the hospital to cross-match."

There was no blood with the supplies. In the rush to comply with Steve's deadline there had been no time for the blood bank to organise any units, but having type-specific readily available at the hospital when they were finally able to move Sam would be critical.

"How's she doing?"

Kate stared at the radio. How's she doing? She's freezing cold and filthy, lying here steadily bleeding out from a wound we could probably fix just fine if we were in a hospital. She's been beaten and dragged around, and I know this because some of the bruises on her arms are shaped just like fingerprints. She's scared and in pain and she's hoping I can save her.

Kate was still staring at the radio. She pressed the button. "She's had better days, Mac." She rested her hand on her forehead, closed her eyes, and managed to make her voice brighter. "So I'm guessing I'm coming to collect everything?"

"Yeah." Mackenzie did well to mask the devastation she knew he was feeling. "Be about twenty minutes, Doc. I think Steve's hashing out the finer points. Keep safe, both of you…Here."

She heard him hand the radio over and followed his cue, offering the set back to Steve. As the negotiator organised the location for the pickup, Kate could hear banging in the background, Mackenzie's voice raised in frustration, and a colleague guiding him out of earshot. Kate quietly opened the barn door, slipped through it unnoticed, and closed it behind her. In the darkness she crouched low, placed her head in her hands, and wept.

❖

Kate allowed herself a whole minute for her breakdown. She decided she had earned the right to have a momentary lapse of self-control, just as long as it was only momentary and her only witness slept through it. She pulled a tissue from her pocket, blew her nose, and wiped her eyes, thankful the light was too dim to show how red she knew they were. Standing up and straightening her clothes, she took a deep breath then returned her focus to her patient. She made her way to Sam's side, pausing to collect blood bottles and a second cannulation kit.

"Here we go again," Kate muttered and drew Sam's left arm gently from its sling. Avoiding the fractured wrist, she secured her tourniquet around Sam's upper arm. The recent improvement in Sam's blood pressure was immediately apparent as her veins flashed blue beneath her pale skin, and the second line was easy to insert. Kate drew off blood samples, scribbling the time and *Samantha* on the labels, unable to remember what surname Sam had gasped on the 999 tape recording.

Kate decided not to remove the cannula. Sam would need more than one IV line once at the hospital when the fluid therapy would be much more aggressive than Kate was able to risk at the moment. Planning ahead for their eventual rescue seemed to clear her thoughts. Looking at Sam's wrist, she realised there was wood lying all over the barn floor, and berating herself for not thinking of it earlier, she hunted around and found a suitably flat piece she could use as a splint. She positioned it on Sam's abdomen and carefully placed the broken wrist on top. Kate hesitated as Sam stirred uneasily, moaning low in her throat, but that was the only protest she managed. After securing the splint with a bandage, Kate eased Sam's arm back down to her side. She gathered up the blood bottles and stowed them safely in her jacket pocket. There was nothing left for her to do then, no other reason for her to delay leaving, and she knelt to take Sam's hand in both of hers.

"Sam?" Her fingers were slender and just a bit smaller than Kate's. "Sam?" They were limp and clammy in Kate's grip; no response when she squeezed them.

"I have to go out and collect some supplies. It'll take me a little while," Kate said, ignoring the way her throat closed on the words. "But I'll be as quick as I can." She watched Sam breathe, the exchange of air too fast and too shallow as Sam struggled to compensate for the blood loss. "I won't leave you, I promise." With her teeth clamped down hard on her bottom lip, she let go of Sam's hand and stood quickly before she talked herself out of going. She knocked on the dividing door, following her routine of not wanting to get herself accidentally shot, and stepped through when Steve grunted.

"Where do you want me to go?"

Chapter Five

A man stood with the box. His shoulders were hunched and covered in snow, his hands thrust deep into the pockets of a coat several sizes too large, apparently borrowed from one of the local farmers. Kate knew it was Mackenzie even before she heard his shout of "Hey, Doc!"

"Hey, Mac," she gasped as she struggled to get within earshot. Her legs trembled when she stopped and she collapsed into an ungainly heap on top of the crate. She had pushed herself too hard, keeping up a punishing pace as she fought her way through snow that was so deep it had enveloped her thighs on more than one occasion.

"Easy, easy." Mackenzie rested a hand on her shoulder, giving her time to catch her breath and regain her composure. Her cheeks were flushed with exertion, beads of sweat crackled into ice droplets at her hairline and fast puffs of white mist revealed just how much effort the quarter-mile trek had taken.

"Here." He rummaged in a bag and pulled out a flask of tea and a Mars bar. He poured a cup and handed it to her.

"No, no. I need to get back."

She was making a move toward standing and wondering whether she would succeed or end up facedown in a snowdrift. Mackenzie spared her the embarrassment, put his hand back on her shoulder, and without the slightest effort, kept her sitting down.

"Here," he repeated in a tone that didn't invite debate.

He had even unwrapped the chocolate for her. Kate's shoulders sagged and she reached for it. She took a huge bite and washed it down with tea. He waited until she had finished the bar. Which took her about another thirty seconds.

"Better?"

She nodded, her mouth full.

"I've brought you all your spare medical gubbins. They said the oxygen cylinder is a lightweight one, which should make it easier to carry. The smaller pack has sandwiches and flasks," Mackenzie told her. Then, quieter, "You both doing okay?"

With her tea cradled in both hands, she flexed her fingers as they slowly defrosted. "I'm fine. Just tired." She hesitated. "Sam's not brilliant, Mac."

On the way to the meeting point she had been holding an internal debate about how much to tell Mackenzie, should he be the one waiting for her, and she had had no doubt that he would be. While the friend in her was desperate to spare him the details, the doctor wanted to give as comprehensive a report as possible to allow the hospital to prepare for Sam's eventual evacuation. She took a breath, tasted crisp, cold air, and swallowed it hungrily, gratefully replacing the thick scent of blood she could sense clinging to her. With a clearer head, the doctor won the debate.

"I've managed to get her blood pressure up somewhat, but I have to keep it relatively low or she starts bleeding heavily again. She has a through and through here." Kate indicated on her own thigh. "Her left wrist is broken but non-displaced, and she has some bruising to her face." Glancing at Mackenzie's face, she decided that mentioning the ligature wounds to Sam's wrists would not be in his best interest. "On the bright side, she smacked the brother, Eric, with a shovel." Kate shook her head with a half-laugh, relieved to see Mackenzie's stricken expression replaced by a proud smile. "She was awake for a short time. She knows you're all right, and she said you were to follow doctor's orders to the letter." She raised an eyebrow at Mackenzie, who chuckled and failed to spot her barefaced lie.

"That sounds about right," he said, unwittingly mimicking Sam. "She always has been the boss." He tapped Kate's empty cup on the box and returned it to the top of the flask. "Speaking of bosses, mine want to know all about the dynamic duo in there."

Kate nodded and told Mackenzie everything she thought was relevant about Steve and Eric. That Steve was unquestionably in charge, that his mood was unpredictable and becoming more inclined toward aggression. No, he didn't seem to care about Sam's safety or her own, although he had shown some semblance of relief when he learned that his hostages at the jeweller's had survived. He cared about Eric and not going to jail, and he was increasingly frustrated by how narrow his options were.

"Has he hurt you?"

Kate met Mackenzie's intense gaze and tried not to think about Steve's tendency to push and shove her at every opportunity, or about Sam's condition when she had found her.

"No. He hasn't hurt me."

He nodded, seemingly satisfied she was being truthful.

"They, um…" He was suddenly fascinated by the straps on the rucksack. "They said to tell you to bail if you wanted to. Y'know, if you felt it was too much for you. That you weren't to be worried about coming back with me. Now."

She took the hand that was fidgeting with the bag's buckle. "I'm fine, Mac. I'm fine and I'm going back to her. You tell them to concentrate on their side of things." She squeezed his hand. "I promised Sam I wouldn't leave her."

She stood and was about to pick up the rucksack when Mackenzie threw his arms around her. She squeaked in surprise but hugged him back, letting out a quiet "oh" as she felt the blood bottles digging into her hip.

"Here." She handed them to him. "Make sure Dr. Tom Delaney gets these. He'll know what to do with them."

"No problem, Doc." Mackenzie stood to one side as she pulled the rucksack onto her back and tested the weight of the box before she picked it up.

"All set?"

"Mmhm."

"Tell Sam I'll see her soon."

"Of course I will."

"Be careful, Doc."

Kate nodded, set her shoulders, and turned her back on him. Her progress was slower with her burden, and she struggled to maintain her footing without her arms to balance her. As she approached a snow bank, she looked toward Mac and waggled her fingers in an attempt at a wave. She saw his hand rise briefly in response. With obvious reluctance, he began to walk in the opposite direction. She didn't look back again.

❖

Something was different when Sam awoke. It wasn't the pain, which hadn't changed at all, deep and constant in her leg, and gnawing in her wrist like the worst kind of toothache. She had woken suddenly, dragging herself from a nightmare, a gasp on her lips, and had automatically reached her good hand out, searching blindly and finding nothing. No gentle pressure on her fingers, no flick of the torch, no quiet voice reassuring her: "See, I'm still here, I'm just saving the batteries." There was just her own breathing, panicked and shallow in the darkness.

"Kate?" she managed to croak. She licked her dry lips and tried again. "Kate?" She looked to her side, just able to distinguish the outline of her IV, the bag three-quarters empty. A slight discomfort when she moved her left arm revealed a second intravenous line in the crook of her elbow. She swallowed against a surge of nausea as she wondered what else had happened while she had been sleeping. She shifted position, tried to sit up, and failed miserably when the effort made her head spin and the nausea intensify.

Beyond frustrated, she pounded her fist on the floor, then, in blind defiance of common sense, grabbed hold of the cane Kate had utilised as a drip stand and attempted to haul herself upright. In an instant, she had made a vague and completely unrealistic plan that involved somehow standing on her ruined leg, making her way to the door, and demanding to know where Kate was. Despite her determination, she succeeded only in turning herself slightly onto her right hand side. The resultant shift in pressure against her leg brought tears to her eyes, and stuck in an awkward position, she couldn't move her hands to wipe them away. She rested her head against the freezing stone and wept hopelessly.

That was how Kate found her, minutes later, when she opened the door and played the torchlight over the barn floor.

"What the hell?" Abandoning her supplies, Kate ran over and dropped to her knees at Sam's side. She placed her hands on Sam's face, felt the wetness there, and used her thumbs to ease it away. "Sam, it's okay. I'm back now. What on earth have you been up to?"

It took an obvious effort, but Sam managed to raise her head. Kate moved to support her and she met Kate's eyes with a smile.

"I thought something had happened to you. So, I, um…I was going to come and find you." Sam's tone implied she was well aware of her own idiocy. "It seemed like a good idea at the time."

Kate's smile widened. She couldn't help it. "Well, it was a lovely gesture," she said, turning Sam onto her back and checking her IV and the dressing around her thigh. "But I'd prefer it if you just stayed put and didn't do anything daft like pull out your drip or set yourself off bleeding all over the place again. Deal?" She held her hand out.

Sam gripped it and shook it weakly. "Deal." She allowed Kate to guide her head back down onto her pillow. "Where were you? Are you okay?" she said to Kate's back as Kate returned to the doorway to collect her equipment.

"Well, I was wading through waist-deep snow to meet some handsome young devil in the middle of a field to pick up snacks for the boys and some spare doctoring stuff for me." Kate put down the box and knelt again. She reached for Sam's wrist and tried not to frown as she counted her pulse. "Mac says hi, by the way. He was modelling the latest in Peak District winter wear. I got the distinct impression he is not a country lad." She kept her voice light as she checked through the drugs in the box. She could see that Sam was trying her best not to move, her body held rigid with her fist clenched at her side. Her pulse had been upward of one thirty and she was drenched in cold sweat.

"How's the pain?" Kate asked in a tone that dared Sam to lie.

Apparently blindsided by the abrupt switch in topic, Sam didn't bother trying to dissemble. "Horrible." She shook her head. "It wasn't too bad before. I mean, it was there, but sort of distant. Now, it's awful. And…" She paused awkwardly and Kate realised she was embarrassed. "I feel sick."

Kate nodded. "Your blood pressure is a little better, which, unfortunately for you, means you're a bit more awake now."

There was morphine in the drugs bag. Kate drew a ten milligram vial into a syringe and mixed it with saline. "I can give you a small dose of morphine. I'll have to be careful because it can knock your blood pressure down, but it should take the edge off. And this is an antiemetic." The second drug went into a separate syringe. Kate hesitated in her preparations as Sam gave her a blank look. "It stops you wanting to throw up."

Sam smiled and watched blearily as Kate labelled syringes, discarded needles, and jotted a note of dosages and times into the small pad she had been using as a chart.

"Right, give me your bad arm. I'll put these through that line. Make sure it stays patent."

Kate suspected Sam didn't really have a clue what that meant, but she straightened her left arm and watched as Kate flushed the line through and then injected the morphine cautiously.

"That's all I can give you for now. We'll see how you go," Kate said, hoping against hope that such a small dose would help ease the pain and not cause any complications. "But you can have the whole lot of this." She injected the antiemetic then flushed the line again. "All done. The morphine might make you a bit drowsy, Sam. Not that you really need any encouragement there. Here, just while it kicks in."

Sam lifted her head and accepted the oxygen mask as Kate connected it to the fresh cylinder.

"This'll feel tight on your arm."

For the first time, Sam's blood pressure was high enough that Kate was able to measure it accurately. "Eighty-four over forty," she announced to Sam who, with her eyes already heavy, clearly wasn't listening. "I can live with that."

❖

While it was a popular urban myth that police officers used their lights and sirens to head back to the station for a cup of tea, it was nevertheless true to say that emergency personnel could hear a kettle being boiled from considerable distances.

"I could murder a cup of tea."

"Bloody hell!" Kate set the flask of tea on the floor before she swiped at the hot liquid she had just spilled onto her hand. "I thought you were asleep."

"Just dozing. I've got a sixth sense where there's tea involved."

Kate laughed. "Yeah, you and every paramedic who comes through our casualty." She screwed the lid back onto the flask. "Oh, Sam, I can't give you any," she sighed, feeling bitterly cruel. "You need surgery on your leg. I have to keep you nil by mouth. I'm sorry."

"S'okay, I'm just really thirsty."

"I bet you are. The oxygen dries your mouth out as well."

Sam nodded. "Mmhm."

Kate could see how chapped Sam's lips were and held an internal debate that only lasted a few seconds. "Hang on, there's a bottle of water somewhere. You can have a couple of sips and just wet your lips." There wasn't really any point in denying Sam that small comfort when she could still, realistically, be hours from reaching a hospital.

"Here, just lift your head a little. Good girl." Kate placed a steadying hand behind Sam's head and brought the bottle to her lips. "Small sips."

The water was slightly stale but freezing cold, and Sam had to force herself not to gulp it down. It was torture to limit herself, but she took a few sips then nodded to Kate that she was finished. The water tracked an icy path straight down to Sam's stomach and she laughed, mortified, when her stomach rumbled like thunder.

"Sorry. I never did get any lunch. We were about to head back for some when the silent alarm call came in. And I guess we both know how that turned out." She closed her eyes, saw Mackenzie's windshield disintegrating frame by frame, and opened them again sharply. In contrast, the dark claustrophobia of the barn was almost a relief, and she stared at the blank walls as she waited for the other images to fade. As if sensing her distress, Kate settled next to her, close enough for Sam to feel a slight warmth where their legs pressed together. That small comfort was all it took to dispel the images completely.

"So you and Mac, you don't work locally, do you?" Kate asked, her voice light and conversational.

Shaking her head, Sam gratefully allowed herself to be distracted as she tried and failed to imagine Mackenzie working in the hills. "No, we're based in Manchester. He lives on the outskirts, but I moved to Stockport three years ago. I can see the foothills of the Peak District from my bedroom. Cally and I would walk there occasionally, but she wasn't really into it."

"That your sister?"

Sam chuckled wryly. "No, my ex. She's a paramedic. Ran off with a nurse." She waited for Kate's reaction; she wasn't in the habit of launching herself out of the closet quite so casually, but it seemed such a trivial issue compared to everything else that was going on.

Kate didn't run away in horror. She just nodded sagely. "Ah ha, living the cliché, was she?"

"Yeah." Romantic liaisons within the National Health Service were the stuff of legend. "I think she broke my heart for a little while." Sam raised an eyebrow at herself, wondering where that had come from. She quickly put it down to drugs, shock, stress, and trauma and knew damn well it was none of the above. She had told Mackenzie, but then he had been working with her for years, while she had only known Kate for a few hours. Sam cleared her throat. "Sorry, I think the morphine is making me maudlin."

Kate gave a low laugh. "I think our current situation is enough to make anyone maudlin. It's so long ago, I barely remember my last ex…I think he was called Christopher and liked chasing me around the schoolyard and pulling my pigtails." She took a sip of her tea, grinning at the giggle she had surprised from Sam. It was the brightest Sam had been since Kate had started treating her. Kate found herself momentarily forgetting where they were and felt some of the burden that she had been shouldering for so long begin to lift slightly. She gratefully allowed herself to enjoy the respite, however brief it might prove to be.

"Well, I only have one love in my life now," Sam declared. "He's clean, eats what I put in front of him, only hogs the bed when it's really cold, and doesn't answer back."

"Cat or dog?" Kate asked, not fooled for a second.

"Cat," Sam said with a laugh. "Mitten. And I really hope he's learned how to open those little packets by now; he'll be starving." She sniffled. "Sorry, can I still blame the drugs?"

"Sure. No problem. My little tabby's called Lotty. She's incredibly pretty, but for some reason will only go through her cat flap in one direction." Kate smiled when she got the desired laugh from Sam. "She'll sit out in all weather waiting to be let back in, no matter how often I try to show her. I thought cats were supposed to be smarter than dogs."

"Mitten can entertain himself for hours playing with one of my socks and then throw up a hairball on my carpet." Sam shrugged. "I think that jury's still out."

"Yep." Kate rested two fingers on the pulse at Sam's wrist. The rate had dropped slightly, suggesting that, for the moment at least, she was stable.

"So," Sam said casually. "Am I going to live, Doctor?"

Kate swallowed hard. There was a desperate plea for honesty beneath Sam's playful tone. Kate had always tried to be truthful with her patients, but she had never been in a situation like this, and she must have missed the class that dealt with keeping up the spirits of your critically injured patient during a hostage crisis with no foreseeable resolution. Kate lifted her head and looked at Sam, who shook her head apologetically.

"Kate, you don't have to…I shouldn't have…" Sam hesitated and took a deep breath. "I just think I'd rather know." Her chin trembled and Kate could see the indentations her teeth were making on her bottom lip, but her gaze didn't falter.

Kate nodded. "It's okay. I understand. I just wish I could give you an absolute answer. I think I've managed to get you stabilised. Your blood pressure is about right, enough to keep you conscious but not high enough to make the bleeding uncontrollable. I'm keeping you cold, which is helping, and that's why that blanket's under your head and not wrapped around you." Kate ran a hand over her face as Sam listened calmly. "You need to be in hospital, Sam. There's no two ways about that. You need surgery, blood, more antibiotics—"

"And a cup of tea," Sam interrupted, taking pity on her.

"And a cup of tea." Kate brushed her fingers lightly over Sam's forehead. "I'm doing my best for you."

Sam nodded as if not entirely sure that she could trust her voice. When she did speak her voice wavered, but she persevered. "I never meant for any of this to happen. I didn't mean to hurt Eric. I thought they were going to kill me and I didn't want it to be on their terms." Her voice did break then. "Kate, I'm so sorry."

Kate fished in her pocket, pulled out a tissue, and handed it to Sam. "Here, wipe your eyes. None of this is your fault. None of it. You can't be blamed for fate getting you stuck in the middle of this mess. I made my own decision to come in here, and the only people accountable are those two idiots in there. As for Eric, he has a few bruises. It's a shame you didn't hit him a bit harder. You might have knocked some sense in."

The fact that her doctor would so casually advocate violence surprised a laugh out of Sam. "Why, Kate, I'm shocked!"

Kate grinned. "Oh, some people are just asking for it!"

❖

Steve was shouting again. His footsteps pounded up and down on the stone, treading the same path over and over. Kate listened as he paused at the window then stamped away, his voice angry, his answers short. She jumped as something thudded against the barn door, and she felt herself tense in readiness, but the door remained shut and she relaxed slightly, not sure exactly what she had been preparing herself to do.

At Kate's side, Sam was sleeping off a second dose of morphine. Kate switched the torch on and moved its light over the length of her, watching her breath fog too quickly on the oxygen mask. Sam's hand clenched and unclenched, and she frowned and murmured at something unseen in the dark. Kate laid her hand on Sam's wrist, to run her thumb back and forth across it. Sam muttered unintelligibly, then gave in and settled.

Beyond the door, Steve had also quietened, his voice low in conversation with Eric. Kate hugged her knees to her chest, knowing that the peace wouldn't last, that sooner or later the negotiations would resume and that, like a rat in a trap, Steve was acutely aware that he had run himself into a corner.

Outside, the light was changing. Thin slivers of grey were now visible through the cracks in the stone walls as dawn struggled to make its presence felt against the storm clouds still massed over the hills. She checked her watch: 7:02 a.m. At some point she seemed to have passed through exhaustion and come out on the other side, running on nothing but raw adrenaline and four cups of caffeine. They couldn't go on like this. The longer Sam remained without proper treatment, the greater her risk of infection, and there was nothing in Kate's supplies that could cope with a combination of blood loss and septic shock. She wondered what the police procedure and protocols were in circumstances such as these. Now they were aware of how critical Sam's condition was, would they eventually decide enough was enough and raid the barn?

She knew she was no match for Steve physically, and after Sam's efforts, he was on his guard for any further attempts. He never entered the barn, instead summoning Kate into the living quarters, always with his gun close at hand. Without really acknowledging why, she reached for her bag. The plastic and glass containers clinked quietly as she sorted through them, half an idea slowly shifting and taking shape. Atropine, amiodarone, paracetamol, adrenaline, benzylpenicillin, Diazemuls, morphine, Narcan, and Oramorph. She hesitated, and then picked up the bottle of Oramorph. Oral morphine. Side effects included respiratory and circulatory depression, nausea, and drowsiness. Next to the drugs bag, a flask of coffee nestled, untouched. Never having liked coffee, she had drunk only the tea, and had been planning to give Steve and Eric her spare flask, a peace offering to let them know she wasn't really a bad person and would prefer it if they didn't decide to shoot her in an attempt to show that they meant business. She unscrewed the safety cap from the Oramorph and sniffed the liquid inside. Her hand shook as she considered whether the coffee would mask the taste of the medicine and how much Oramorph it would take to counteract the caffeine and incapacitate the two men without resulting in any dangerous side effects.

First do no harm. She returned the cap to the bottle and placed it back into the drugs pack. She ran her hands through her hair and then buried her face in them, hiding away, wishing she were braver.

"Shit." She shook her head, her teeth working furiously on her bottom lip. "Shit." She made a space for the drugs pack in her box of equipment. She closed her hand on a plastic case. The shape was immediately familiar to her, and her stomach lurched violently as she pulled it out. An AED. Now located in every major public place and every hospital corridor, an Automated External Defibrillator delivered measured shocks to a person in cardiac arrest. Acid rose to the back of her throat and she swallowed against it. She heard cloth rustling as Sam sensed the incremental change in the barn's light, and without thinking Kate reached out a hand to reassure her. The hand she clasped was cold, the bones slender and fragile under her touch. Tears burned in her eyes and Kate, defeated, let them fall.

"Sam, I'm so sorry. I just can't."

❖

"Why did you want to be a doctor?"

Kate reached for the bottle of water as she considered her answer. She soaked a piece of gauze and eased it gently over Sam's lips.

"Thanks," Sam whispered. She hadn't been awake long, but she had been restless, unable to find a comfortable position, and Kate had been trying to distract her by telling her about the hospital, its staff, and some of the patients that had passed through its doors over the years. For some reason, an answer to Sam's question wasn't easily forthcoming.

"I'm not sure. I've never really thought about it. I was in and out of hospital with asthma as a kid. I spent a lot of time chatting to the nurses and doctors, and I became interested in medicine. I was good at science at school." Kate hesitated, thought of the bottle of Oramorph buried away in its bag, and looked at Sam, whose face was now just about visible without the torchlight and whose exhausted eyes were watching her intently. She swallowed hard. "I um…I wanted to help people. I know that's a terrible cliché but it's true."

A flicker of recognition in Sam's expression implied that she had picked up on the undercurrent of tension, and when she spoke the lightness of her tone seemed deliberate. "That's pretty much why I joined the police. Well, that and the uniform is really cool."

Grateful for the deflection, Kate looked at the huge rent in Sam's trousers where she had attacked them with her scissors. "Sorry about your pants. I'm sure they'd be cool if they were in one piece."

"No problem." Sam lifted her good leg slightly, trying to shift her weight off a sore spot. "Hey, why'd you pinch my boot?" Her right foot had been bare for hours, but this was the first time she had commented on it.

"Oh, I did it before, when you were asleep. I needed to check the pulse in your foot." There was an X marked in Biro on Sam's foot where, thanks to the improvement in Sam's blood pressure, Kate had been able to locate its pulse. "It means the blood supply is still getting past your injury, which is obviously good news."

"Otherwise the whole damn thing might fall off?" There was real fear beneath Sam's flippancy; her career depended on her being able-bodied, and Kate wondered for how long she had been letting that fact eat away at her.

Kate wrapped her hand around Sam's exposed foot. "Give your toes a wiggle for me, hon," she said softly.

It obviously hurt, but Sam managed to move all five. "Well, would you look at that?" She had managed to raise her head slightly, and waggled her toes a second time just for her own entertainment. "Hey, they still work!"

Kate's grin was broad. "Yes, yes they do. Now lie back down."

Too relieved to protest, Sam relaxed her head against the blanket. "You know my work boots have a public health warning attached to them, don't you?"

Kate nodded wryly. "Yes, it's a good thing I was wearing gloves. The boot and what's left of your sock are in a clinical waste bag over in the corner." She gestured to the far side of the barn. "I tell you what. When we get out of here in one piece and you get back on your feet, I'll treat you to a new pair. I'll even throw in a pair of decent socks."

Sam laughed and gave Kate a thumbs-up with her good hand. "You certainly know how to motivate a girl!"

❖

Her head nestled on her arms, Kate was dozing when the banging started. Instantly alert, she looked at Sam, who was watching the door with frightened eyes.

"He was just on the radio," Sam said, her voice tense. "I think they must have crapped all over his plans again."

"Well, he will keep asking for a helicopter in a snowstorm." Kate tried hard for levity, but frustration bit into the words. Beyond the door, glass smashed against the stone and she could hear Eric trying to reason with Steve, who seemed to have given up on forming sentences and was just yelling incoherently. Without thinking, Kate positioned herself in front of Sam, sensing an escalation but not knowing what form it would take.

It was heralded by words Kate had been dreading hearing.

"I'll show them. I'll fucking show them!"

The barn was flooded with a sudden blast of light as Steve wrenched the door open and, without hesitating, strode over to Kate and jerked her to her feet.

"No, don't, please." Sam was struggling to sit up, pushing desperately with her good arm. Her voice broke. "Please, don't."

Kate was trying to keep her feet beneath her, shocked by Steve's force as he dragged her toward the door. She struggled against him briefly and he lost his grip on her arm. She quickly turned back to Sam.

"Sam, stay still!" It came out harsher than she had intended and she softened her tone. "I'll be okay. Just stay still."

With a grunt, Steve tightened his hold. Kate allowed herself to be taken into the adjoining room, trying not to panic as he kicked the door shut and threw her forward. Off balance, she fell and landed heavily on her hands and knees. She cursed under her breath as she felt the coarse stone abrade her skin. It seemed safer on the floor, so she remained where she had fallen, watching Steve warily as he stalked toward Eric and grabbed hold of the radio handset.

When he spoke into it, his voice was low and controlled. "I know you're out there. I know you're closer. You need to know not to fuck with me." Through a burst of static, Kate heard someone attempt a reply, but he flicked the handset off and turned to face her. "Get up."

She stood slowly, unsure if her knees would hold her weight; her entire body was trembling, her breathing rapid, her eyes wide. If he killed her, he was effectively killing Sam as well.

"Steve, please. Just think about this for a—"

In a few short strides he was beside her, his gun hand rising then falling in a blur of motion as he backhanded her across the face. The pistol caught her hard, slicing into her cheek, and the force of the blow took her onto her knees once more.

"Oh, shit." The words were muffled by a groan as she automatically raised her hands to her face. Her vision blurred and she struggled to remain conscious against a wash of dizziness. She distantly heard Eric voice a weak protest, but the room spun again as Steve pulled her upright. He looped his arm across her throat and half-carried, half-dragged her to the front door.

The freezing air took her breath as he opened the door, but it cleared the dizziness slightly, and she managed to gain her footing, raising her head to look out onto a vast expanse of white. On the horizon, the hills stood as mute witnesses, the sky still fierce, grey storm clouds whipping overhead, heavy with the threat of more snow. It was beautiful. She took deep breaths of the fresh air, ignoring the blood cooling on her cheek and the stinging pain from the skin the gun had split. When Steve pushed the gun under her chin, forcing her to raise her head, she watched the sky shift and surge, and remembered lying on warm grass beside her brother David, making him laugh as she named the shapes the clouds made and he refused to agree with any of her suggestions.

Steve was shouting across the fields. He gave the police a two-hour deadline to accede to his demands. Kate listened as he threatened to kill her and Sam, because he had nothing left to lose and he was tired of being treated like an idiot. She wondered at the type of person who would murder two people to provide a salve to his ego, and she thought of Sam smiling at one of her bad jokes, desperate not to let Kate see how much she was hurting.

As suddenly as he had pulled her out of the barn, Steve was pushing her back inside, full of bravado at the chaos he was sure he had sown amongst his tormentors. He closed the dividing door on his gloating, leaving her choking air back into her bruised throat.

"Kate?" Sam sounded frantic.

"I'm okay, I'm okay. Just give me a second." Kate made her way into a corner of the barn, dropped to her knees, and vomited cold tea into the dust. "Shit," she whispered, wiping her mouth with her hand. But at least now she knew what she had to do.

CHAPTER SIX

A cross a bit. To the left. No, your other left…"
It was next to impossible for Kate to apply the thin
dressing strips to herself in half-light with no mirror, and she shook
her head as she struggled to follow Sam's instructions and close the
wound on her cheek.

"Here, give me the gauze." Sam held her hand out.

"No, no. I'll manage." Kate dabbed at the cut, which was still
bleeding thickly down her face.

Beside her, Sam laughed shortly and held her hand out again.
"Bloody doctors! Give me the gauze and bend down a little, Kate.
You have me at a slight height disadvantage."

"Okay, okay." Kate soaked a fresh pad in saline and handed it
to Sam, then lowered herself within reach. "Just remember, you're
still my patient…ow!" The salt cut into the laceration and brought
tears to her eyes. "Shit! Oh, ow! You know, I do this to patients all
the time and never realised it stung so bloody much."

Sam winced in sympathy as she eased the blood away and
cleaned around the wound. "Okay. All done. Now you need a strip
here." Cold fingers touched Kate's cheek gently. "Good, that's it.
And another one here." Again, the feather-light touch. "Last one
here, and you're all finished." Sam left her hand in place until Kate
placed the strip correctly, then she cupped Kate's chin, turning
Kate's face toward the light to appraise her handiwork.

"Oh, Kate, it looks sore," she murmured.

Kate leaned her head briefly onto Sam's hand "Mm, it is." She pulled her head up with reluctance. It had been a relief to just let someone take care of her for a few minutes. "I'll take some paracetamol. Thanks, Sam. I'll be fine." She taped a dressing in place and washed the tablets down with bottled water.

"How long has it been?" Sam asked quietly.

The dividing door had been left ajar when Steve had dragged Kate outside and she realised that Sam had heard everything that had transpired.

Kate glanced at her watch. "About ten minutes." After returning the paracetamol to the bag, she pulled out the flask of coffee and the Oramorph and set them on the ground beside Sam. "Sam, I had an idea…" She explained about the drug, about adding it to the coffee in the hope that the men would drink it, that it might make them so drowsy they wouldn't be able to follow through on their threats or react quickly enough if the police decided to pre-empt the deadline.

"Won't they be able to taste it?"

"I don't think so. The coffee smells pretty strong. Besides, hospital coffee usually tastes awful. You could spike it with paraffin and no one would know the difference." Kate sighed. "There's no guarantee they'd drink it anyway, but I can't just sit here and do nothing but watch the clock tick down."

Sam was shaking her head. "Is it really worth the risk? What if Steve suspects something? He doesn't seem to care who gets hurt now."

Kate touched her hand to her cheek where it was throbbing. She was so tired. "I'm hoping he'll just think I'm trying to butter him up, that he's so wound up he won't be thinking that logically. Eric's due his check-up in twenty minutes. I was going to pretend I'd just found the flask, offer it to them because I don't like coffee."

"Might it harm them?"

"I'm not sure," Kate admitted. "There's a chance they might overdose, but if I don't put enough of the Oramorph in, it won't have any effect. I can still make my checks on Eric and keep the Narcan handy as an antidote."

"Oh, just like with heroin overdoses? One shot of Narcan and they're up, punching, kicking, and moaning over their ruined fix," Sam said with the obvious insight of someone who had encountered her fair share of drug addicts during her career with the police.

"Exactly. Look, we have to try something. There's no way I'm having a cup of tea and a Mars bar as my last meal."

Sam laughed quietly then checked herself. "Hey, when the hell did you manage to sneak a Mars bar?"

❖

"I've never been a good liar. When we were young, David— that's my brother—would tell the most outrageous lies to get himself out of trouble and I just never could. I mean, I'd try, but I blush at the slightest provocation, and for some reason my throat does this closing up on words thing. And sometimes I stammer even though I don't stammer. And I—"

"Kate!"

Kate stopped in the middle of screwing the lid back onto the flask and turned to Sam. "—babble on," she finished with a self-deprecating laugh.

Sam was laughing helplessly. "We're doomed," she declared. "You ready?"

Kate looked at her watch. She had waited until Eric's check-up was due, not wanting to break the routine and draw undue suspicion onto herself. "Yep. Wish me luck."

Sam nodded. "You're right, you know. We have to do some-thing. I don't want us to die here." She managed a tremulous smile. "Good luck."

❖

Eric could barely meet Kate's eyes. She went through her routine of taking his blood pressure and pulse and assessing his coordination and strength. He mumbled answers to her questions as he stole glances at the dressing on her cheek, before looking away sharply in the hope Steve wouldn't catch him showing any concern. He waited until she leaned in close to check the reaction of his pupils with her pen torch, then he whispered, so quietly that she barely heard him, "I'm sorry he hit you, Doctor."

Kate nodded. "Yeah, me too. Not your fault, Eric." Not your fault that your brother is a psychotic thug, but it is your fault you were stupid enough to follow him into all this and that you're too much of a coward to do anything to stop him now. She kept her face neutral, and he was too preoccupied with his own misery to sense any of the anger she was currently attempting to conceal. She replaced her equipment piece by piece and, just as she had mentally rehearsed, she pulled the flask of coffee from her bag as if it were an afterthought.

"Oh, Eric, I found this in with my supplies. It's coffee and I only drink tea. I wondered if you and Steve would like it." She shrugged, giving the impression it made no difference to her one way or the other. "It's still hot."

His face lit up with a smile, sure now that his redemption was complete. "Yeah, thanks. Steve used all ours up."

"Okay then. I'll, um...I'll get back. You take another dose of paracetamol in an hour if your head's still hurting, and you know where I am if you need me."

"Yep, thanks, Doctor." He was clutching the flask like a lifeline.

Kate resisted the urge to run to the door, forcing herself to open it and step through calmly. She managed to shut it behind her before her legs gave way and she sat down heavily on the step.

"Kate?"

"I'm fine, Sam. It's done."

❖

Sam lay quietly, watching as Kate checked her IV, measured her blood pressure, and felt methodically around her bandaged thigh to assess any further bleeding. Kate was pale, her cheek swollen and raw beneath the blood-stained dressing, and Sam didn't comment when her hands shook as they adjusted the flow regulator on the drip.

Sam looked away quickly as tears burned her eyes, and she blinked them back, refusing to let them fall and cause Kate any further distress. She looked toward the wall instead, where the light in the cracks was brightening as day broke and ate incrementally into the two-hour deadline Steve had set.

She was scared. She had never seriously considered dying, although there had been the odd occasion when Mackenzie was driving that the possibility had crossed her mind. Never having subscribed to any religion, she wondered exactly how she went about making her peace, then felt Kate's cold fingers resting on her wrist and cursed herself under her breath.

"Sam? Any particular reason you're a 'fucking idiot'?" Kate sounded worried, which only made Sam more furious that she had even thought about lying back and quitting when Kate had fought so hard to keep her alive.

"I'm okay. I'm just giving myself a polite little pep talk."

Kate nodded, a half-smile crossing her lips. "You too, huh?"

Sam returned the smile sheepishly. "I wish I'd taken the *Self-motivation and Betterment* course they offered us last year."

"They never did!"

"Yeah." The smile was easier this time. "They must've had some surplus in the budget they needed to use up in a hurry. I opted for a day on an army assault course and an introduction to firearms instead." She looked at the bandage tight around her leg. "Oh, the irony."

They both laughed, Sam gladly banishing her morbid thoughts if only temporarily.

"So what was my score?" she asked, gesturing to Kate's notes. Her vision had been blurring intermittently, which she suspected wasn't a positive sign.

"Well," Kate sighed. "Your blood pressure is down slightly. So I've increased your fluids a little. How are you feeling?"

"Oh, you know. This wasn't exactly what was promised in the brochure," Sam said lightly. She had noted Kate's reluctance to give her an exact blood pressure reading and decided that she could skirt around bad news just as effectively. "The food's rubbish and the central heating leaves a lot to be desired. And don't get me started on this bloody pillow."

The woeful expression on Sam's face had the desired effect of making Kate laugh and she played along. "I tried to source the finest goose down, but it was surprisingly scarce."

"I think two bricks in a sack would be more comfortable."

Still laughing quietly, Kate moved to sit behind Sam. She eased the folded blanket from beneath Sam's head. "C'mere." She patted her lap and wriggled closer, allowing Sam to rest back against her leg with a soft sigh. "Any better?"

"Mmhm." Sam closed her eyes as she felt Kate's fingers gently stroking a path through her hair. "You do this for all your patients?" she mumbled, lassitude eating into her speech.

"No. Not all of them. Just the ones I pick up in barns."

Sam smiled, keeping her eyes closed and pretending, just for a minute, that nothing else was happening. There was no deadline, no bullet hole in her leg, no armed men next door, no snowstorm or wind whistling through the gaps in the stone. Nothing mattered but the rhythmic pass of Kate's fingers and the warmth of her leg beneath Sam's head.

"Kate, don't let me fall asleep."

"I won't. I'll poke you the minute you start snoring."

"I want to be awake. Just in case."

"Mmhm. How about I wake you in twenty minutes?"

"Okay. Twenty. No more."

"No more, I promise. Shush now, Sam. Close your eyes."

❖

"Sam? Sam? C'mon, sleepyhead, wake up for me."

Sam groaned and raised a hand to protest. She was still so tired and had been enjoying the sweetest of dreams.

"Sam? It's Kate. Open your eyes."

The dream and the pleasant calm it had evoked receded as Kate's voice became more insistent. Sam relented and obeyed her instructions. "I'm awake. See?" She forced her eyes open, blinking in the half-light until the blurriness faded.

"You look about as awake as I feel," Kate said, entirely unconvinced. She was watching the dividing door, listening intently.

More alert now, Sam pushed herself up slightly. "What did I miss?"

"I'm not sure. I think I heard someone throwing up a minute or so ago. I'm going to go and check on Eric, see how they both are."

"Did I oversleep?"

Kate chuckled. "Yeah, right through your alarm clock. I let you have an extra five minutes. You were smiling and it seemed a shame to interrupt."

If Sam had had sufficient blood pressure, she would have blushed. She couldn't remember what she had been dreaming about, but it had certainly been relaxing. She decided a change of subject was in order. "I'm sure I don't know what you're talking about. Will you be all right in there?"

"I think so. Eric's due his check-up so it's a good excuse to see what's going on. Sorry, hon, it means you get the breeze block back."

Kate ignored Sam's theatrical moaning and replaced the folded blanket that really did feel as hard as a rock. "I'll be as quick as I can."

"Stay out of trouble, will you?"

"I'll do my very best." Kate gave Sam a nervous grin, knocked on the door, and stepped through.

❖

Eric lay still on the bed as Kate made quick progress through his baseline observations. He was pale, his blood pressure had dropped slightly, and there was fresh vomit on his shirt. With her heart pounding, she noted his condition and tried not to focus on the empty mug at his bedside.

"Not feeling too good, Eric?"

"He's been puking again." Steve sounded disgusted rather than concerned and remained in his place at the window.

"That can happen with a concussion. Just take it easy. Try and sleep if you can, and be sure to shout if you need me."

She was packing her equipment away, trying not to rush, trying to keep her voice steady. Eric had closed his eyes and she watched him closely, relieved to see him taking full breaths at a regular rate. With the head injury and the Oramorph he seemed suitably docile. One down. She glanced at Steve, who remained oblivious at the window. He raised a mug to his lips and swallowed deeply. One to go.

❖

They sat in silence. The last time Sam had asked "how long?" they had had less than half an hour left. She hadn't spoken since.

Having refused a further dose of morphine, she endured the pain, determined to be awake, to do whatever she could to resist when Steve came for them. She closed her eyes and listened to the rhythmic thud of something loose on the roof, its movement in the wind as pronounced and unwelcome as the tick of a clock.

There were a thousand things she wanted to say to Kate, memories and stories she wanted to share before it was too late, but mostly there was a simple thank you and sorry. She opened her mouth to speak and found herself silent, tears blinding her. She choked back a sob, her hand dropping onto the filthy stone of the floor. She reached out her fingers. They were taken up by Kate's immediately and the tears finally streamed down her cheeks as she held on tight.

❖

Kate heard Steve retching and froze at Sam's side. Her palms were suddenly clammy and she let go of Sam's hand, realising with a sick sense of dread that this was where her plan had ended, that she didn't have a clue what happened next. The men were certainly being affected by the drug, but in her ideal scenario, this was when the cavalry had stormed in, finding the men easy prey. The cavalry weren't storming in. They were still attempting to negotiate over the radio, a tactic that had quite clearly reached the limits of its effectiveness. Steve was no longer paying the negotiator any attention and had just threatened to drag Sam outside and finish her off in front of anyone who had encroached upon the barn. There were only ten minutes left on the clock. If the police had any other ideas, they were leaving them awfully late.

The retching stopped abruptly and liquid splattered onto the stone. Steve gagged and then coughed twice. A stream of muttered curse words slowly became more audible and Kate heard her own name being spat out, along with a remark that something had been done to his "fucking coffee." She knew they were out of time.

"I'm going to fucking kill them."

Steve's declaration sounded clear in the silence. Kate looked down at Sam and took a deep breath. "Whatever happens, Sam, you just keep your head down and stay put, okay?"

Sam was shaking her head, her eyes wide. "Why? What are you going to do, Kate?" She put her hand out to grab hold of Kate and stop her from moving away, but Kate had already scrambled to her feet.

"I'll be right back."

It took every ounce of her resolve, but she ignored Sam's pleas, looking around frantically for something, anything she could use as a weapon, before giving up and moving to stand in front of Sam, hoping Steve would focus on her long enough for help to arrive. The crash of the dividing door made them both jump. Kate instinctively raised her hands in a defensive gesture as Steve stalked toward her, his face pale and furious, his gun clenched in his fist.

"What did you do to me, you bitch?"

She took a step backward, her eyes fixed on the gun. "Nothing. I don't know what you're—"

He punched her hard, smashing her bottom lip against her teeth, blood spraying as it split, but she managed to stay on her feet, maintaining her position between the gun and Sam.

"What. Did. You. Do?" He sounded every word slowly, then, by way of final punctuation, he raised the gun and pointed it at Kate's chest.

She spat blood onto the floor and wondered what the safety range of a bullet-proof vest was and how much of a delay she could cause by just letting him punch her repeatedly. Behind her, Sam was quietly hyperventilating, and anger boiled in Kate that they had got so far, managed for so long, only for everything to go to hell at the final hurdle. She licked at the blood on her lip and looked him straight in the eye.

"You kill me and you'll never know."

This time it was a backhand, the gun catching her across her bandaged cheek, and she lost her balance despite her best efforts. She dropped to her knees in a haze of pain, no longer sure her decision to piss him off and keep him distracted was one of her best.

The force Steve had put into his blow unbalanced him slightly, but he recovered more quickly than she, kicking her in her side to knock her onto the floor. He stood over her, gun pointed at her head as she struggled to draw in a breath, his face impassive, his finger playing with the gun's safety catch. He stayed like that until she could focus on him again, then he leaned down low and spoke directly into her ear.

"I guess I'll just kill your little friend then."

He rose too abruptly and swayed against the resultant dizziness but didn't fall down, and Kate could only watch as he strode over to Sam and stood above her, one foot on either side of her thighs.

Sam could see Kate fighting to steady herself and get to her feet, and she allowed herself to relax slightly, not concerned that Steve had turned his attention to her, just relieved that Kate was moving. Looking up at him as he towered over her, she decided she was damned if she was going to make it easy for him. Summoning all her strength, she lifted her good leg and kicked him as hard as she could in his groin, her steel-toe capped boot making satisfying contact. He certainly hadn't been expecting that, and let out a howl of pain, forgetting everything for an instant except the agony between his legs.

Unable to move and exhausted by the brief effort, Sam could only wait for his retribution, but at least he had stopped using Kate as a punching bag. Bent over with one hand on his knee, he pointed the gun at Sam's head.

"You'll fucking pay for that." Breathing heavily, an idea seemed to occur to him and he smiled grimly at her. "But not here."

He leaned down to grab Sam's wrist, and she let out a strangled cry as he began to drag her toward the door. She dimly heard Kate shouting her name as she felt something tear in her injured leg and a thick warmth begin to spread out from the core of her wound.

"Sam! No, no, don't. You're hurting her, don't…"

Kate watched helplessly as Steve pulled Sam inch by inch toward the door, determined to carry out his threat and kill her in front of an audience. Still on her hands and knees, she searched around on the floor, picking up and discarding a flimsy piece of wood and half a brick that crumbled beneath her fingers. Then her hand closed around the cold regulator of the oxygen cylinder. Although it had been emptied within the first two hours, the cylinder's metal casing gave it a considerable weight. She lifted it in both hands before staggering to her feet.

With her eyes closed against the pain, Sam was trying to use her broken wrist to knock Steve's gun from his grip, and Kate watched as he paused to hit her hard across the face, stunning her into compliance, before he began to drag her once more. Kate saw the despair in Sam's eyes as, exhausted, she finally stopped trying to fight him. In contrast, Steve's lip was curled in a snarl of determination. He was certain now that no one was going to stop him from enjoying his moment of glory.

Without a sound, Kate crossed the short distance between them, raising the cylinder in her hands before bringing the curved end down hard onto the side of Steve's skull. The skin on his temple split on impact and he froze as blood began to run down his cheek. It took mere seconds for him to collapse, but he still had time to look at Kate, the anger set in his features gradually replaced by disbelief and bitter accusation. Then he went down, landing heavily as his head, unprotected, cracked against the stone floor with a wet thud.

He lay unmoving. With a shudder, Kate threw the cylinder away from her and cautiously approached him. The gun lay loose by his slack fingers and she picked it up gingerly with one hand, feeling for the pulse at the side of his throat with the other. There was nothing. Blood spread darkly from beneath his head, collecting in rivulets in the stone, but it was the only indication that he had been alive. There was no pulse, no rise and fall of his chest, no puff of breath on her palm as she held it over his mouth. She considered attempting resuscitation and was about to give her first breath when she noticed the thick matter collecting like jelly at the side of his head, and with a choked sob, she turned away, turned to Sam, who wasn't moving either.

"Sam? Sam?" With a desperation bordering on panic, Kate applied painful stimuli, rubbing her knuckles along Sam's sternum and letting out a gasp when Sam weakly tried to bat her hand away.

"Sam, open your eyes. Good, now keep them open. Oh shit."

There was blood everywhere, staining the dressing on Sam's leg and pooling beneath her. A deep red smear mapped exactly how far Steve had managed to drag her.

"Oh fuck. No, no, no. Not now."

The length of IV tubing was strained to its utmost. Kate pulled the makeshift stand closer to Sam, checked the line hadn't been wrenched from her arm and—caution no longer an option—opened the flow as fast as it would go.

"Sam! Sam, listen to me." The oxygen mask went back on, chilled air blasting out, and Sam looked at her with a silent protest. "I need you to press here." She grabbed Sam's arm, balled her cold hand into a fist, and pressed it firmly into her groin. "It's your femoral artery, Sam. I need you to press hard to try and stop the bleeding."

Tears were running freely down Sam's cheeks, but she tried, forcing her fist to stay where Kate had put it, trying to ignore the seductive pull of sleep.

"Keep it like that, Sam. I'll be right back."

Sam shook her head, her eyes imploring Kate to stay. Kate knelt close to her, cupping her cheek gently.

"He's dead, Sam. He can't hurt us anymore. Two minutes. I'll be two minutes. Just hang on. I have to get help, okay?"

Sam nodded once, digging harder into her leg, the pain working to keep her alert as she watched Kate give Steve's body a wide berth and hurry to the door.

❖

The only sound in the room was Eric's snoring. Kate stood on the threshold for a few seconds, the gun shaking in her hand, but the pattern of his breathing didn't falter, and she stepped through and looked around the room with more confidence. The radio was on the table where Steve had tossed it. She scooped it up but didn't dare to switch it on until she had restrained Eric. The men's holdalls were under the table and she quietly rifled through them. She winced as stolen jewellery slipped from her hands and clattered onto the floor, a reminder of what exactly had set all of this into motion. The jewels glittered, exquisite, obviously expensive and utterly useless now to the two men. Everyone had paid too high a price for them.

Beneath the gems and a bag of money, Kate found boxes of spare ammunition and a change of clothes, then finally closed her fingers around something more valuable to her than anything she had discovered so far—several pre-cut lengths of rope.

"Oh thank you," she muttered as she selected the longest piece. Without giving herself time to hesitate, she took hold of Eric's hands and bound them tightly before fastening the remaining length of rope to the bedstead. Despite the rough treatment, he barely twitched in his sleep.

Kate looked down at him, waiting for something to happen. Seconds passed and nothing did. She started to shake, a fierce tremor that spread uncontrollably, making her legs collapse from underneath her and sending her to the floor. Her breath was coming in gasps and she bent her head, fighting not to hyperventilate. She didn't have time for this; she needed to get back to Sam. Tears blurred her vision, but she managed to turn the radio on, not bothered now about waking Eric.

"Come in, please. Someone, please? Mac?" She was trying so hard not to sound hysterical. "This is Kate Myles. We need help in here."

"Dr. Myles, what is your situation?" A voice she didn't recognise.

"I killed him. I killed Steve. I didn't mean to, I didn't mean to, but he's dead." She was crying freely now, tears running off the end of her nose. "His brother's secure. I tied him up to the bed. Officer…" She tried but still couldn't remember Sam's surname. "Sam's bleeding everywhere." She took a deep breath and some sensible part of her realised they might need proof that they weren't going to walk into a trap. "I'm going to open the door. There's only me here."

She pulled the front door open slowly and stepped through into the snow. Almost immediately she saw movement, much closer than she had expected, and not knowing what else to do, she raised a hand and waved at them.

"I have to go back in to Sam." Her throat closed and she let out a soft sob. "It's safe for you to come in. Please. Oh God, please come in now."

❖

Kate dropped to her knees beside Sam.

"It's okay, honey. I'm here, I'm here."

Sam turned her head toward Kate and managed a small smile. For the first time, Kate had been able to leave the door open, and a gentle light from the embers in the fireplace helped dispel some of the bleak terror of the situation. Sam's fist was still where Kate had positioned it, held in place only by sheer stubbornness and a sense of obligation to a woman who had consistently risked her own life to help a complete stranger. She could see tracks on Kate's cheeks where tears had left a mark through dust and blood, and rougher, scrubbed patches where Kate had attempted to hide the fact with the back of her sleeve. Sam pretended not to have noticed, as Kate changed the IV bag, her fingers moving deftly in a well-practised routine. She wrapped a fresh bandage around Sam's thigh, an automatic apology on her lips as she pulled it tight then raised Sam's leg back up onto the crate.

"They're coming, Sam," she whispered, and took hold of Sam's clenched fist. The fingers stayed locked in place even when Kate lifted the hand clear. She unfurled them gently and tucked Sam's hand back down beneath the blanket. She took up the pressure herself, pushing down hard against Sam's femoral artery to try to slow the blood flow to the rest of her leg. It was little more than a crude tourniquet, but there was nothing else she could do.

"Just relax. You've done really well. We're safe now. Just hold on a little longer."

CHAPTER SEVEN

C"lear?"
"One down. Main room."
"Dr. Myles?"
"Main room clear."
"Dr. Myles?"
"In here." Kate could barely speak.
"Doc? Kate?" Mackenzie sounded frantic.

Kate found the energy to raise her voice. "We're in here, Mac."

The silhouettes of two armed officers appeared in the doorway, guns raised, ready for the action they had missed by a good ten minutes. They took stock of the scene before them and loosened their stance slightly, moving forward to assess the room systematically, torchlight cutting into every corner. Joint declarations of "clear" had barely passed their lips when Mackenzie stepped into the room.

Kate had no idea how he had managed to designate himself a role in the rescue team. Perhaps he had just remained inconspicuous in the chaos. Now, as he walked forward, the sickened expression on his face told her he wished he had stayed outside.

The air in the barn was thick with the smell of blood and, underneath the coppery sweetness, a more foetid odour that always seemed to accompany violent death. Well-accustomed to it, Kate no longer paid it any heed, but Mackenzie brought his hand up to cover his nose and mouth. He barely afforded the dark outline of Steve's body a second glance; he was already moving toward

Sam. Kate saw him fumble for his radio and raise it to his lips. "Get those paramedics in here now! Confirmed safe. Get them in here!" There was an affirmative response he didn't respond to as he pushed himself forward.

"Doc?" he said quietly as if afraid that he would startle her.

She looked up at him and he couldn't stop the gasp that escaped him as he saw the injuries on her face.

"Oh Jesus, Doc."

"Hi, Mac." Kate could only imagine how bad she looked, and even though smiling was painful, she managed to grimace briefly.

"What do you need?"

She was grateful for his logical question. It allowed her to focus on practicalities and not just give in to the urge to curl up and weep. He knelt at her side, and when she adjusted her position slightly to allow him to see Sam for the first time, she wondered whether Mackenzie would break before she did. Sam was looking right at him, and although her face was obscured by an oxygen mask, Kate saw the relief in her eyes just before she smiled.

"Hi, sweetheart." Mackenzie took the hand that she had lifted weakly to wave at him and enveloped it in his own. "Samantha Lucas, I can't leave you alone for a minute, can I?"

Her hand twitched as if she was trying to return the pressure of his, but her eyes closed involuntarily and her fingers fell slack.

"We need to get her out of here, now," Kate said firmly. She had given Mackenzie time to compose himself, but Sam couldn't afford to wait any longer.

Mackenzie nodded, still staring at Sam. "Paramedics are on their way in. They brought extra kit and a stretcher. They should only be a minute." He gave Sam a last look and ran to the door to check on their progress. Kate heard him shouting urgently and she bowed her head again. Her hands burned with cramp, but she ignored the pain, telling herself help was on the way and that she wouldn't have to do this alone for much longer.

It had only been minutes since the first men had stepped across the threshold, but the barn was full of activity as Scene of Crime officers snapped photographs and began to bag evidence. Steve still lay where he had fallen, but Kate heard Eric protest and struggle briefly as he was led away. There were two officers shielding her from the commotion, maintaining a respectful distance whilst providing her with much needed light as they shone their torches toward Sam, careful to avoid dazzling them after so long in the darkness. They offered more assistance, but Kate shook her head, not willing to relinquish her position in order to start delegating to others.

She watched as blood blossomed on the new dressing around Sam's thigh, a small red flower that spread insidiously to take over the expanse of white, and she pushed her fist harder into Sam's groin, desperately trying to reduce the blood loss and give Sam time to reach the hospital. Sam moaned, shifting uneasily at the increased discomfort, and Kate set her jaw, unable to relent.

A clatter at the door announced the arrival of the paramedics. Kate was relieved to see faces she recognised, their expressions tense as they made their way across the room.

"Hey, Kate." Danny knelt beside her and began unzipping his bags. "You look like hell." He never had been one to stand on ceremony, but he touched her arm gently.

"Thanks, Danny. That was just what I needed to hear."

Kate felt a tiny part of herself relax a fraction as Danny immediately changed the oxygen cylinder for a fresh one and his partner Rachel began to set up a scoop stretcher. Mackenzie assisted, his bandaged hands fumbling as he followed her instructions to the letter.

"Dr. Delaney was all for coming himself, but he was needed at the hospital. He sent you a present instead," Rachel said, pushing a polystyrene box over to Kate. "Here, let me take over there for you."

Kate nodded, unable to speak as she stared at the box of typed and cross-matched blood. It seemed like several lifetimes ago that she had sent Sam's blood samples across the field with Mackenzie, a decision that had been more of an afterthought. She shook her head as she realised that her afterthought might just have given Sam the time she needed. She felt soft hands on hers as Rachel eased her from her position.

"You set the blood up, Kate," Rachel said quietly, taking over where Kate had left off. "Who do we have here?"

"Sam," Kate choked out, brushing away tears with her fingertips. She was fighting for self-control, and she reached for the blood box, trying to focus on clinical facts. "Her name's Sam. She has a through-and-through bullet wound to her right thigh. I think it clipped an artery. She's hypothermic, which was helping to control the bleeding, but then Steve, he moved her and she's haemorrhaging again." Kate was finding it hard to multitask, so she sacrificed her handover to concentrate on attaching a giving set to a unit of blood. "I need a flush, Danny."

Danny nodded and unhooked the stethoscope from his ears. "Approximately sixty-six systolic and tachycardic at around one forty." He unwrapped the blood pressure cuff from Sam's arm and drew saline into a small syringe. "It might be worth getting a unit into her before we move. Mountain Rescue are here to help with the stretcher, but we have a twenty-minute hike to the ambulance."

Kate connected the transfusion to the line in Sam's arm, setting the flow to a fast rate and handing the bag to one of the obliging police officers. She wanted to leave, to get Sam out, run across the fields and not pause for breath until they were at the hospital. She also knew Danny was right.

"We could try direct pressure on her leg. I don't think there's an underlying fracture." She hesitated. "There can't be, or she'd be…" She trailed off, unable to complete the thought, and Danny nodded in understanding, wrapping his gloved hands around the patch of blood on Sam's thigh and squeezing hard.

Sam reacted immediately to this fresh insult. With a weak cry, she tried to inch away, her good hand grasping at her thigh trying to dislodge whatever it was that was hurting so much.

"Shit, sorry!" Danny said, mortified. "I thought she was out for the count."

"Not likely. Sam, easy, it's okay." Kate took hold of Sam's flailing hand and cradled it in hers. It was enough to calm Sam's frantic efforts, and she turned her head to the side to reassure herself Kate was still there.

Kate met Sam's eyes with a smile, her voice soft. "You're just too bloody stubborn to pass out, aren't you?"

Sam managed a nod. She looked frightened by the light, noise, and unfamiliar faces that surrounded her.

Sensing her disorientation, Kate squeezed her hand. "The guys in green getting up close and personal with your leg are paramedics. The rest of the rabble is your lot. You're safe, and we're going to be moving you as soon as you're stable."

Sam mouthed "okay" behind the mask, her eyes drooping again, and Kate rested a hand against her cheek.

"If we ask them nicely, I'm sure they'll put the sirens on for us…"

❖

"I think we might be winning here, Kate." Danny carefully released his grip on the bandage and nodded to Rachel to ease the indirect pressure she had been maintaining. Kate stared at the bloodstain on the dressing, willing it not to spread. Thirty seconds ticked past, then a full minute, and there was only the tiniest change in the pattern.

"That's good enough for me," she declared, the dreadful fear that had been pressing on her ribcage and making it hard for her to breathe abating slightly. She glanced at the blood bag, now three-quarters empty. "Check her BP, Danny. Mac, can you tell the Mountain Rescue team we're about ready?" She turned her attention back to Sam. "Sam?"

"Mmhm?"

"Sam, we're going to get ready to move. I need you to lie still and let us do everything for you, okay?"

Sam raised an eyebrow, implying her options for dissent were at best rather limited.

Kate chuckled. "Yeah, I know, stupid thing to say. We have quite a hike out of here. It's going to be uncomfortable, but we'll do the best we can." She swallowed hard. "Trust me?"

Sam nodded immediately, reached up, and pulled her oxygen mask away. "You staying with me?"

"Of course I am. I might have to get a piggyback from Mackenzie to keep up with the pace, but I'm not going anywhere, Sam."

"Mmm. He'd probably drop you, y'know." Sam sighed. She sounded frustrated by the amount of trouble she was causing. "Thanks, Kate."

"Shh, you just rest now." Kate put the mask back in place and gestured to the four Mountain Rescue men hovering at a diplomatic distance who started unravelling a cocoon sleeping bag they'd brought with them to protect Sam from the worst of the elements. Kate hung a fresh unit of blood and looked to Danny for his verdict on Sam's blood pressure.

"Seventy-six over forty-two, tachy's down to around one thirty."

"Fabulous, thank you." Kate dropped her head to her chest and just breathed for a couple of seconds. "Right, um, can we get this bag under her if we roll her onto her good leg? Sam, grit your teeth, honey. Ready? On three."

There were more than enough willing volunteers, and they handled Sam as if she were precious, all of them aware of what she had already been through and how precarious her condition was. Kate supervised the threading of IV lines from the depths of the cocoon's fastenings and ruffled Sam's hair as she pulled the hood snug around her face.

"That all right for you?"

Sam gave her a contented smile as Rachel and Mackenzie clipped the scoop stretcher together and began to fasten its straps into place.

"Come here, Kate." Danny was pulling dressings and swabs from his bag.

"No, no, Danny. Really, I'm fine."

Danny moved to her side and took her upper arm firmly. "They can strap a scoop up, Kate. Let me look at your cheek. It's a mess."

"It's okay," she mumbled, eyes cast to the floor to hide the blatant lie.

"Of course it is. You know it's still bleeding, don't you?"

Kate touched a hand to her cheek and was surprised when it came away warm and wet. "Shit."

"Yeah, shit. Come on. It'll only take me a minute." He guided her to sit beside him and she complied, resistance drained away by his gentle perseverance. He peeled the soaked dressing loose and scowled at the injury it revealed. "Did he hit you twice?"

"Yes," she whispered. "He used his gun." She didn't want to think about it. Not the sound of the flesh splitting, not the pain or the terror or the weakness she had felt. She didn't want to think about Steve or how long it had taken for him to collapse after she had pounded the metal cylinder against his skull.

Danny probed her cheek with careful fingers. "I think you have a fracture here."

"Probably."

"You'll need stitches."

"I know."

"This'll do till you get to the hospital." He smoothed a clean dressing into place. "You want any painkillers?"

"I had a gram of paracetamol." Kate had no idea how long ago that had been, but Danny didn't push the issue.

"You're all set, Doctor." He turned to pack his kit away, and she touched his arm briefly.

"Thanks, Danny."

"Any time. Now what do you say we get the hell out of here?"

❖

"Here, swap this for the Kevlar."

Kate gratefully accepted the thick waterproof jacket Mackenzie was offering and rearranged her many layers of clothing, rotating her neck and shoulders as they were released from the weight of the protective vest. The new jacket was huge, dropping to her knees, but it was warm and dry and felt wonderful. She pulled the hood up, and then knelt beside Sam, who, at least to the untrained eye, looked like she was sleeping peacefully.

"Sam?" Kate touched her hand to Sam's forehead. The skin was marble-cold beneath her fingers. Sam opened her eyes slowly and seemed to take a long time to realise that it was Kate bundled up in the unfamiliar coat. When she did, her smile reached her eyes.

"You ready to leave all this luxury behind then?"

She surprised a laugh out of Sam, who played the game, shrugging as if to say "only if we really have to."

Kate grinned. "You just want to see me fall on my backside in the snow." She let her hand linger on Sam's cheek a moment, and then looked up to the rescue party.

"Right then, on three…"

❖

Kate felt a steadying hand on her arm as she stumbled over something unseen in the snow. She had lost count of the number of times Mackenzie had stopped her falling flat on her face, as—unable to help carry Sam with his hands stitched and bandaged—he had adopted the unofficial task of keeping Kate on her feet.

A few metres ahead of them, the team with the stretcher paused to negotiate a stone wall. Kate took the opportunity to push herself and catch up to them. Without needing to be asked, the team, as they had several times before, lowered their burden slightly, and Kate brushed snow from Sam's face and rested two fingers on the side of her neck to count her pulse. Sam shifted at the cold touch but kept her eyes closed. Kate murmured reassurance before standing aside to allow the team to continue.

The sky was grey, undercut with that strange glow that always accompanied snowfall, and it was glaringly bright to Kate's gloom-accustomed eyes. The discomfort at having to squint was more than offset by the crispness of the air and the austere beauty of the hills. Kate had always loved the snow; it brought out the child in her, making her yearn to do stupid juvenile things like pelting colleagues with snowballs and sledging down Kinder Scout's immaculate ridges. Now, with it soaking into her boots and her trousers, freezing her toes into senseless blocks and sapping what little energy she had left, she cursed the stuff under her breath and offered up wild promises in exchange for a sudden and complete thaw.

It never happened. Swapping amongst themselves to allow for rest, the stretcher bearers made good progress, keeping up a punishing pace for Kate to try to maintain. Mackenzie hovered close by, poised to deal with the collapse Kate was fighting tooth and nail to avoid. Her breath rasped harshly, aided by a heart pounding too quickly to count, and her legs trembled with the effort of keeping her upright. But she didn't fall, and it was only when she glanced up to see the blue strobes of an ambulance sparking off the snow that she realised Danny and Rachel had gone on ahead, that they had fired up the vehicle's engine, and that they were now less than twenty metres away, waiting for them.

❖

The last of the Mountain Rescue team to leave the ambulance had closed the doors behind them. Kate stood wavering in the sudden quiet as her legs threatened to give way beneath her. She knew she needed to be doing something but was unable to move or to do anything at that point other than concentrate on remaining vertical.

Danny and Rachel unclipped the ends of the scoop and carefully pulled its two halves out from underneath Sam, leaving her lying on the ambulance stretcher's thin mattress, the sleeping bag still snug around her. Holding the scoop, Rachel eased herself past Kate and secured it in its place by the back door. She seemed to be moving in slow motion; Kate blinked furiously, wiped her face with snow-soaked gloves, and wondered what the hell was happening to her.

The back doors slammed again, there was a pause, then the engine revved, and the ambulance slowly pulled away. There were hands on her arms and she flinched at the contact, but it was only Danny, talking to her softly and guiding her to sit in a seat behind the head of the stretcher. She sat down numbly, staring at Sam's face: grey and blue with cold, framed by dirty, sodden streaks of blond hair, a livid bruise on her cheek.

"I never noticed this one in there," she muttered, reaching out to touch the contusion. "It was so dark."

Danny nodded, unfurling a blanket and wrapping it around Kate's shoulders.

She shivered involuntarily. "We need to keep the heater off. She needs warming gradually." Clarity was returning to her slowly as she watched Danny reconnect oxygen, hang the IV and blood bags, and pull the leads from the ECG monitor.

"It's off, Kate." He held the leads out to her, an unspoken question in his eyes.

She took them gratefully and managed to stand up in the lurching vehicle without falling straight back down. "Thanks."

"No problem. I'll do a BP and a blood sugar, and then we can really get moving."

Kate unzipped the side of the sleeping bag and opened it enough to allow her access to Sam's torso. "Sam?"

There was a mumble of recognition, but Sam's eyes didn't open.

"Sam, I need to put these stickers on your chest. They'll feel a little cold at first." Kate shook her head with a smile. "Yes, I know that was a stupid thing to say." She unbuttoned the top of Sam's shirt and slipped her hand toward Sam's left clavicle. Once that lead was placed, she repeated the action on the right. "I'm going to untuck your shirt. Just bear with me." Two more stickers just below Sam's rib cage, and Kate felt a shudder beneath her hands as the chilled gel hit flesh that had barely managed to get warm. It was strangely intimate and she smoothed the shirt back into place as a surge of emotion made her dizzy. Tears blinded her as Sam's heart rate sang out fast and shrill on the monitor.

"Eighty-two over forty-six and three point seven," Danny announced, then leaned into the front of the cab and told Rachel she could put her foot down.

"You're doing okay, Sam." Kate zipped the bag up again and wished she could hold her hand, needing the contact that had become such a natural comfort. Multiple sirens wailed, and Kate realised that the police had provided them with an escort.

"We're almost there. Don't you dare give up on me now."

❖

The ambulance had barely stopped when the back doors flew open, freezing air rushing in just before the onslaught of voices.

"Get the suspension down, then you can drop the ramp."

"No, it's the other button."

"Shit, sorry. Got it."

Then Tom's voice, clear and controlled above the mêlée. "Leave Rachel and Danny to get the stretcher out. Everyone else make some space, thank you."

Kate had her back to the door, pulling leads out of the monitor. When Tom spoke, she looked around, and she saw how hard he fought to keep his face neutral. She swayed unsteadily when she straightened. He took a step toward her as if afraid she was going to faint, but she took a deep breath and instead surprised the hell out of him by smiling.

"Hey, Tom."

He helped her unhook the bags of fluid with a wry shake of his head.

"Hey yourself." He took her arm gently, and she allowed herself to lean on him as she walked down the ambulance ramp into the snow. Her eyes were fixed on the stretcher, which the paramedics were guiding out and steering quickly toward the hospital entrance.

"She needs theatre."

"There's one on standby. Quick assessment in resus, then we're all set and ready to go. How're her vitals?"

"They're…Her BP is…"

The rush of heat in the hospital made Kate's head swim. She bit down hard on her swollen lip, the sharp pain clearing her vision and allowing her to regain her focus. She heard Sam cry out softly as the stretcher came to a halt in the resus bay, and she hurried to her side, everyone else forgotten in an instant.

"Sam?" She placed her hand on Sam's cheek.

Sam turned to look at her, and Kate saw her relief at finding a recognisable face amongst the chaos.

"You're at the hospital, Sam. We're going to move you across to a bed, and we need to get you undressed and take some X-rays. Then you're going to go to sleep while we fix your leg, and I'm going to be with you when you wake up. Is that okay?" Simple facts, because she knew Sam wasn't well enough to process anything more complicated.

Sam mumbled an affirmative sounding reply and managed not to make a sound as she was moved onto the hospital bed. She could hear Kate reeling off a succession of figures, drugs given, injuries sustained, and she raised an eyebrow because in all the fuss about her leg she had forgotten that she'd fractured her wrist. Someone was cutting her shirt and trousers off, and she whimpered as they inadvertently pulled at the fabric that had been sucked deeply into her bullet wound. She heard a quick apology and felt them adjust their course, cutting widely around the area.

The pain subsided to a manageable level. A gown and warm blankets replaced her uniform, there was a soft pillow beneath her head, and she felt herself drifting, fuzzily aware of being poked and prodded, but not able to rouse herself enough to care. Time passed, but she couldn't gauge it accurately.

Suddenly the bed was moving. White tiles passed rapidly overhead, before the bed came to a halt in a smaller room redolent with the sickly smell of gas. The terror returned as she remembered Kate telling her she would go to sleep while they fixed her. She didn't want to go to sleep. She had fought for so long to stay awake. Kate had woken her so many times, and each time it had been harder to force her eyes open. She didn't know if she had the strength to do it again.

"No, I don't...Kate?"

Kate was there immediately. Her hand, when she took hold of Sam's, was warmer than it had ever been, and Sam clung on to it. It seemed difficult to draw in enough breath to speak.

"Kate, don't let me fall asleep. I want to be awake."

"Oh, honey, it's not like that this time," Kate said quickly, but she looked sick with fear, and Sam suddenly understood that there was a real chance she might not even survive the anaesthetic, let alone wake up after it. The words seemed to be sticking in Kate's throat, but she managed to continue. "You need an operation to stop your bleeding. When you wake up, you'll be warm and safe and I will be there waiting for you. I promise."

Sam blinked against the stark light of the anaesthetist's room. She knew that, despite Kate's assurances, Kate was as terrified as she was, but they had both been so scared for so long it was becoming second nature for them to bluff their way through.

"You need to get some rest, Kate," Sam muttered by way of changing the subject. She surprised a strangled half-laugh, half-sob from Kate.

The voice of another doctor made Sam jump slightly. Dr. Tom Delaney, the man who had taken control in the ambulance bay, placed his hands on Kate's shoulders as he spoke to Sam. "Don't worry, Officer Lucas, we'll take good care of you both." He passed a syringe full of milky liquid to a man standing behind Sam's head. "We need to send you off to sleep now. Is that okay?"

Sam nodded, her eyes fixed on Kate's, as Tom explained something about a burning in her arm, but she wasn't really listening. She just watched Kate smile reassuringly and forgot to be frightened as she let the drugs take her under.

Chapter Eight

S hit." The anaesthetist had thirty years of experience and was a man of few words, none of them usually expletives. "Shit." Kate watched the figures on the monitors in horror. Sam's blood pressure was plummeting rapidly in response to the anaesthetic, as her heart rate raced in an effort to compensate. Then, just as suddenly, her heart rate began to decrease. The numbers fell gradually at first, followed by a precipitous decline into a profound bradycardia. Kate knew it even before Tom announced it.

"She's going to arrest. Get the pads on her."

Kate was already moving, pulling Sam's gown down her chest and slapping two defibrillator pads into place as the anaesthetist demanded a succession of drugs and then readjusted their levels, fighting to achieve a tenuous balance between keeping Sam unconscious and keeping her alive.

"That's better. Good girl."

Kate felt the trembling begin at her knees and heard herself gulping great gasps of air as spots swam in her vision.

"Kate?" Then sharper. "Kate?" There were hands on her arms, taking some of her weight and trying to move her toward a small stool at the side of the room. "Kate, let go. Come on, before you faint all over your patient."

It was only then, as she stared at the now-stable vital signs dancing across the monitor, that she realised she had Sam's hand in a death grip.

"Head between your knees. Slow, regular breaths." Somehow, Tom had got her onto the stool.

"I'm fine, Tom."

"You will be. Just have a minute. You're paler than she is."

Kate smiled wanly and ran her hand across her face, managing to wipe away the cold sweat without anyone offering further comment. She watched as the anaesthetist hyperventilated Sam with the bag and mask and then intubated her without difficulty. Having ensured the placement of the tube was correct, he tied it in place and connected the ventilator, altering the machine's settings slightly as he muttered encouragement to Sam.

Everyone had settled into a relaxed routine, working with quiet efficiency to finalise preparations for theatre. Kate, her head much clearer, took a minute longer to watch the steady rise and fall of Sam's chest, grateful that someone had taken the time to pull her gown back into place so she was no longer exposed.

"Okay, central and arterial lines. Laura, can you do a catheter? Kate?" Tom held a central line kit out to her.

She smiled, grateful to be able to do something constructive. After so many hours of struggling on her own, she was surprised at how difficult it was to hand Sam over to someone else's care.

"Simon's seen the X-rays. He'll be scrubbing in as soon as Kingston has been moved to the high dependency bed."

Kate nodded as she threaded a guide wire through the needle in the side of Sam's neck. "Are he and Emma okay?"

"Emma's absolutely fine. She's been spending a lot of time wondering what to wear for her first press interview. Kingston's awake and stable. Simon's very pleased with himself and, oh, speak of the devil…"

The doors swung open as Kate secured her line in place. She glanced up to see a brief look of horror flit across Simon's face before he hid it behind a smile and enveloped her in a huge bear hug.

"Oof. Good to see you too, Simon." Kate winced slightly as he pressed against her sore ribs. He released her with a quick kiss to the top of her head, switching smoothly into surgeon mode.

"We almost set? Good. I'll get scrubbed and meet you in there."

Without being told, Kate settled back on the stool. For the moment at least, Sam's treatment was out of her hands.

"Kate?" Tom lifted her chin gently.

"Mmhm?"

"You go with Laura now and get cleaned up."

She shook her head. It hurt. "No, I want to be in there…" Her voice trailed off because she knew she was being foolish.

"You go with Laura. There's nothing you can do in theatre besides make me worry that you'll pass out and fall off your perch. Get something to eat and then get your head down for a few hours. I promise you can have her back as soon as she's in the ITU."

Kate laughed softly. "Thanks, Tom."

"Hey, I didn't spend the last goodness knows how many hours wading back and forth through snowdrifts or stuck freezing in a barn. She's definitely your patient, and I will let you know how she's doing, so long as you promise to let us look after you for a while."

"Okay. I promise." Kate stood as Simon propped open the theatre doors. She let her hand rest on Sam's forehead. "Take good care of her."

"Of course they will. Come on." Laura took Kate's hand in hers as Sam was wheeled slowly into theatre. The theatre doors shut, and Kate, too tired to pretend anymore, sank to her knees and sobbed.

❖

"Come on, darling. Blow your nose. You look like my four-year-old after I've told him to eat his peas."

Laura handed Kate a paper towel. She managed a shaky smile and wiped her face clean.

"Sorry," she said, not quite ready to make eye contact.

"There's nothing to be sorry about. What you've just been through…" Laura shook her head, her voice quiet. "Kate, I can't even imagine what it must have been like, but you're both safe now and you have to let someone take care of you for a while, okay?"

Kate nodded. She didn't feel strong enough to argue.

"Think you can stand?" Laura got to her feet and held her hand out.

"Oh God, I hope so. There's no way in hell I'm going in a wheelchair."

Laughing, Laura managed to half-drag, half-wrestle Kate up from the floor. "Just wait till you've got your sea legs," she said as Kate sagged against her, breathing heavily.

"I'm fine. Just a bit dizzy."

"Okay then, shall we go while the going is good?" Laura linked arms with Kate, managing to take some of her weight without making it obvious, and together they made their way slowly to an examination cubicle.

"I don't mind if you bleed on me, Kate, but you vomit on me and I'll never forgive you." Laura pushed the cubicle's curtain aside, grinning when Kate chuckled. "Right, no arguments, now. Get those clothes off before they stand up and walk off by themselves. There's a set of scrubs here, and then you are getting on the bed."

Kate opened her mouth, a protest starting to form on her lips, but she was silenced by Laura waggling her finger like a stern schoolmistress.

"Ah, ah, don't—"

"But I just—"

"I don't want to hear it, Kate. You will be examined, X-rayed, stitched, bandaged, rewarmed, fed, and watered. Then you will sleep. No ifs, ands, or buts."

Kate nodded and sheepishly looked Laura in the eye. "I know. But I don't think I can bend down to take my boots off without throwing up."

"Oh." Laura's cheeks reddened. "Well, why the bloody hell didn't you just say so?"

❖

"Sorry, Kate, just a minute longer." Laura winced in sympathy as she ran a swab across the lacerations on Kate's cheek, where an X-ray had shown a hairline fracture to her cheekbone. Kate had gratefully swallowed the painkillers suggested by the locum doctor before Laura had started the task of cleaning the wounds ready for suturing.

"I hate local anaesthetic," Kate muttered, her knuckles white from clutching the blanket across her lap.

"Yeah, but I recommend it for these. Shit. Grit your teeth. There's a bit of dirt in here."

"I don't think they can get any more gritted," Kate said, trying anyway. "You know, I'd say that to Sam, 'grit your teeth, honey,' and she'd not make a sound. She must have been hurting like hell and so scared, but she just put up with everything I had to do to her."

Laura discarded her final swab and pulled her gloves off, resting one hand over Kate's. "I'm sure you don't want platitudes, Kate, but they said everything was going okay, and if she's as tough as you reckon, well, I'm guessing she'll be giving you a run for your money before you know it."

Kate squeezed Laura's hand gratefully. It had been half an hour since their last update from theatre and she was fervently hoping that no news was good news.

"Okay, we're all done here. I'll see if I can track down the good doctor for you. How about a cup of tea and some toast? Your first blood pressure was crap and your sugars could be higher."

"Mmm, that'd be lovely, thanks." Kate rested her head against the pillow, the painkillers having helped the throbbing subside to a dull ache. Laura piled another blanket on top of her, and Kate let out a slow breath, the constant feeling of anxiety beginning to release its grip on her. The police had asked for a statement but were willing to wait. They were busy enough with Eric, who had been given a dose of Narcan on Kate's instruction and was under observation in a side ward. Her mother had been contacted and assured of her safety, while a villager had volunteered to feed her cat and Mackenzie had arranged for someone to feed Sam's. Meanwhile, Laura was making her tea and toast.

She closed her eyes and the sounds of the hospital faded. She instantly saw the interior of the barn. The smell of blood was everywhere but couldn't mask the putrid stench of the man she had killed. Sam's hand was limp and lifeless in hers and Kate couldn't move as Sam's eyes rolled and her breathing slowed. Kate could hear herself hyperventilating and she yelped as a voice broke sharply through the images.

"Kate!"

Her eyes flew open and she took in the familiar white walls of the hospital cubicle and Laura's worried face. "Sorry," she whispered, her mouth bone dry. "Shit." When she touched a hand to her face it came away damp with tears and sweat.

"You dozed off. Here."

Laura gave her a cool flannel and she wiped her face carefully.

"Too soon to talk about it?" Laura was pulling the bed's tray up. Tea and toast were arranged alongside a tetanus shot and a dose of antibiotics.

Kate nodded, cradling her mug in hands she couldn't quite seem to get warm. She took a sip and sighed, feeling her heart rate steadying to a normal level. "Oh, I never thought hospital tea could taste so good."

"You really think I'd give you hospital tea? I used my own stash, and that's real butter on your toast." Laura accepted the change of subject easily. "Latest word from theatre is that she's stable. They're packing her leg and leaving it open for forty-eight hours or so, to monitor infection, and she should be in recovery as soon as they've set her wrist."

"Thank you." There was nothing else Kate could manage to say.

"So drink and eat up. The doc is on his way to stitch you, and we can get you to ITU just as soon as you decide whether you want your tetanus in your arm or your bum."

Kate didn't deign to answer. She took a bite of toast and washed it down with tea, then held her arm out to Laura, who sniggered.

"Chicken."

❖

Sam's hand lay in Kate's. Her fingers didn't exert any pressure of their own or curl around to hold on to Kate's. Someone had tried to clean them, but the flecks of blood under her nails had proved too stubborn, a testament to how much effort she had made to stop herself from bleeding to death. Kate clasped her hand tightly, not caring about anything other than one fact: it was warm. Although Sam was still pale, the faintest glow of pink was sketched on both cheeks and her face was relaxed as she slept.

Tom was talking, telling Kate that Sam had done well, that there had been an arterial bleed, but once it had been located it had been easy to repair. He told her about debris along the bullet's track and inflammation and the strong likelihood of infection. They had packed the cavity and would need to operate again to further debride then close the wound. They were giving her antibiotics, painkillers, blood, and more fluids.

Kate nodded in where she hoped were the right places. She stared at Sam, who lay motionless beneath a tangle of tubing and wires. The light in the ITU was too bright. She had a sudden urge to dim it so it wouldn't startle Sam when she woke up. It was only when Tom touched her gently on her arm that Kate realised he had asked her opinion.

"Sorry, Tom. What?"

"The vent. I think we should keep her on the vent for another twenty-four hours. Give her time to rest and give the antibiotics a chance to start working. What do you think?"

Twenty-four hours. She stared blankly at him. It seemed like an awfully long time. She shook her head, but then checked herself, wondering when the hell her priorities and common sense as a doctor had been usurped by her need to see Sam wake up. Tom was doing exactly what he had promised, handing Sam back into her care, and she was finding that her abilities as a doctor were currently somewhat lacking.

She ran a hand through her hair with a sigh and nodded. "I think that would be best." She took a deep breath and choked down her pride. "Tom?" It was hard for her to look at him. "Could you? I don't…" She watched Sam's chest rise and fall in accordance with the breathy hiss of the ventilator. "Oh shit. Look, I'm knackered. I can barely think straight, let alone make clinical decisions." She was so tired, her voice was breaking. "I promised I'd be here when she woke up, but I don't think I'm safe to be taking care of her medically right now."

He nodded, seemingly relieved that she had conceded the point before he had needed to raise it. He pulled a reclining chair over to the bedside. "Sit down before you fall down."

Kate lowered herself gratefully and rested her head back.

"You should be tucked up in a bed too," he said. "Stay here with her. I'll get her through ITU, and because I know damn well you won't take any sick leave, you can get her through the rest. The other patients are out of bounds. Try to do anything besides getting yourself and Sam well again and…" He paused, trying to conjure up a suitable punishment. He threw his hands into the air as she raised an expectant eyebrow at him. "Oh, I don't know, but I'll think of something, and believe me when I tell you I can be very creative."

She laughed. "I know when I'm beaten. Thanks, Tom."

"No problem at all." He knelt and cupped her chin in his hand, tilting her cheek into the light to assess the swelling. "How's the pain?"

"Manageable."

"Still dizzy?"

"Mmm, only when I move too quickly."

"What was the score?"

"Eighteen." Eighteen individual sharp little knots of pain, one for each stitch. "And a hairline fracture."

He shook his head, his thumb brushing her good cheek before he dropped his hand. "You did a great job with Sam. You know that, don't you?"

"I was terrified," she whispered.

He gave a low laugh, one eyebrow arched in disbelief. "I think that was the normal response to the situation, Kate. You might have been terrified, but you got yourself and your patient out alive. So what do you say you have a rest and let us do a bit of the work. That sound okay?"

"Sounds lovely." Kate's eyes were already closing. She distantly felt Tom tuck a blanket around her as she let the soothing rhythm of the ventilator take her into sleep.

❖

The beeping was shrill and insistent, and it pulled Kate from an interminable dream of following spatters of blood through a field of snow, desperately trying to locate their source.

"Sorry, sorry." Tom's voice, and the beeping stopped.

Kate blinked, completely disorientated, as she wondered why the hell Tom was there to switch her alarm clock off. A few seconds of utter confusion cleared with a hammer blow of recollection, and she sat up, stifling a groan as the movement jarred her ribs and made her head spin.

"Is she okay? What time is it?"

Tom was correcting a setting on a medication pump—the source of the alarm. "It's four in the morning. You managed about five hours and only woke up once."

"I don't remember that," she mumbled. She was scanning Sam's monitors, assessing her vital signs.

"You screamed. I don't think you were really awake. You settled again pretty quickly."

"I've been having nightmares." She could only recall flashes, but the sickening fear was the one constant. "Every time I close my eyes, I'm back there." She sighed. "I suppose it'll get easier." Her tone drew a line under the subject.

He nodded. "Yes, it will."

Kate barely heard him. Her attention was focused on Sam. Kate hunched forward, closer to the bed rail, and absently splinted her torso with her hand when something there pulled uncomfortably.

"Sam's doing okay," Tom said. "We're getting her core temp up slowly, her pressure is good, urine output has picked up, and there's no sign of any further haemorrhage." He cleared his throat and Kate reluctantly raised her head. Tom never had been one for overlooking small details. "Did you hurt your side? It wasn't mentioned on your chart."

It wasn't mentioned on her chart because the only injuries she had told Laura about were the obvious ones on her face. She considered lying. She didn't want the fuss, she didn't want to be exposed and examined, but mostly, she didn't want her friends to know how bad it had been. Tom was watching her expectantly, and she realised he already had a damn good idea of what she and Sam had been through. He had seen her face when he'd opened the ambulance doors, he had read her chart, and only just coaxed her back to sleep after a nightmare.

"Let me see." His voice was quiet, but he wasn't giving her an option.

Without looking at him, Kate raised the hem of her scrubs top, found the start of a deep purple contusion, and lifted the fabric until the full extent of the bruising was revealed.

"He kicked you." It wasn't a question, but she nodded in confirmation anyway, studying the injury for the first time herself. A mess of blue and red flared out from an epicentre of deep purple, the shape clearly defining the arc at the front of Steve's boot.

"I don't think anything's broken." She hitched in a breath as she touched the area with a tentative hand. Nothing felt out of place beneath her probing. It was just stiff and very sore.

"Here, let me." Tom moved her hand and carefully assessed the wound himself. He was thorough and Kate winced as he flexed her ribs. "Sorry. I think you're right, no fractures, but you could do with an ice pack for the swelling."

An involuntary shudder ran through Kate and she shook her head vehemently. "No. No ice." She couldn't bear to think about being that cold again. She pulled her top down hurriedly. It was warm in the ITU, but her skin was suddenly covered in goose pimples.

Tom had the grace to look guilty. "No ice. Sorry, I wasn't thinking. I'll get you some ibuprofen, but you should have something to eat with them."

That really wasn't a problem. She was craving a hot meal. "The kitchen's shut, Tom."

"Yeah, I know. How does lasagne sound? Shirley Jones brought round enough to feed an army. It'll just need five minutes in the microwave."

It sounded fantastic and she smiled as her stomach rumbled.

"Right then, I'll take that as a yes. Don't go anywhere."

"Well, I don't have anywhere else to be right now."

❖

The doors swung closed behind Tom as he left the room. The nurse on duty was scribbling notes behind her desk. For the first time in hours, Kate was alone with Sam. She stood, closed the gap between them with a tentative step, and then bent low over Sam's forehead and kissed her softly.

"We made it, Sam."

She could feel tears trickling down her nose. Abashed, she wiped them from Sam's face. The ventilator hissed with its quiet cadence as lights blinked on IV pumps and monitors. The figures and numbers were gibberish to the untrained eye, but to Kate they were like a balm on her shredded nerves, consistently reassuring her that Sam's condition was stable.

"We're going to let you sleep a little while longer, honey," she said, her voice hushed by the prevailing sense of calm in the ITU. She brushed her hand across Sam's forehead, moving strands of blond hair still filthy with dirt and blood. "You're doing really well, but you need your rest, and knowing you, you're going to be an absolute bugger to try and keep in bed." She took a piece of gauze from the drawers at the bedside, ran warm water over it, and carefully began to clean Sam's face. Beneath the grime of dried tears and sweat, more bruises lay hidden, injuries that hadn't been mentioned in the dark and had been neglected in the rush to treat more urgent ones. They were superficial and wouldn't leave any scars, given time to heal. Kate swallowed hard, wondering how long it would take for both of them to claw their way back to some semblance of normality. She took a deep breath and decided there was no time like the present.

"Mackenzie found someone to feed Mitten. He misses you, but I think he's coping." She grinned. "And your cat is fine too…"

❖

"I was on the floor, on my hands and knees. I couldn't get my breath, and he leaned down right next to me and told me he was going to kill Sam instead."

Kate stared at the tape recorder as it slowly recorded her statement for posterity. It would be there for the detectives to rewind, analyse, and transcribe, and for the Crown Prosecution Service to listen to and make decisions about justifiable force, self-defence, manslaughter, or murder. She didn't have the energy to care. Right now, she just wanted it to be over, to tell the detective everything she knew so she could get back to the ITU and Sam.

"Can you remember his exact words?"

"Yes." She closed her eyes. She could remember his words, the tone of his voice, and the sourness of vomit on his breath. "He said, 'I guess I'll just kill your little friend then.'"

"Meaning Officer Lucas?"

"Yes."

"Can you tell me what happened next?"

"He stood up. He seemed slightly unsteady, but he righted himself and stood over Sam. She…" Kate smiled briefly and shook her head. "She kicked him."

"Officer Lucas kicked him?"

"Yes. With her good leg. Right in the bollocks. Sorry, testicles."

Unable to help himself, the detective grinned, a look of admiration flitting across his face before he composed himself and gestured to Kate to continue. She took a sip of water. "The pain made him yell out, but it didn't stop him, and Sam couldn't move away from him. He grabbed her by her arm and he started to drag her. I could see…" She sipped the water again, the tremor in her hand betraying her as she put the glass back on the desk.

"Do you want to take a break?"

"No! No, I'm okay. I want this done."

She told him how she could only watch as Sam, crying in pain and bleeding heavily again, desperately clawed at Steve's gun hand with her broken wrist.

"That was when I picked up the cylinder." Kate sucked in a breath. The air seemed to have gone from the room. "He hit her.

He hit her across the face and she went still. She was too exhausted to fight him anymore, and he was pulling her again. He wasn't watching me. I lifted the cylinder and I brought it down on his head." Her throat felt raw as if she had been screaming for days. "I didn't know what else to do. He was taking her to kill her and I just wanted him to stop. I didn't mean for him to die, but when he fell his skull cracked against the stone. I checked him, but he wasn't breathing, and he…he didn't have a pulse."

"Did you attempt to resuscitate?"

She closed her eyes, smelled blood and faeces and saw thick, wet clumps of tissue. "No. I was going to try, but his skull had fractured and there was brain matter on the floor."

The detective nodded, his pen scribbling furiously on his notepad. "So what did you do?"

"I left him and I went back to Sam. I knew I had a chance of helping *her*."

"She was bleeding?"

"Yes."

Sam's blood had been everywhere—soaking into Kate's trousers and hot on her freezing hands as she pushed them against Sam's leg. She told the detective as much as she could remember, ignoring the way her voice cracked as she detailed those last frantic efforts to keep Sam alive.

The detective, uncomfortable with the distress he was causing, wouldn't meet her eyes, focusing instead on taking his notes. The words rushed out of her now that the end of her testimony was within reach. She fought to keep her voice from faltering as the detective listened without comment and the tape recorder continued to rotate steadily.

❖

The detective, still looking stricken, had thanked Kate and offered her an arm to lean on as she stood shakily. He had tried to reassure her, but without Sam to corroborate her statement and with evidence still being gathered, his words sounded hollow. She declined his assistance, and although her head swam, she managed to leave the room without staggering. She shut the door behind her and leant on it, breathing heavily.

"Hey."

Kate hadn't noticed Laura sitting waiting outside the office, her work bag beside her and her coat on.

"Haven't you got a home to go to?" Kate's voice was soft, as if speaking for so many hours had robbed it of its strength. She sat beside Laura and rested her head against the wall.

"Ben's picking me up, but the roads are still bad. Tom told me where you were. I thought you might need a shoulder."

"Mmm." Kate nodded and gratefully accepted the arm Laura tucked around her, feeling her body betray her as she relaxed and started to tremble. "I killed him, Laura."

"I know, Kate. I know, but the way I see it, he didn't give you a choice."

"I keep feeling the metal hitting his head. Sometimes, I hit him differently, and he falls but not so badly. But most of the time, I feel the crunch and then there's the smell..." She trailed off but she couldn't suppress a shudder.

She knew his full name now: Steven Garrett. The detective had told her that the family had been known to the police for years; that Steve, together with his cousin Tony, had already served jail sentences for aggravated burglary. The police suspected that this robbery had initially been planned by Steve and his cousin, with Eric only intended to feature as a driver. When Tony had found himself in the hospital after breaking his jaw in a bar fight badly enough to require surgery, Steve had apparently gone ahead with the plan regardless. The cousin had vehemently denied any involvement. Eric was terrified and keeping quiet, and the police had nothing to go on but supposition. Tony, believing himself to be untouchable, had subsequently given several interviews in the press demanding that Kate be prosecuted for murder.

While the detective hadn't gone so far as to produce the articles, he had felt duty-bound to let Kate know what had been happening whilst she had been isolated within the confines of the hospital.

It was one more thing for her to worry about, and she felt herself begin to shake uncontrollably as the weight of everything began to bear down on her. Laura tightened her hold in response. Kate heard her take a breath to speak, hesitate, then start all over again as she floundered for the right words.

"It's a cliché, Kate, but it'll take time. You did what you had to do to keep yourself and Sam safe. You didn't make Garrett open fire in a jeweller's. You didn't make him take Sam as a hostage and threaten to leave her to bleed to death." Laura's voice was rising with anger. "You volunteered to go into a horrendous situation, something most people would never have had the balls to do." She turned slightly and looked at Kate directly. "He can't have been expecting the fight you two put up. He'd lost control and he probably would have killed you both without blinking."

Kate nodded slowly, her memory busy smashing through images of Steve: his fists and his gun, the snarl on his face, a boot pounding into her side. They were finally replaced by that first shock of seeing Sam left alone to die in the freezing dark with her hands bound behind her and her blood coating the floor. Kate sat up straighter. "I need to be with Sam."

Laura smiled. "Of course you do. Come on."

Taking the hand that was offered, Kate got to her feet and walked with Laura toward the ITU. "You ever think about a career in motivational speaking?"

Laura snorted. "What? And give up the vast fortune I'm making in nursing?"

Kate laughed at the incredulous look on her face.

Laura squeezed her hand. "You know, you should go back to laughing. It suits you." She kissed Kate on her uninjured cheek. "I'm going to see if my better half has fought his way manfully through the blizzard to take me home to bed. I will see you in the morning."

"Thanks, Laura."

"Any time. Go on then."

She gestured with her head in the direction of the ITU entrance. Kate didn't need further prompting. She pushed the door open and with a nod and a brief wave, hurried down the corridor.

❖

Through the small window at the side of Sam's bed, Kate could see the snow falling again, the flakes drifting down and accumulating steadily on the sill. As long as she watched, she could ignore how desperately nervous she was and concentrate instead on the silent storm beyond the glass.

"Okay, we're all set. You ready?"

She turned away from the window toward Tom, who smiled reassuringly; the anaesthetist, who was making final adjustments to the tools on his trolley; and Sam, who slept on, unaware of what was to come.

"She'll be fine, Kate. She's doing well, but if she can't manage we'll just put her under again."

Kate nodded and moved closer to Sam's side, taking hold of her hand. She didn't want her to wake up and be surrounded by strangers.

"Right, Tom, you can knock the propafol off."

The pump alarmed briefly as the drug keeping Sam asleep was disconnected. The anaesthetist ensured her airway was clear of secretions, using the suction with a steady hand, his confidence borne of his professional detachment.

Kate—unable even to try to distance herself from her patient—interlaced Sam's fingers with her own and willed her to move. She didn't have to wait long. After a brief twitch of Sam's arm, the monitor recorded a steady elevation in pulse rate as she became increasingly aware of her surroundings. It only took seconds for her to try to draw a breath, a different alarm sounding as the ventilator detected changes in pressure.

"Sam, I'm going to take the tube out of your throat now. Try and take a good, deep breath in for me." The anaesthetist's voice was pitched perfectly to cut through the drugs and confusion and fear, and Kate watched as Sam relaxed slightly and after one failed attempt, took the required breath.

The tube came out in a mess of saliva and blood, quickly suctioned clear as Sam gagged and coughed.

"Good, good. Deep breaths now." The anaesthetist held an oxygen mask tightly over Sam's face, his eyes flicking between Sam and her vital signs. He nodded briefly to Kate, a tacit acknowledgement that it would be her voice that Sam expected to hear, and she smiled gratefully, having been unwilling to intrude on his procedure.

Sam was struggling weakly, fighting against the suffocating sensation of the mask.

Kate rubbed the back of her hand. "Sam, it's okay. Just lie still. You're in the hospital and you're safe."

The effect was instantaneous. Sam stopped moving and tried instead to open her eyes. It was obviously an effort for her, but she forced them open and blinked against the dim light.

Kate was smiling at her. A proper smile, one that reached her eyes and made the tears in them shimmer and dance. Sam tried and failed miserably to speak; it was taking all her strength just to breathe. By means of compensation, she managed to return Kate's pressure on her hand, watching mesmerised as the smile grew even broader. She wanted so much to stay awake, and there were so many questions she wanted to ask, but instead she gasped as the pain in her thigh cut through the hangover from the anaesthetic and hit her with the force of a sledgehammer. She sobbed hoarsely against the rawness of her throat.

Kate's hand was on her forehead, stroking gently, and she was telling her to hang on for just another few seconds. Then there was a flush of warmth in her wrist and she fell back into the darkness.

CHAPTER NINE

It was easier the second time. Awareness returned gradually, without the sensation of slow suffocation, and the pain in her leg, although still there, had been tempered by strong narcotics. Moving was difficult; everything seemed to be fettered by a tube, a wire, a dressing, or a cast. The fingers of her unbroken wrist were wrapped snugly by a hand, and Sam decided that wriggling them was as good a place to start as any. There was an immediate reaction. The hand jerked in surprise, and Sam could hear the relief in Kate's voice when she spoke.

"Sam? Come on, stop playing possum. I just felt you move."

Sam opened her eyes and waited until the shapes and shadows coalesced into recognisable objects. Her head rolled drunkenly to the side and she saw Kate perched on the edge of a chair, watching her intently and smiling that smile again when she realised Sam was awake.

"Hi there."

Sam tried to reply, but her throat felt like she had been gargling with razor blades and the only sound that emerged was a groan.

"Sam, easy. You're going to be sore from the ventilator." Kate poured water into a cup. "Here you go. Just sip it slowly."

Most of the first mouthful ended up down Sam's chin, but her coordination improved after that, and the cool water tasted wonderful. She swallowed the last of it and licked her dry lips. "Are you…" It came out croaky and quiet, but at least it was recognisable as speech. With an effort, she pushed aside the discomfort and the languor that was already pulling her back to sleep. "Are you okay?"

Kate shook her head with a laugh. "I'm fine, you idiot. How're you feeling?"

"Mmm, sleepy."

"That'll be the drugs. You need to sleep. It's good for you."

Now it was Sam's turn to laugh. "You been to bed since we… since we got back?"

At least Kate had the grace to look sheepish. "Touché. Well, it's still snowing so I can't go home, and these chairs are surprisingly comfortable." She gently brushed her fingers across Sam's forehead. "Besides, I had a promise to keep."

Sam's eyes were closing. "Thank you," she mumbled. "Thank you for saving my life."

It was such a simple statement, but it knocked the breath out of Kate and she choked back a sob. Sam fumbled for Kate's hand, her grip unexpectedly strong.

"Don't cry. You know, you have a gorgeous smile."

The words were barely uttered before Sam was asleep, but Kate smiled, slightly flustered. She felt heat rise to her cheeks and an unfamiliar flutter made her heart rate skip and quicken. She sat back in the chair and shook her head in bemusement as she considered the last few days. She had no desire to go home. Her clothes were a random variety of ill-fitting surgical scrubs, and her appetite depended on whatever Tom had to tell her about Sam's latest blood test results. She rubbed a hand over her face, too tired to come up with any answers, and not sure she would know what to do with them if she did. Sam was deeply asleep, her breathing soft and regular, her fingers twitching occasionally, reacting to a dream. Kate watched her, sure of something: there was nowhere else she wanted to be.

❖

"Sam, leave it alone."

"I can't help it. It itches."

With a sigh, Kate moved the thin oxygen tubing back below Sam's nose. "It might itch, but you need it. The morphine makes your breathing too shallow. Course, we could always take that little button away from you if you'd prefer?"

Sam narrowed her eyes at Kate and attempted a scowl, but that made her nose itch and she sneezed instead. Kate stifled a laugh and found something intriguing to look at out the window. After the second surgery on her leg, Sam had been given a pump to control her own pain relief, and Kate was well aware that she wasn't using it enough. Nobody doped up on a decent dose of morphine would have been able to force a drinking straw beneath a plaster cast, but that was what Sam had been trying to do earlier when Kate had returned from the shower. Apparently, the plaster cast itched too.

"I'm being a pain in the arse, aren't I?"

Sam looked so remorseful, Kate didn't know whether to laugh or cry. Sam had only just regained consciousness fully when Simon had taken her back to theatre to remove any remaining dead tissue and then close the wound on her leg. Struggling out from under a second anaesthetic had taken its toll, and she had spent a day alternately vomiting and sleeping. She was awake for longer periods now and was gradually losing the various tethers and tubes of the ITU. The bruises on her face were tracking time at the same pace as Kate's, the deep purple gradually being replaced by a wider spread of blue and green.

Kate looked at Sam, whose eyes were still doleful, although there was now more than a hint of mischief in them. They had managed to wash Sam's hair for the first time that morning, and the simple act of removing the last vestiges of filth from the barn had made her laugh freer and her smile a little easier.

"I'm just glad you have the energy to be a pain in my arse."

"I have to say, it's taking a lot out of me." Sam sighed melo-dramatically.

"And yet it seems so effortless." Kate stopped midway through pouring a cup of juice. "Oh, speaking of effort, the physio is due tomorrow morning. We can't have you sitting around in bed forever." She kept her voice light, but when she thought of Sam not being around it felt like she had been punched in the guts.

Sam didn't seem to be thinking that far ahead. "If I can get out of bed, can I get rid of the catheter?"

Maudlin thoughts were banished instantly by the look of pure, expectant joy on Sam's face, and Kate laughed. "If you can get into a chair without splitting your stitches or using such innovative swear words that Tom has to look them up in the dictionary, then I don't see why not."

Sam grinned and gave a thumbs-up with her good hand. "Excellent."

❖

The letter had been sent recorded delivery, requiring a signature for receipt of its collection. It bore a return address that clearly identified its sender. Slush seeped into the thin fabric of Kate's shoes as she stood outside the post office and stared at the brown envelope in her hands. She hadn't really dressed appropriately for the weather, having only intended to go home to check on Lotty and pick up a few things to take back to the hospital. The *sorry we missed you* notification from the postman had been lying in the pile of junk mail on her mat. The envelope was small, the letter inside apparently no more than a page or two in length. Even though she had a very good idea of what the document would say, her stomach still turned over as she started to walk back to her Land Rover. The pedestrian crossing was on red and she waited at the side of the road. She flinched when the person beside her reached out to her.

"Oh hell, sorry, Doc." The hand was withdrawn immediately and Eddie Capper nodded instead, his arms now folded. "Just wanted to say I'm glad you're okay."

"Thanks, Cap." She didn't feel okay. Every noise on the High Street seemed far too loud, the sky was too bright and too big, and she longed to get back to the sanctuary of the hospital. The crossing turned to green, sounding a high-pitched beep, and Eddie hurried over the road with her.

"If you need anything…"

She nodded. "I'll know where to call."

His shop was in the opposite direction to the car park. She waved once to him, relieved to be on her own again. The Land Rover was still warm but she started the engine regardless and cranked the heater up as far as it would go. Condensation clouded the windows, concealing her from the few shoppers who were out taking advantage of a freshly ploughed main road. Her hand shook as she opened the envelope.

The letter comprised one neatly folded sheet of paper. In three short paragraphs, the representative from the Crown Prosecution Service detailed the events that had occurred in the barn. He wrote that the physical evidence and the preliminary statement of witness Samantha Lucas corroborated Kate's own version of events, and presented a clear-cut case of self-defence and justifiable force, with no grounds for a prosecution. He confirmed that they would be in touch should the case against Eric Garrett proceed to trial and concluded by providing the contact details for the victim support service.

Kate carefully folded the letter along its original creases and slid it back into its envelope. Using her sleeve, she cleared the mist from the windows. A fresh smattering of snow coated the car park and small flakes were melting the instant they landed on the heated windscreen. She manoeuvred the Land Rover carefully out of its parking space and turned left to head toward the hospital.

❖

Sam was stirring a spoon in a bowl of cold rice pudding when the door to her room opened. She waved the spoon enthusiastically at Kate, grey stodge flying off it to land with wet thuds on her table.

"Not hungry?" Kate set a large paper bag down on one of the chairs and came to stand by the bed.

"Not really." Sam pulled a disgusted face, but the quality of the food was only a small part of the problem. The amount of antibiotics and painkillers that were being pumped into her were effectively wiping out what little appetite she might have had. She pushed the table aside and watched Kate settle into a chair. The light above her bed was dim, but it didn't mask the troubled expression on Kate's face.

"What's wrong?"

Kate immediately shook her head. "Nothing. Well, aside from that rice pud, that's very wrong." She attempted a smile at her weak joke, but Sam wasn't at all convinced.

"You have a pretty good poker face, Kate, and I'm quite drugged, but you look terrible, if you don't mind me being blunt."

"I don't mind, but I'm fine, Sam. Really."

"You're not fine. Don't make me come over there." Sam made a move to throw off her sheets and Kate did smile then.

When Sam patted the small space beside her on the mattress, Kate sighed but obediently perched on the bed. After a moment she brought out a letter from her coat pocket and handed it over. Hindered by a plaster cast and an IV line, Sam struggled to pull out the letter. The official stamp on the envelope had already made what little she had eaten settle like cement in the pit of her stomach and she waited impatiently as Kate took the envelope back and straightened out the sheet of paper for her.

Its contents were succinct and politely worded. Sam skimmed it quickly and then reread it to make sure she was understanding it properly. The numbers on the monitor at her side switched from amber to red as relief made her pulse race.

"Kate, this is good news." She set the letter aside and rested her hand on Kate's leg.

"I know," Kate said quietly. "I just don't really feel like it's something to celebrate."

"No, I'm sure you don't."

It was never silent in Sam's room. An IV pump measured its dosage out in steady ticks and oxygen bubbled as it passed through a humidifier, but those background sounds became even more prominent as Sam waited for Kate to reply. Kate's fingers toyed with the edge of the envelope and she finally tucked it into her pocket.

"I feel like I've got away with it too easily." She looked and sounded sickened. The only colour left in her face was from the ugly lines of sutures and the bruising that surrounded them. "I killed a man and they've taken less than a page to tell me that what I did was okay."

"They're not telling you it's okay, Kate. They're telling you that you didn't break the law," Sam said reasonably. "The only people who can tell you it was okay are the ones who were there in that room."

"I can't." Kate's voice broke and tears dripped off the end of her nose to splatter softly onto the mattress.

Anger on Kate's behalf rose too abruptly in Sam for her to be able to damp it down. "I can," she countered quickly, and the vehemence in her voice shocked Kate into looking up. "I couldn't stop him, Kate. He was dragging me outside to execute me and I tried, I really fucking tried, but I just didn't have the strength left to fight him. I know you didn't mean to kill him. I know that because I know a little bit about you." She took hold of Kate's hand as if the contact alone would be enough to persuade Kate to see things from her perspective. "When you hit him, all I felt was relief."

"I'm a doctor," Kate whispered. "I'm not supposed to take a life."

"I would have died hours before that if you'd not been there," Sam said. "I *owe* you my life." For her, the balance was simple to appreciate. There was no way she would still be alive had Kate not set foot in the barn.

"You did most of the work yourself, Sam." Kate sounded less certain of herself now and Sam could see that she was seriously considering what she was being told.

"No, I'd already given up," Sam admitted, desperate for Kate to understand what it had been like, for her to understand exactly how crucial her intervention had been. "Everything I'd done had just made things worse. When he shot me and I was lying there, I could feel the blood pumping out and I remember thinking 'well, that's that' and I know I should've been scared, but mostly, I was just so tired."

Kate sniffled and swiped at her cheeks with the back of her hand, but her face no longer looked so ashen. "Don't remind me. You were a bugger to try to wake up."

"I remember that too. I could hear someone talking to me and she sounded pretty, so I thought I'd have a little peek." Sam winked at Kate and succeeded in surprising a laugh out of her.

"You're a daft sod."

"Maybe, but I decided if you'd risked your life to try to help me then the least I could do was put a bit of effort into sticking around." Sam wondered whether she had said enough, and whether any of it would help Kate eventually to come to terms with the guilt she was shouldering, guilt Sam knew was partly her own to bear. She was heartened to see Kate sit up a little straighter, the ghost of a smile playing on her lips.

"You did that for me, huh?"

"Yes," Sam answered honestly. "I did that for you." She was the first to look away, sure that every one of her secrets would come tumbling forth if Kate continued to smile at her like that.

The mattress creaked as Kate stood, and Sam heard the rustle of the paper bag.

"Thought you might appreciate this." Kate turned back to the bed and held out an egg custard from the village bakery.

Sam felt her mouth begin to water in anticipation. "How did you know those were my favourite?" A quirk of Kate's lips was all the response she needed. "Mac. Of course. He knows all my bad food habits," she said with a laugh.

"It's all yours if you answer me one thing."

"What?" It came out slightly squeakier than Sam had intended. She would do a lot for the sake of an egg custard, but she was harbouring a mass of thoughts and feelings she simply wasn't ready to bring out into the open just yet.

"What's my tell?"

"What's your what now?"

"My tell," Kate repeated with emphasis. "I'm crap at lying generally. You already know that, but you said I have a pretty good poker face and I have, with my patients, and yet you see straight through me. So," she fixed Sam with a look, "what's my tell?"

Sam held out her hand and beckoned Kate closer. She waited until Kate had sat back down on the bed and then touched her fingers to Kate's cheek.

"You get a tiny little crease right here." She grazed the skin with the tips of her fingers. "I noticed it in the barn when you told me I was doing fine even though I felt worse."

"Oh," Kate said softly. "Not a lot I can do about that then, is there?"

"Nope." Sam reluctantly lowered her hand.

"Can it be our secret?"

"Can I have my egg custard?" Kate placed the small pastry in Sam's hand and Sam grinned. "Your secret's safe with me," she said, and offered Kate the first bite.

❖

"Nearly done, Sam. Just another minute."

"I'm not having a very good day, am I?" She could feel beads of sweat breaking out on her forehead. She lay on her side, knuckles white from gripping the bed's side rail, while Kate changed the dressing on her leg. After sitting in a chair for the first time, she had endured an hour of physiotherapy, and this latest round of torture was to check whether the physio had opened any of her stitches.

"Oh, I don't know, you graduated to using a bed pan. Hmm…"

"Hmm, what? Jesus! Ow!"

Sam tried to twist around to see whether Kate really was pushing a rusty dagger into her wound. She couldn't move far enough, but she could see Kate's frown.

"Sorry, hon. This is a bit more inflamed than I'd like." Kate must have realised belatedly that she was being watched because she attempted a smile and then forced brightness into her voice. "We'll just start you on some stronger antibiotics. It'll be fine, Sam."

Before Sam could reply, the curtains around her bed opened a crack.

"Is she decent?" Mackenzie's eyes were screwed shut as he poked his head into the gap.

"No, my arse is hanging out. You have perfect timing." Sam pushed herself onto her back, and held her arms out. "Get over here, you big idiot."

Mackenzie winked at Kate before enveloping Sam in a hug that almost crushed the breath out of her. "Well, look who's back in the land of the living and not-drooling."

He kissed her on the cheek and pulled up a chair at her side.

"It's good to see you, Officer Lucas."

She smiled, almost shy when she thought of all the other times he had seen her recently. Kate had told her that in between trips home and helping with the investigation, Mackenzie had visited her numerous times. Sam had no recollection of any of those visits, largely because she had been drugged into a stupor for several days. "We got into a bit of a mess, didn't we?"

He laughed at the understatement of the century. "Yeah, well, we got out of it again. Oh, brought you a present." He fished in his pockets and pulled out three bags of Haribo sweets. "Jack picked them. They're his favourites. He's been making a scrapbook of all the news clippings."

"Oh, bloody hell." Isolated in the ITU, it had been easy for Sam to forget that the incident would have been a big news item, and the hospital staff, aided by the snow, had battled successfully to keep the media at bay.

"I'll leave you two in peace for a bit. Mac, you want a cuppa?"

"No, I'm fine, thanks."

Kate pulled the curtain shut behind her.

"So you wanna play 'who's got the biggest scar?'" Sam looked up at Mackenzie and grinned. "'Cause mine'll kick any of yours in the arse…"

❖

Ice cracked beneath Kate's boots as she stepped out of her Land Rover. She stood still and took a minute just to look at the hills and breathe deeply. Frosty air rushed into her lungs. She could smell the musk of silage from the fields surrounding her cottage and hear sheep bleating their disapproval of the freezing weather. It was all completely familiar and tranquil, and yet the flutter of nervousness would not relent.

Earlier that day, it had been Sam who insisted she go home for the afternoon. "Go, have a hot bath. Eat something that doesn't take five minutes to cook in the microwave. I'll still be here when you get back. It's not like I can run very far at the moment." But as Kate pushed the front door of her cottage open, she felt like a stranger in her own life.

The stillness of the hallway was broken almost immediately. The rapid approach of tiny footsteps heralded the arrival of Lotty, who herded Kate into the kitchen and then began to lick her empty dish expectantly. Kate regarded her with scepticism.

"Don't try and tell me you've not been fed, miss. I can see how round your tummy is from here."

When Kate opened the cat food cupboard, packets of treats scattered onto the tiles and the volume of Lotty's purring became even more impressive. Unable to say no to such enthusiasm, Kate dropped a generous handful of biscuits into the dish. Then she turned her attention to the pile of mail her neighbour had left on the kitchen table: glossy take-away menus, supermarket special offers, and entreaties guaranteeing lottery cash prizes. She dumped it all into her recycling bin, glad to find there was nothing urgent that she would actually have to deal with. The message counter on her answer phone seemed to have reached its limit of twenty. She ignored it and headed upstairs to run a bath instead, to which she added a generous amount of a bubble bath that rather optimistically promised her "total relaxation."

Having had nothing for over a week but tepid hospital showers, the hot water felt wonderful. Kate sank down into the bath, the bubbles frothing right up to her chin. The persistent aches and pains—in her back from sleeping in hospital chairs, and in her side where the bruising was still tender—gradually faded. She ducked her head beneath the water and tried to convince herself that this was a big step toward her life returning to normal: her cat welcoming her home from the hospital and a hot bath after a long shift. That had been her life for years, and she had always considered herself content, had always thought that that was enough for her. She realised now that it wasn't enough and that, although she had only been away from Sam for a matter of hours, she was already longing to go back to her. Kate knew something was changing, something fundamental in herself. It wasn't the post-traumatic response Tom had been warning her to expect, although that was there in the nightmares and the flashbacks and the way she jumped at sudden noises. This was something different, something deeper, and it didn't feel traumatic at all.

Pulling on her favourite old baggy sweater and then brewing tea in her usual mug made her feel slightly more at ease. She made a bacon sandwich, took it over to the sofa, and left space on her knee for Lotty to sit and help her eat. As Kate was licking the grease from her fingers, the phone rang for the fourth time.

"Hello?"

"*Finally*, darling. I've been calling for days now!" Kate's mother sounded upset and more than a little aggrieved. Kate had spoken to her since the rescue but possibly not as often as her mother would have liked.

"Sorry, Mum, it's been a bit crazy here. I've been at the hospital a lot."

"Oh my God, are you okay? You said you were okay."

It took Kate a fair amount of time to calm her mother down and as much again to persuade her that recuperating with her in London was not a good idea.

"Are you eating properly?"

Kate looked at the crusts and ketchup on her plate and shrugged, glad that her mother couldn't see her. "Yep, I'm eating fine."

"You always were too thin, Kate. If you lose any more weight, you'll look so wan on the television when you finally give a press conference."

There was a dull thud as Kate's head hit the back of the sofa. She closed her eyes in despair.

"Don't worry, the camera always adds a few pounds, Mum," she said, having learned from an early age that humouring her mother was far less stressful than contradicting her.

It seemed to work, and after a little subtle hinting on Kate's part, her mother only briefly returned to the idea of a nice, relaxing trip to London before leaving her in peace.

Kate picked up the bag she had packed and added a selection of books she thought Sam might enjoy. After a quick search, she found Lotty snoozing on her pillow and kissed the top of her head.

"I'll see you soon, little one."

The phone was ringing again, but when Kate answered it all she heard was the dial tone. Relieved not to have to delay any further, she dropped the handset back into its cradle and all but ran out the front door.

❖

The nurse at the desk shook her head sternly as Kate walked into the ITU.

"I thought you were taking a break, Doctor."

"I took a break. I had a bath and everything." Kate smiled when the nurse threw up her hands in surrender. "How's she doing?"

The nurse glanced down at the chart in front of her. "Her temp is up slightly. She's had some paracetamol, and Dr. Delaney is going to switch her to a different antibiotic." Kate nodded, but her attempt to appear impassive apparently failed. "Don't look so worried," the nurse continued. "She seems okay in herself. Mostly she's just bored, I think. I daresay she'll be better for seeing you."

Kate didn't really know how to reply to that and settled for thanking the nurse. When she knocked on Sam's door, she was greeted by a faint "come in unless you have needles."

"Hey!" Sam's eyes widened, surprise and then delight brightening her face as Kate stepped into the room. It took her a few seconds before she managed a scolding look that put the nurse to shame. "I thought I sent you home."

"You did. I went home. Then I came back. I really feel very rested," Kate said. By way of changing the subject, she lifted the books from her bag and set them on Sam's table. "Here, I didn't know what you'd like, so I brought a selection."

"Compared to this gift from Mrs. Mullineux, who escaped from Gynae and wandered in here an hour ago"—Sam hefted a large print bodice ripper aloft—"anything is going to be a classic."

She displayed the lurid cover for Kate to admire. "I actually read the first chapter. I suspect the hunky cowboy and the beautiful but vulnerable young widow will live happily ever after."

Laughing, Kate pulled her chair closer to the bed. "Such a cynic."

"Goes with the job," Sam conceded. "So how was your trip home? Aside from brief."

"Fine. I suspect several of my neighbours might be feeding Lotty. She gets any bigger and I'm going to have to widen her cat flap." Kate stared at the crisp white of the bed sheet. She could feel her smile slipping away. "Nothing had changed, Sam. It should have been great to be back; my own things, my own bed and bathroom, but it all felt…" She paused, struggling to find the right words. "I didn't want to be there. I was at home and I felt homesick." She looked up at Sam. "I missed you," she said simply.

"I missed you too." Sam's quiet reply came without hesitation.

Kate held Sam's gaze, wondering how someone she had known for little more than a week could feel like such a vital part of her life. The slightly confused expression on Sam's face suggested she was thinking along the same lines. They both looked away at the same time and Kate heard Sam exhale shakily.

"It's still snow—"

"What's the weather—Oh." Sam started to laugh and Kate relaxed back into her chair as the tension in the small room eased.

"Still snowy and bloody freezing," Kate said with a grin. She pulled four bars of chocolate out of her bag and held them up for Sam to choose from. "Wasn't sure if you were a Cadbury or a Galaxy girl, so I bought a few of each." She tore the wrapper from the one Sam indicated and handed it to her.

"Mainly I think I'm just a chocolate girl," Sam mumbled around a mouthful.

"Mmm, it has to be said I'm not terribly fussy either," Kate agreed.

"So how long have you lived here?" Sam shifted onto her side and held out a piece of her chocolate to swap with Kate. "The village looked lovely. Well, what little Mac and I managed to see of it."

"I've lived here all my life, pretty much. I left to go to university and then I spent a few years working my way around some of the larger city hospitals. I moved back to Birchenlow…" Kate paused as she tried to gauge the time correctly. "Five years ago. My mum's originally from London and she never really settled up here. She and David went back to live down south after my dad died. I stayed in the village and then bought my own cottage. My dad always said I had the hills in my blood. I can't imagine opening my curtains in the morning and not being able to look out onto them."

"You walk up there a lot?"

"Every chance I get," Kate said. The question stirred a memory in her and she wiped her hands on her jeans as she mentally debated whether she should mention it. "Back in the barn, you said you liked hiking," she ventured cautiously. Sam nodded, but she looked slightly lost, as if she were struggling to remember the conversation. "You had an ex who wasn't so keen," Kate prompted gently.

"Oh, yeah." Sam screwed her chocolate wrapper up and pushed it around her table with her finger. "Cally didn't much like getting her boots wet."

"Well." Kate took a breath, still uncertain of herself. "If you'd like, once you're back on your feet, I could show you some of the walks around here. There are some really good routes up on Kinder. I usually walk on my own, but it'd be great to have company." The words seemed to leave her in a rush, and Sam, having apparently sensed her apprehension, reached out to squeeze her hand.

"I would love that," Sam said and smiled broadly.

Kate forgot to feel awkward and smiled with her. It felt good to be making plans together, plans that would see them staying in touch even after Sam was discharged from the hospital.

"Have to warn you about the sheep up there, though. They've got a really mean streak." Kate managed to keep her voice completely serious. "Hard as nails, they are. They'll gang up on you and mug you for your butties as soon as look at you."

Sam tilted her head to one side, as if considering the warning. "We got held hostage in the middle of a snowstorm, Kate," she said slowly and then lowered her voice to a confidential whisper. "I think we can outwit a few sheep, no matter how well organised they are."

Kate stifled a giggle behind her hand. "I'll remind you of that when they've stolen your lunch and you're trying to get me to share mine."

Sam was laughing freely. Kate found herself struck by the blue-grey of Sam's eyes and the way the colours seemed to intensify when she smiled.

"Kate?"

Kate suddenly realised that Sam had been asking her something. "Yep." She cleared her throat. "What's up?"

"Nothing, I was just wondering if you could pass me some juice, but you seemed to have left the room there for a while."

"Sorry," Kate mumbled, hoping Sam wouldn't press her for details.

Sam, however, didn't seem willing to let her off the hook. "You were staring at me."

"Yeah, I was." Kate squirmed a little. "It was your eyes. They do something a bit strange when you laugh."

"Oh, the shifty colour thing." Sam nodded sagely. "My mum used to tell me it made me look devious."

"It does not!" Kate said, aghast. "It's really pretty."

"My mum's no longer on my Christmas card list, if that helps any."

Kate winced. "Sorry."

"She lives in Australia with her boyfriend, who…" Sam counted up on her fingers, "will probably be about twenty-five by now."

"Ouch."

"Better off without her, I think. She all but arranged an exorcism when I came out to her." Sam was obviously trying to keep her tone light, but there was hurt in her eyes.

Kate went to sit on the side of the bed. She leaned forward and tucked a loose strand of hair behind Sam's ear. "I am sorry, Sam."

"Yeah, me too sometimes." Sam sipped the juice that Kate held for her, their fingers overlapping on the glass.

"Can you stay for a while?" she asked as Kate set the glass down.

"Of course I can."

"You could help me choose something to read." Sam gestured at the stack of books on her table.

"Oh my." Kate picked one off the top of the pile but then swapped it for Mrs. Mullineux's romance novel. "I think we should start with this," she said as Sam shook her head in horror. "Aww, come on." Kate's shoulders shook as she laughed. "I really want to know if the cowboy and the widow get their happy ending."

❖

The cold air made the stitches in her cheek ache, but Kate knew it wouldn't last for long; the sub-zero temperatures would soon numb the pain into submission, and the peace and solitude of her vantage point was worth the temporary discomfort. For once, her nightmare hadn't disturbed Sam. She had woken, sweating and trembling, a scream on her lips, and tip-toed from Sam's bedside, to inevitably end up here: a tree stump in the corner of the hospital grounds where she could name constellations or watch the thin winter sun slowly wash the hills with light.

Tipping her head back, Kate traced the shape of Orion, and then twisted around until she spotted the twins, Castor and Pollux. There was reassurance in their familiarity, that they were always where she expected them to be. Despite the freezing temperature leaching the sensation from her fingers and toes, she felt herself relax slightly.

She was considering hot chocolate and toast when she heard the noise. It was completely incongruous in the silence, an insistent, shrill beeping, and initially she had no idea what could be causing it. Then she pressed a hand to her hip where her pager rested. For a second she was stunned, trying to work out why anyone would be paging her in the earliest hours of the morning, when her only patient was Sam, who was fast asleep less than fifty yards away.

Her only patient was Sam.

Kate pulled the pager from her belt and hammered on the button to silence the alarm. The display bore three letters: ITU. She didn't even realise she was running.

❖

Tom, covering the night shift, reached the ITU at the same time as Kate, his pager still gripped in his hand.

"What is it? What's wrong?" She felt sick with dread, terrified that she already knew what his answer would be.

"I'm not sure. They said she'd spiked a fever and she was vomiting."

"Shit. I thought we'd got the antibiotics into her in time."

"Yeah, so did I."

He held the door open for her, heading off to speak to the nurse while Kate hurried to Sam's bedside. She attempted to hide her concern behind a smile, but she faltered as she saw Sam's flushed face and heard her heart rate sing out far too rapidly from a hastily-reattached monitor.

"Hey," Kate said softly.

Sam was sitting bolt upright against her pillows, clutching a grey cardboard bowl. She looked thoroughly pissed off. "Sorry about this," she muttered, before the colour drained from her face and she dry-heaved into the bowl. "Oh, God, sorry."

"Stop apologising. C'mere." Kate cupped Sam's chin in her hand and wiped a cool washcloth over a face that burned beneath her touch.

Sam gasped as Kate's still-freezing hands made contact with her skin, and then she pushed against them until Kate got the message and rested one hand on her forehead.

"Nice?"

"Perfect." She sipped from the glass Kate held to her lips, rinsed her mouth, and spat the liquid into the bowl without needing to be told. They were both well-practised in this routine by now.

"My leg really hurts." She spoke so quietly Kate had to strain to hear her, acutely aware how much the admission had cost.

"I know, honey. We're going to have a look at it, and we'll need to restart an IV so we can manage the infection."

Sam nodded and held her arms out obediently.

Tom pushed a trolley stacked with equipment and drugs across to her bedside. "You're certainly keeping us on our toes, Sam," he said. His brow creased in a frown as he took hold of her right wrist and turned it over. "Christ, we've made a mess of you, haven't we?" Kate bit her lip at his comment. Sam's arms were mottled with bruises where previous IV lines had been sited and re-sited. Sam tried to smile, but it turned into a groan as she reached for the bowl again.

"We're going to give you something for that, Sam," Tom said, then in an undertone. "Kate, I've got this."

Kate nodded gratefully. She moved to the opposite side of the bed and wrapped her arms around Sam, who sank into them and shivered miserably.

"Sharp scratch here."

Sam didn't flinch as the needle pierced her forearm and dug deeply to locate the vein; she just shuddered and tried to push deeper into Kate's arms, her breath coming in quick gasps.

"All over, Sam. You're doing really well." Tom was taping the line in place, conferring with the nurse, who drew drugs into syringes methodically and handed them over in the order he requested.

"Her BP's dropped." Kate was watching the monitors with a terrible sense of déjà vu.

"Hang a litre of saline. Keep an eye on her fluid balance." The nurse was nodding and making notes on a chart. "Quarter-hourly obs and see if we can pinch a fan from paeds." He took Sam's hand and gave it a squeeze. "Sam, your temperature's through the roof, but I think you figured that one out for yourself. We've given you something for the pain and the sickness, and that little IV bag is more antibiotics, so you should start to feel better soon."

"Is it MRSA?" Sam was the first to voice the obvious question. Everyone had heard about hospital acquired infections, and MRSA was the bogeyman of the National Health Service.

Tom glanced across to Kate in an unspoken request for guidance. She gave him a barely perceptible nod. In the barn, Sam had always sought an honest answer, and Kate knew she would want to be told the truth. "We don't know, Sam. It could be." He sighed.

"Given how long you had muck in your leg, it's more likely to be an infection from something that was dragged in there, but we're going to cover our bases, and the antibiotics we're giving you are effective against MRSA as well. How does your leg feel?"

"Mmm, bit numb…I'm all a bit numb, actually."

"That'll be the morphine, Sam." The look of bleary surprise on Sam's face had made Kate smile, but her expression sobered quickly when she thought about what they had to do next. "We need to take some swabs from your leg, send them off to the lab."

"Crap." Sam sounded too tired to offer any real resistance.

"My sentiments exactly," Tom said, washing his hands and pulling on fresh gloves. "Shall we just get it over with?"

Sam nodded, and Kate helped her to roll onto her left side, trying to ignore the small noises of discomfort that escaped despite her best efforts.

Standing behind her, Tom pulled the sheet free. He and Kate winced simultaneously at the inflammation that had spread beyond the boundaries of the dressing on the back of Sam's thigh.

"It's the exit wound," he muttered, pressing a hand over the reddened skin and apologising when Sam moaned. "I'm going to take the dressing off. Try and stay still for me."

Without being asked, Kate knelt in front of Sam. "Just watch me, Sam."

Sam raised her head. She was biting her lip as she fought to stop herself from crying. Kate swallowed hard, trying not to betray the fact that her own heart was aching. They had already been through enough. Was it too much to expect a fucking break? Taking a deep breath, she managed not to rant at the injustice of it all. Instead she smiled and ran a hand lightly across Sam's forehead.

"You know Lotty tried to convince me she was on the verge of starvation earlier? She even managed to con me out of half my bacon butty…"

In the periphery of her vision, Kate could see Tom begin to take his samples. Plastic clinked gently against glass as he dropped the swabs into tubes. He drew a Biro outline of the inflammation to track its progression and then redressed the wound. As he worked, Kate continued to tell her story, pulling Sam's attention away from what Tom was doing to her. As Sam's eyes grew heavy, Kate lowered her voice. Still running her hand through Sam's hair, she watched as Sam slowly surrendered to the pull of the morphine and drifted to sleep.

❖

"Kate! Kate!"

Sam's voice bordered on hysterical, and Kate, as she had several times already, took hold of Sam's hands to stop her thrashing. Despite the antibiotics, the paracetamol, the fan, and cool sponges, her temperature had continued to rise, and Kate could do nothing but attempt to calm her as her delirium deepened.

"Kate! Please. Please…" She was wrestling with the oxygen mask, her eyes wide with terror. "Please don't let them cut my leg off."

"Oh God," Kate whispered, horrified at the torment on Sam's face, not knowing whether anything she could say would be able to break through the fever and offer any comfort. She placed her hand on Sam's cheek and waited until Sam met her eyes, a brief flash of lucidity in them as recognition held for an instant.

"You are going to get better, Sam. You hear me? And you are going to walk out of this hospital."

"Promise?" Sam was trying so desperately hard to stay conscious.

There was a warning voice spinning in her head, shouting at her not to make promises she couldn't keep, but Kate ignored it and nodded. "I promise." Her conviction was absolute because the alternative was unthinkable.

Sam's eyes closed immediately and she settled into a relatively peaceful sleep. Kate sank back into her chair and willed the trembling to subside.

❖

"If you don't stop being so bloody awkward, I'm just going to roll your bed out into the snow and cool you down that way!"

Kate dropped the thermometer onto the side table and reached for the flannel and bowl of water. There was no reaction from Sam, who remained asleep, oblivious to her exasperation. The labs had identified staphylococcal bacteria in the wound swab distinctive to MRSA, but Sam's temperature had dropped only slightly in twenty-four hours, and the infection refused to release its hold on her.

As Kate ran the flannel across her face and down her arms, Sam opened her eyes slightly. Kate dropped the flannel back into the bowl with a splash and a quiet "oh" of shock.

"You with me?" she asked her usual question and was surprised when Sam nodded and licked her lips tentatively, seemingly as bewildered as Kate was.

"I...I heard shouting...were you yelling at me?"

Sam looked so worried that Kate shook her head forcefully. "Oh no, not at you. Well, not really. More at the fact that I can't fix all this quickly enough."

Sam relaxed a little, the tension leaving her face. "I thought you were mad at me. You'll fix me. You got me this far."

The trust in her brought a lump to Kate's throat and she smiled shyly. "You're doing all the work."

"I'm mostly sleeping." Sam looked sheepish, then swallowed and moaned hoarsely. "Ow, you been feeding me sandpaper?"

"Only when you're unconscious. Here, use the straw. You ended up wearing most of it last time."

The iced water obviously eased some of the soreness in Sam's throat because she sighed with relief. "Don't remember that."

"No, you were muttering something about frogs in spandex at the time."

"Liar." A smile, a small one, but a smile all the same.

Kate grinned. "Think you can stay awake while I change your gown?"

"Probably not."

"Well, at least you're honest."

Sam raised a lazy hand to the vague vicinity of Kate's face. "You look tired." The hand waved around and Kate took hold of it, guiding it to her cheek.

"Been looking out for you."

"Tired…" Kate felt Sam's fingers trace the outline of the bruise on her cheek. "But you are beautiful, Kate." There were tears in Sam's eyes as she closed them. "I could fall in love with you," she whispered.

Stunned, Kate gasped softly. Tears streamed down Sam's cheeks and she kept her eyes tightly shut, turning her face into her pillow as if she hadn't intended to say so much and was afraid now of what the consequences might be. Kate pressed a kiss to Sam's forehead and then eased the tears away with the cloth. She had no intention of bolting for the nearest exit.

"Don't cry, Sam. I'm staying right here."

Kate stared unblinking as Sam's hand fell slackly onto the sheets and her breathing became deep and regular.

"Right then…um…gown…" Kate stood, looked around herself, forgot instantly what she was looking for, and sat back down again. She ran her hands over her face and stared at Sam. "Well, I'm glad you can sleep after that little bombshell." Breathing slowly to try to steady her pounding heart, she wondered whether it really had been a bombshell after all. They had been so close over the past weeks, and had suffered through an ordeal most people would be unable to imagine, wasn't it natural that they would form a close bond, and that Sam, still being so unwell, might interpret that bond as something more?

Kate listened to the rationalisations playing out in her head and laughed. Her theory worked right up to the point where she came into it. It didn't explain why she had spent practically every hour at Sam's side. It didn't explain the wrenching ache she had felt on the few occasions she had gone home, or the way her heart had leapt when she had returned to the hospital and Sam had greeted her with one of *those* smiles. It certainly didn't explain how damn giddy she felt right now. There was no anger, no embarrassment, or feeling that Sam had put her on the spot and made her react inappropriately. There was just an overwhelming sense of relief and nervous anticipation for whatever was to happen next.

With a smile, Kate shook her head. "You probably won't remember a damn thing anyway, will you?" She rested her hand on

Sam's forehead and decided it might be safer to get back to business as usual. "Okay, so where was I? Gown. Oh, Sam, this never goes well when you're asleep."

She was unfastening the tie at the back of Sam's neck when Laura poked her head through the curtains.

"Well, fancy meeting you here," Laura said with a grin. "I came in early to take you to tea and it looks like my timing is exemplary as ever." She moved to the opposite side of the bed and carefully drew Sam forward, allowing Kate to reach the gown's lower ties.

Still somewhat preoccupied, Kate just nodded her thanks and allowed Laura to help her out by threading IV bags and lines precariously through the arms of the gown as she eased it from Sam's shoulders.

"Jesus, it's like playing cat's cradle. Why were you doing this on your own?"

Kate barely heard Laura's question and she didn't give an answer. With a quiet apology to Sam, Kate folded the sheet to her waist and sponged her upper body with cool water. It was so much easier to change her with a second pair of hands helping, but Kate was always keenly aware of how vulnerable Sam had been made to feel since being taken hostage, so she had tried to expose her as little as possible.

"Hello? Earth to Kate?"

Kate was wringing the cloth in the water. Glancing down at the screwed up piece of fabric, she realised it was well and truly wrung. "Sorry, Laura, what were you saying?"

Laura laughed and held out the clean gown. "Let's just get this on her for now."

Together, they reversed the process they had just been through and then leaned Sam back against the pillows, where she mumbled and screwed her nose up at something unseen before settling into a deeper sleep. Kate took her temperature and held the thermometer screen up for Laura to read.

"Thirty-eight point four. Is that on the way down?"

"It's certainly better than it was. She was awake just before you came in."

"She recognise you this time?"

Kate nodded, loath to remember the numerous occasions when Sam had woken, terrified, screaming for Kate and not realising she was right by her side. Instead, Kate thought of their most recent conversation, and was unable to stop the warmth she could feel creeping into her cheeks. "Yep. Yes." She seemed to have developed a stutter and cleared her throat. "She knew who I was this time."

Laura was eyeing her with a worried frown. "I think you need a break. What say I take you away from all this and we go for a slap-up meal?"

"A slap-up meal in the hospital café?"

"I only promised a slap-up meal. I didn't promise it would be edible or digestible."

Kate smiled but then bit down on the skin at the side of her fingernails as she looked at Sam.

"Sam would want you to have a break. Tom said he'd be around in an hour or so. I can have you back for then. There's a nurse chomping at the bit for something to do, and you have your pager."

Kate relented. "I really fancy egg and chips."

Laura sniggered. "Wow. When you push the boat out, you just don't know when to stop, do you?"

CHAPTER TEN

K ate dipped the last of her chips in her second egg, mopped up the yolk with a piece of bread, and then reached for her dish of chocolate sponge and custard.

She had made it halfway through her pudding by the time she paused for breath and realised Laura was grinning at her. "What?" Her eyes narrowed with suspicion and she checked her chin and shirt for custard. Finding none, she was genuinely puzzled. "Okay, I give up. What's so funny?"

Laura's tea slopped over the edge of her mug as she laughed, and she set it down. "It's nothing, Kate. I just don't think I've ever seen anyone eat the food here with such relish."

"Oh." Kate hesitated with a spoonful of pudding halfway to her lips. She looked at what she was about to eat—brown, fluffy sponge and a generous helping of institutional custard—then shrugged and swallowed the lot. "It has to be said, though"—she tapped her spoon on the rim of the bowl—"they do make a damn fine chocolate pud."

"If you say so. I'm just happy to see you eating."

"I've been eating." Kate was indignant, but she couldn't remember the last meal that hadn't been snatched at Sam's bedside and hadn't comprised a sandwich and a yoghurt. She wondered if the bacon sandwich she had shared with Lotty counted as a hot meal. Eventually, she came up with what sounded like a reasonable excuse. "Well, my face has been sore…"

"You need to take better care of yourself, Kate. You're too thin, and to be brutally honest, you look knackered."

Kate pushed her empty dish aside and picked up her mug. "That *was* a bit brutal," she muttered, mostly into the drink, because she knew damn well Laura was right.

When she had looked in the bathroom mirror that morning, dark shadows had marred the skin beneath her eyes. The bruises on her face had faded to yellow, but the criss-crossed scar on her cheek was still livid and starker somehow without the artificiality of the sutures to conceal it. The fact that she had looked as dreadful as she felt had been no comfort to her.

Laura took her hand and seemed relieved when she didn't snatch it away.

"I'm just worried about you. Someone needs to look out for you too."

"I think I'm okay," Kate said slowly, considering. "It's just hard to sleep sometimes."

Laura swallowed deliberately, and Kate saw her set her jaw as if she had decided that now she had started with the hard truths she was going to push her reservations aside and go for broke.

"Maybe you should go home for a while. Take a proper break, sleep in your own bed, and cook yourself some decent meals. What you're doing for Sam, it's a really good thing, Kate, but do you think you might be a bit too involved?"

Kate put her mug down. Her palms were clammy and she gently extricated her hand from Laura's. Laura looked pale and worried, scared that now she really had said too much.

Kate managed a smile she hoped was reassuring. "I probably am," she whispered. The words needed to come out, but her voice felt as tremulous as she did. "I don't know what's happening to me."

Laura nodded, seemingly encouraged by what she must have perceived as agreement. "You both shared something terrible and you feel obliged to keep promises you made while you were under incredible stress."

But she looked confused, her confidence faltering, when Kate shook her head. "No. No. I've thought about all that. That's what I put it down to at first. Stress and the pressure and everything that we went through. I mean, of course we became close. There was just the two of us and we had to fight so hard just to get out and we both did things we never thought we'd have to do. But now I think there's something else..." Kate looked down at the table, afraid to look at Laura, sure she would give everything away if she did. She clutched at the mug in front of her, oblivious to the heat as her grip turned her knuckles white.

She felt bewildered, as if the disparate pieces of a puzzle had fallen together and given her an answer that she was now terrified of saying out loud. An endless minute dragged on. She could sense Laura's silent scrutiny and looked up just in time to see Laura's eyes widen. Apparently, the penny had dropped for her.

"You have feelings for her, haven't you?" Laura said quietly, so quietly she could barely be heard above the clanking of pots in the kitchen and a voice telling someone they were nearly all out of baked beans.

Kate closed her eyes, relief and terror almost choking her, as hot tears fell down her cheeks. She hadn't meant it to be like this, this revelation. Not in a café full of cooking smells and muted conversations and the ping of the cash register. All reminders that life was going on, even if hers was changing irrevocably. She raised her head and met Laura's eyes, seeing the shock and understanding there as everything fell into place, even before she answered the question.

"Yes. Yes, I have."

"Holy shit." Laura blew her breath out in a whistle, opened her mouth, and then clamped it shut again.

Kate stayed silent as well, toying nervously with the handle of her mug, and Laura reached out a hand to cover hers, stilling the restless motion. Kate knew Laura would have a thousand questions, but for now at least she was keeping them to herself. In all the years Kate had been friends with Laura, Kate had never had a boyfriend. The absolute dearth of eligible bachelors in Birchenlow had become a running joke between them, and Kate had been happy to remain single, never having had the inclination or motivation to closely examine her reasons for that. She could only imagine how difficult it was for Laura to adjust herself to the idea that her closest friend, whom she must have thought she knew better than anyone, might actually be gay.

Kate used a paper napkin to dry her face. She felt exhausted, as if the enormity of her admission had drained the little energy she had to spare. She drew in a breath. "I'm sorry. I didn't mean to put all this on you."

"No." Laura squeezed her hand and Kate squeezed back as if that alone would be enough to stop Laura from running away. "I'm glad you told me. I think you needed to tell someone. Does Sam know?"

Kate shook her head helplessly. "I don't know. She may have an idea, but she's been so ill. I just...*I* barely even know. I don't know what I'm doing, what I'm feeling. I don't know what it all means." She looked to Laura, desperate for guidance. "I know I've never felt this before and it's scaring the hell out of me."

Laura smiled softly. "In a good way?"

"In a scary way." Then a smile of her own. "In a good way."

"Bloody hell. You've gone and done it, haven't you? You've finally gone and fallen for someone."

"I wasn't looking to."

"Yeah, it's a bit of a mess isn't it?" Laura's face creased with sympathy as Kate nodded miserably. "Oh Kate, I don't know what you want me to say. You're her doctor, and you're right, she's been so ill. Maybe you need to step away a little, for the sake of both of you."

It was nothing Kate hadn't already considered, but hearing the words spoken out loud made her feel physically sick.

"I can't just leave her." A sudden surge of emotion closed her throat, and she choked back fresh tears. "I can't."

"I'm not saying you should. But you definitely need to give up being her doctor. And you need to put a bit of space between you and take some time to think everything through. To make sure that this is right for both of you."

In other words, make sure you know what the hell you are doing before you ease yourself out of the closet. Through the sleepless nights and the hours at Sam's bedside, Kate had imagined every possible scenario a thousand times over. She had thought what it would mean to be gay in a small, rural village. Telling friends who had always assumed she was straight because she had never given them cause to believe otherwise. Telling her mother, for whom it was likely to signal the end of the world. Facing the possibility that patients who liked and trusted her would reveal prejudices she had never known they harboured. She ran her hands over her face, wincing at the pull on the still-healing scars.

"I'll speak to Tom. Ask him to carry on as Sam's doctor."

"Will you tell him why?"

"No. No, not just yet. I think he'll be glad I'm asking him. I know he's been worrying about me."

"Well, that's a start."

There was a gulf lying unspoken between them. Sam. Laura would probably advise her to run a mile, to cut her losses now, before she got herself in any deeper and made a mistake that had the potential to wreck everything she had worked so hard for. It would be sound advice, and she would mean well, but she didn't say it, and Kate was profoundly grateful for her restraint.

"You'd better be getting back there." The wry smile on Laura's lips implied she suspected Kate was already a lost cause.

❖

Sam wasn't sure if it was the pain or the thirst that had woken her. She opened her eyes slowly, blinking twice before she realised she was able to focus clearly. The pain in her thigh nagged constantly, her head throbbed, and her throat was parched, but the mere fact that she could rationally consider her numerous complaints was a definite, if somewhat unfortunate, improvement.

She was cold, but it wasn't the bone-aching cold of a high fever, just a chill from being in the draught of a fan whilst only covered by a light sheet. She turned to the side Kate always sat on, to find an empty chair. The door to her room was ajar and she could see a nurse sitting behind the desk, but she was reading something with her head bent low, and she hadn't noticed that Sam was awake.

Sam didn't call for her. She reached out with her good hand and managed a trembling grip around a beaker of water. The straw was more of a challenge, but she finally captured it between her lips and felt quite triumphant as she swallowed careful sips. The rattle of the fan masked any noise she made, and she was content just to lie quietly, enjoying the novelty of being awake and alert for the first time in...

She shook her head. She had no idea what day or time it was. It was dark outside, but there was no clock, and she struggled against the disorientation of not knowing how much time had passed, or exactly what had happened while she had been delirious or unconscious. Not trusting her voice, she moved her hand toward her buzzer, sure that Kate wouldn't be too far away, with all the answers. She touched the smooth plastic, but she didn't press down, halted by a vague memory that slowly took shape and formed an insidious little ball of unease in her stomach.

Kate. She had said something to Kate. It was difficult to distinguish true memories from the vivid drug and fever induced dreams. Sam closed her eyes, trying to sort out the reality from what she had only imagined.

She had called Kate beautiful, but that wasn't it. She was sure that wasn't all of it, and then it all came back in a rush.

"I could fall in love with you."

Shit. Sam closed her eyes. Shit.

She remembered that Kate had kissed her chastely and reassured her. She had a dim recollection of being moved and a dry gown replacing a soaked one, and then nothing, until now.

If she had possessed the energy and hadn't had the headache, she would have slapped herself for being so bloody stupid. Kate was her doctor, a professional with a reputation and a career that she had no right to just waltz into and attempt to commandeer. It was enough that Kate had risked her own life to save Sam's, and that she had been with her tirelessly ever since. She didn't need the added burden of a declaration of love, even if she could explain it away as being influenced by delirium.

Sam only realised she was crying when she felt the tears splash off her nose. She had tangled her IV reaching for the water, and she snagged her wrist as she tried to wipe her face, swearing in pain and frustration. It brought the nurse over, who mistook the tears for deterioration and looked blankly terrified, as if she had been caught slacking on the job.

"I'm okay," Sam whispered, her voice hoarse with misuse. "I just..." She held her arm up as far as it would go.

The nurse smiled with relief. "Oh, come here..." Careful hands unwound the tubing and ensured the line hadn't been dislodged. "You look better. How are you feeling, love?"

"Um, not too bad. A bit clearer."

The nurse rested her hand on Sam's forehead, the old-fashioned way of checking for a fever, and nodded reassuringly. "You feel much cooler. I'll get you a fresh drink, and I'll let Dr. Myles know you're awake. She's just nipped out for something to eat." She picked up the water jug and hurried off.

Sam watched her go and wiped her face with her newly-freed hand. She didn't want Kate asking questions, didn't want Kate to worry or try to work out why she was upset. She closed her eyes, feeling weary and sick. She did love Kate. She felt it every time she saw her, that little jump in her chest, and the rush of blood that made her smile even as it made her head spin. She loved her, but it was just too much to ask that Kate love her back.

❖

Sam hadn't heard the door open. Standing in the doorway, Kate watched her wriggling in the bed. She was trying to turn herself over, and swearing quietly but vehemently at her many encumbrances, starting with the cast on her wrist, saving particular ire for the IV tangling up her good arm, and ending with the leg that apparently still wouldn't obey any of her instructions. She finally flopped against the pillows and spotted Kate as she looked up.

"Oh, hello!" Sam's snarl of frustration was immediately replaced by a broad smile. The pure, unguarded happiness on her face made Kate instantly forget the conversation she had been rehearsing so she wouldn't accidentally blurt out what was really on her mind. Instead, she laughed softly and made her way to the bedside.

"I counted fourteen."

"Fourteen?"

"Expletives. I was waiting to see if you could hit twenty, but you started to re-use a few."

Sam grinned. "What can I say? I've been ill."

"You have the eloquence of a sailor."

"Why, thank you, madam."

Kate rested her hand on Sam's forehead. "You know that wasn't a compliment, don't you?"

"I had my suspicions." Sam closed her eyes at Kate's touch. "So am I still hot?"

Kate smiled and shook her head; she wasn't going to go near that one. "Your temperature is lower, which I'm sure is what you meant." She couldn't keep her face straight, with Sam playing along and feigning innocence, and she decided a change in subject would be safer. "What were you trying to achieve when I came in?"

"Oh." Sam paused, obviously struggling to remember that far back. "Oh, I was trying to turn over. My bum is numb."

Kate put her bag on the chair and slipped her jacket off. "Nothing worse than a numb bum. C'mere."

It took a fair bit of manoeuvring, but she managed to help Sam into a position that didn't leave her grimacing and gave her easy access to her side table and the bed's remote control.

"Ahh, that's better. I love you! You're a lifesaver."

Kate laughed. "I only helped to un-numb your backside." But Sam's face was pale and serious as she realised what she had said, and Kate, pushing aside her carefully made plans, hesitated in the middle of straightening the bedding and made a snap decision. "Not now, Sam. I think we probably need to talk. But not right now."

Sam nodded. She looked relieved to have been granted a reprieve. "Okay. Not now."

Kate dipped her hand into the bag. "I wasn't sure what flavour you liked, but I figured you couldn't go wrong with vanilla."

"Vanilla is perfect." Sam took the spoon Kate held out to her. "You sharing?" She laughed as Kate produced a second spoon with a flourish and snapped the lid off the ice cream tub.

Kate watched Sam dig into the ice cream and sat down with a relaxed sigh. This absolutely wasn't the right time. She felt emotionally wrung-out, and Sam had barely had the chance to wake up. The Talk would just have to wait until they were both good and ready.

"So what did I sleep through this time? Oh, bugger." Ice cream slid off Sam's spoon and she tried to catch what had fallen with her tongue.

"Not an awful lot. It's still cold outside and…Oh, Sam, you're wearing most of that."

Kate used her finger to scoop up the ice cream that had dripped off Sam's chin and landed in the hollow of her throat, then she wondered what the hell to do with it. There was no way she was licking it off her fingers. There was no way she was letting Sam lick it off her fingers. In the end, she hurriedly wiped it on a napkin and fought, with only partial success, not to blush. To her credit, Sam made no comment, and was slightly more dextrous with her next effort.

Kate watched her furrow her brow with concentration and settled back into the chair. "Apparently, Mackenzie is quite the local celebrity. He cut the ribbon at the grand opening of a new butcher's shop in the village the other day." Kate started to giggle.

Sam looked at her in disbelief and then started to giggle too. She snorted loudly and started to shake. Then she dropped ice cream down her chest again.

"Oh, bollocks."

Kate shook her head in despair and reached for another napkin.

❖

"You made that up. That's not a word."

"It is. It's a Siberian tent made out of animal skins."

"Yurt?" Sam shook her head in disbelief as Kate scribbled the word into the last space in the crossword.

"It is a word. It fits, and we have finished." She displayed the puzzle with a grin.

Sam gave her a one-handed round of applause before yawning hugely. "I think it was mostly down to you."

"Mmhm. You tired?"

"Yeah, it's past my bedtime." Sam smiled, recognising the irony of her statement. "Okay, so it's pretty much always my bedtime at the moment."

Kate, tidying away the newspaper and the empty ice cream carton, turned at Sam's despondent tone. "You should start feeling stronger, now the infection's on the way out. We can get you back on the physio, get you up and walking, and you'll be out of here before you know it."

Her optimism was genuine. She really did want Sam to make a full recovery and go home, back to her life and her career, but Kate's positive tone belied the leaden feeling in her chest as she contemplated that prospect. She knew she was being selfish and entirely unrealistic. Sam would leave the hospital eventually, but the thought of not being able to see her every day filled Kate with dread.

Sam was watching her with heavy eyes. Kate smiled fondly, brushed her hand through Sam's hair, and drew in a deep breath. "I thought I might head home tonight." She didn't want to. She didn't want to go back to her cold house and sleep alone in her cold bed. Laura had said it would be for the best, but she felt miserable. Sam now looked miserable, and Kate wasn't convinced it was best for either of them. "Will you be okay?"

Sam nodded. "Shouldn't *I* be asking *you* that? I'm never on my own in here."

"I'll be fine." Kate sounded surer than she felt. She still had the nightmares and still woke like clockwork at three a.m., sweat-soaked and terrified. Most of those nights, Sam had woken with her. It would only take a touch or a quiet word of reassurance to allow

Kate to settle and sleep on undisturbed. Sam had always tried to give as much comfort and support as she had received.

"Okay then." Sam managed a smile. "Give Lotty a cuddle from me."

"I will." Kate looked around. "Right. Do you have everything you need?"

There was an obvious answer to that question, but Sam managed to nod. "See you tomorrow?"

"Definitely." Kate picked up her coat and left the room before she could change her mind. The door swung shut behind her and she leaned back on it for a moment. "Sleep well, sweetheart." She kept her voice to a whisper, but there was no one there to hear her anyway.

❖

The phone was ringing insistently, pulling Kate from a restless sleep. Her hands shook as she answered it, the shock of being woken so suddenly making her heart pound.

"Hello?"

Silence. Then one word: "Bitch." Then the dial tone.

She stared at the receiver as the tone became shriller and then dropped it onto its stand as if it had burned her.

"Jesus."

In the morning, she wondered whether she had dreamt it, and not entirely certain that she hadn't, she didn't say a thing to anyone.

CHAPTER ELEVEN

Kate quickly ushered Mackenzie to stand on the opposite side of the empty bed. He opened the door when they heard voices outside and they both applauded as Sam was wheeled into her new room. She blushed, giving a mock bow in the wheelchair, before she took hold of the crutches Kate held out to her and struggled to her feet. The cast on her wrist had been changed to a new lightweight one, and she had been able to hobble about for a whole day before Tom had declared her fit to leave the ITU. He had told her that he would continue to oversee her care and, not having been aware of any alternative arrangements, she had made no mention of it to Kate.

Kate held her breath as Sam steeled herself and then managed to cross the six-foot gap between the wheelchair and the chair at the side of her bed. She made a hasty grab for its arms and collapsed into it with a sigh of relief.

"You both just wanted to see me fall on my arse, didn't you?"

Her audience of two made shocked noises of indignation, and Sam laughed, looking out the window at her new view of rolling hills that were still white at the very tops.

"Big day." Kate smiled proudly as Mackenzie planted a kiss on Sam's cheek.

After the infection had finally left her system, Sam had told Kate that enough was enough, that there would be no more setbacks. She had eaten everything she had been given, performed her exercises with rigid discipline, and abandoned painkillers in the daytime because they made her fall off her crutches. The Talk had never happened. The lingering sense of things left unsaid had faded as they studiously avoided the subject and any potentially damaging fallout. Sam looked so much stronger, her cheeks pinker than Kate had ever seen them, and with a little of the weight she had lost regained, she no longer had the pinched, sickly look of the desperately ill.

"I feel knackered now." Sam took a deep breath and rested her head against the chair.

Mackenzie perched on the side of the bed and leaned down to pull something from beneath it. "Here." He presented a bunch of freesias to Sam. "Happy new room!"

"Thanks, Mac. Mmm, they smell gorgeous."

"I'll see if I can find a vase." Kate took the flowers and headed out into the corridor. When she returned to the room, Sam's face was serious and Mackenzie had his hands out in a *don't shoot the messenger* gesture.

"She wanted to come and see you. She's called for updates twice a week."

"Okay, okay. I suppose it'll be nice to catch up." Sam spotted Kate and looked relieved to be able to change the subject. "Oh, those look lovely."

Kate put the flowers on the side table. "Problems?"

"No." Sam sighed. "Cally, my ex. She's been giving Mac earache for not letting her come here."

"You weren't well enough." Mackenzie shrugged. "Cally upsets her," he added by way of explanation.

"She doesn't upset me. Well, she did. But that was a while ago."

Kate sat on the bed beside Mackenzie. "The heartbreaker."

"What? How did you? Oh, the barn. You have a good memory." The tone of Sam's voice implied that she wished Kate's memory of that conversation wasn't quite so acute. "I'm sure I'll be fine. Will you both stop looking so worried, please?" Her smile convinced neither of them.

Mackenzie patted her shoulder. "She gives you any crap, you just let me know." He winked at Sam confidentially. "And I'll set Kate on her."

❖

Sam counted quietly to ten and then lowered her right leg to rest on the bed. She was exhausted, covered in sweat, and her leg ached continuously, but she had managed to complete the exercise routine her physio had designed for her. She was getting better at it, but the muscles in her injured leg had been considerably weakened and it was taking longer than she had anticipated to build the strength back up. She was debating buzzing for assistance to shower, when there was a soft knock at the door, and it swung open before she had called out an answer.

"Anybody home?"

In the three seconds between Sam realising whom the voice belonged to and Cally stepping into the room, her reaction flipped between fear, dread, and joy, before finally settling on an overwhelming self-consciousness, a sense reinforced by the fleeting look of shock that passed over Cally's face before she hid it behind a smile and a smothering hug.

"You look great."

"And you never could lie for shit."

Cally released her and laughed. "No, I couldn't." Her eyes narrowed and she sat on the edge of the bed. "Mac warned me you'd had a rough time. You still look a bit pale."

A rough time. Sam shook her head wryly at the understatement. "Yeah, I've had better months."

Cally really did look great. Her cheeks were flushed from the cold air, her hair was styled slightly differently again and darker this time than that day in the old lady's garden. Sam smiled easily, genuinely pleased to see her and pleasantly surprised at the lack of turbulent emotions that traditionally assailed her in Cally's presence.

"So." Cally took Sam's hand and held it in hers, bouncing it gently in her lap. "What've you been up to then?"

The question was so absurd that Sam hesitated, trying to think up a pithy response, before she realised Cally was taking the piss and started to laugh. "Well, it all happened the day after our encounter in the snow…"

It took over an hour to recount. Cally sat and listened quietly, prompting when Sam faltered, and squeezing her hand in tacit understanding when her voice broke or shook. It was so much easier talking to Kate. Kate had been there. She knew how cold the barn had been, had heard the wind banging the roof and howling through the crumbling mortar. She had pressed her hands into Sam's blood, splinted Sam's fractured wrist with discarded pieces of wood, and finally, in those dreadful few minutes, she had killed a man to save them both.

Telling the story to Cally, Sam had barely been able to find the words for any of it, and in the end had adopted a clinical sense of detachment to describe her own experiences. But there was one part of the story she simply could not remain detached from, and that was Kate. Sam had been careful not to say too much about Kate. She was all too aware Cally had an uncanny ability to read her like an open book.

When she had finished, Cally let out a low whistle and poured her a glass of juice. "You all right?"

Sam nodded, sipping the juice and feeling drained.

"So where's this doctor of yours? Have you kept in touch since it all happened?"

The juice instantly went down the wrong way, making Sam cough. She coughed even harder when Cally thumped her on the back, but the unexpected diversion at least gave her time to try to think how she was going to respond.

"Uh." She was still stalling. "Kate's actually been here quite a lot," she hedged, in a vain hope Cally would just allow the subject to drop.

"What's she like?" Cally clearly had no intention of doing anything of the sort. "I don't think any of the papers have managed to get an interview with her yet."

Sam set the juice down and looked at Cally. She had been twenty-three and fresh out of the closet when she had first met Cally on an emergency call involving teenagers, a large amount of illicit substances, and an unfortunate incident in a cemetery. Their three-year relationship had eventually fallen apart in a mess of infidelity that, despite Cally's reputation, Sam had never seen coming.

The trace of a smile on her lips, Sam gave a slight, bemused shake of her head. At the time, she had wondered whether she would ever be able to love anyone else quite so completely. She realised now that what she had felt for Cally had barely been the tip of the iceberg, and that infatuation was not the same thing as falling in love.

Cally was still waiting for Sam to say something, her expression puzzled.

"You'd like her," Sam ventured cagily, and then her voice softened. "She's lovely."

"Yeah? Tall? Short? Old? Young?" Cally waggled her eyebrows. "Exactly how lovely are we talking, Officer Lucas?"

"Slightly taller than me, two years older than me and—"

"And lovely enough to have made you redder than a lobster." Cally raised her feet to rest them on the bed frame and folded her arms. "Sam?"

"What?" It came out as a mumble. Sam could feel her cheeks burning and with Cally apparently scenting blood in the water, Sam absolutely did not want to meet her gaze. There was a touch on Sam's arm and she caught her bottom lip between her teeth. "I'm fine, Cal."

"Yeah, you look it. What the hell's going on?"

Sam dared a glance up and her guard slipped ever so slightly when she saw the genuine concern on Cally's face. She was so desperate to confide in someone.

"I think, I mean...It's complicated, Cal. I don't know but I think—"

"Oh my God, you fancy her!" Cally blurted out, but the grin faded from her face as Sam shook her head.

"No, it's more than that," Sam said. Her stomach did a flip-flop and nervous adrenaline made her palms slick. She closed her eyes.

"I've fallen in love with her." The words came out with the release of a confession pent up for far too long. She felt lighter just for having said them out loud and she managed a shy smile at Cally's wide-eyed look of shock.

Cally picked up Sam's juice and finished it in a couple of gulps. "So let me get this right. You got taken hostage, got shot. Got rescued, got fixed, and managed to get smitten with your lady doctor and all-round, all-conquering heroine?"

Sam shrugged and nodded. It sounded absurd when it was put like that.

"Does Kate know?"

"I think she has an idea."

"But you haven't talked about it?"

"No. We've been meaning to, I think. But we never really get around to it."

"Is she gay?"

Sam lowered her eyes, and toyed nervously with the sheet. "I don't know."

"Oh bloody hell, Sam!"

"I didn't mean for this to happen." It sounded pathetic even to her.

"She's a doctor. A doctor in a small village. I doubt it has a thriving gay scene. Hell, it probably doesn't even have a gay!"

Sam knew that was only partly true, that some rural villages had a disproportionately large population of lesbian couples, but she conceded the point about Kate's position, because it was nothing that she hadn't already considered.

"You think I'm being unfair?"

"I think you're being unrealistic." Cally leaned forward and ran her hand through Sam's hair. "Maybe Kate hasn't spoken to you because she doesn't know how to let you down gently."

Sam felt her stomach twist as the juice threatened to make a reappearance. That possibility had also been playing on her mind, and the fact that Cally had immediately voiced it made it seem all the more likely to be true.

"What do you think I should do?"

Cally sat up straight and sighed, her hands open. "Oh, Sam, I don't know." She hesitated, considering. "If I were you, I would put a little distance between you both and see what's left when things are back to normal. This..." Cally gestured at the hospital room. "This isn't normal, Sam. You've been hidden away here for so long, I think you may've forgotten that. Have you thought about what you're going to do when you get out of here?"

Sam hadn't. She had tried to think about anything *but* that. The thought of leaving Kate and the familiar security of the hospital was beginning to give her sleepless nights, but Cally, as ever, had effortlessly pinpointed and then subtly tweaked every one of her exposed nerves.

"Well, no pressure or anything, but you could always come and recuperate at mine. It's familiar, safe. I don't think you should be on your own straight away."

"I don't know, Cal. I...I haven't...I just don't know if it'd be a good idea."

Cally's answering smile was sincere. "Hey, it's just an idea. No strings." She stood and kissed Sam on the cheek. "I should let you get some rest. Promise me you'll at least think about it?"

Sam nodded warily but managed to smile. "I will."

"I'll see you soon. Anything you need?"

"No. No thanks."

Cally shut the door with a click. Sam leaned her head back heavily, more confused than ever. She closed her eyes, too weary now for a shower, and tried to stop her thoughts jumping about so rapidly. As she rubbed her forehead to stave off the throbbing that had started there, she remembered Cally's hand brushing through her hair. Cally hadn't been wearing her commitment ring, and she hadn't mentioned her partner once. Sam groaned as the throbbing in her head intensified and she wondered how her life—which had been played out entirely in a hospital for a month—had managed to become so damn complicated.

❖

The spin cycle of the washing machine had been loud enough to smother the first few rings of the telephone. Kate had been busy scrubbing the remnants of porridge from a pan and just managed to dry her hands and snatch up the handset before the answering machine could intervene.

"Hello?"

The scream was as sudden as it was piercing, like a sound effect from a horror movie amplified for maximum impact. Startled, Kate lost her grip on the handset, and it landed on the carpet, one of its batteries flying loose as the plastic cover separated.

"Jesus Christ." She struggled to clip the battery back into place with fingers that seemed to have lost their dexterity. As soon as she had fixed it, the phone began to ring. She stared at it with dread, fear making her heart pound.

She accepted the call, but held the handset a safe distance away from her ear and said nothing. Even so, she could hear the masculine breathing, the sound harsh and deliberate. When he said her name in that same controlled tone, she lowered the handset and cut him off. Cold sweat ran down her neck and chilled her throat. The phone was ringing again. She knelt and unplugged it, then drew her knees to her chest and wrapped her arms around them. She felt hot and cold simultaneously, and when a tingling sensation started in her fingers she realised she was breathing too fast.

"Shit." Using the sofa for leverage, she clambered to her feet. Sparks of light dotted her vision, but she managed to walk to her front door and check that it was locked. One by one, she made sure her windows were closed, peering out of each to try to spot any unusual movement in the fields. There was nothing out there, however, and the only sound in the cottage was the washing machine stuttering to the end of its load.

Kate collected the DVD player she had packed up to take to the hospital. Before she left the cottage, she went back into the living room and reconnected the phone. As she went out the front door and locked it behind her, the phone was already ringing.

❖

"So we're freezing cold, it's pouring with rain, and it's dark. Gary pulls this idiot upright, and as soon as he does, the guy's trousers fall down around his ankles. Gary can't let go because this guy is having severe alcohol-related issues with gravity, so it's left to yours truly to get down and wrestle his pants back up over his arse. Seriously, I do not get paid enough for this crap."

Sam laughed as Cally leaned back into the bench with a melodramatic pout. "Oh, you know you love it."

Cally shrugged. "Beats working in an office, although I'd probably come home smelling a little fresher if I did that. You do not want to know what that chap had been rolling in before we rushed in to save his life."

"I can imagine." Sam cradled her mug of tea in her hands. "It's certainly fresh out here."

Cally looked up, concerned. "Are you cold? We could go back inside."

"No, I'm fine. It's lovely here."

They were in the grounds. Cally, having decided that hospital air made her sneeze, had suggested a walk, and Sam had managed a new record of ten minutes on her crutches before collapsing onto a conveniently situated bench.

"Mmm, you always were one for a bit of wilderness." Cally was eyeing the surrounding hills with disdain.

"And you never wanted to get your boots muddy."

"Those boots cost me a hundred and twenty pounds."

"Cal, they were walking boots. You were supposed to walk in them."

"And I could walk around Manchester in them just fine."

Sam shook her head with a despairing laugh. "You useless bugger."

Cally grinned, then her face turned serious and she squeezed Sam's hand. "I've missed this."

"Cal…" Sam meant it as a warning, but Cally was undeterred.

"I have. I've missed you. Missed having you around. Just chatting like this."

"We could've chatted all you wanted, but you seemed to prefer chatting to Joanne."

"Ouch." Cally dropped Sam's hand and put hers to her heart as if she had been wounded.

"You deserved it."

"I did." She nodded. "She left me, you know."

"Yeah, I noticed your ring was missing."

"I think I went a little bit nuts when I heard about you. I was on shift that day and the rumours were flying around that something major had happened. When I found out it was you, they had to take me off duty." She was looking at her shoes where they shuffled on the grass, and wouldn't meet Sam's eyes. "I phoned Mac, obviously, and couldn't get through, so I had to watch it all play out on the news. I finally managed to speak to Mac when you'd been here for a couple of days. Jo put up with me for another week, but we'd been pretty rocky before all this happened."

Sam watched Cally scuff her feet back and forth, trying to remember if she had ever looked so defeated or sounded so sincere. Sam took hold of her hand and squeezed it gently until she looked up.

"I am sorry, Cal." Sam put her hand on Cally's cold cheek and Cally leaned into it, her eyes brimming with tears. She pressed a kiss into Sam's palm.

Neither of them noticed Kate until she cleared her throat softly. Sam reacted as if she had been burned, dropping her hand into her lap as she felt her cheeks flush. Kate tried a smile, but it failed to reach her eyes and she had difficulty looking at Sam.

"I, er…I looked in your room, but Marcus said you'd come out here." She drew her coat closer around herself. "I brought that movie you wanted to see." She checked herself and shook her head, holding her hand out. "I'm sorry. I'm guessing you must be Cally."

"Yes. Kate, right? Nice to finally meet you. Sam's told me a lot about you."

"All good, I hope?" The standard response, only Kate didn't seem to have the heart to put any humour into it.

"All good." Sam took the answer away from Cally, but Kate still wouldn't meet her eyes.

"Well, um…I should go. Don't get cold, Sam."

Sam shook her head. "I won't. We were just about to head back inside. Will I see you tomorrow?"

"Yes. Yes. Probably. Maybe not for too long, though, because I…Someone's coming to the house to have a look at my water tank." Kate sighed and then, as if unsure whether her lie had been convincing enough, she added, "It leaks."

"With a bit of luck, it'll just need a patch," Cally said, her voice cheerful and seemingly oblivious, and Sam resisted the urge to try to throttle her.

"Yeah, hopefully." Kate didn't seem to know or care what she was agreeing to. "I'll see you later."

"Yes." It was all Sam could manage.

Kate nodded, then crossed the grass and headed for the car park. She didn't look back, and her shoulders were stiff and set.

"She seemed nice." Cally was playing with the zip on her jacket, frowning as it snagged and caught in the fabric. "Damn!"

Sam ignored her and clambered to her feet. Nothing seemed to be working properly and she swayed on her crutches. "I'm going back inside."

"Oh, okay."

It seemed to take forever, that ten minute walk. Cally, sensing Sam's mood, kept quiet. She pecked Sam on the cheek and made a getaway before they reached her room. Relieved to be alone, Sam struggled on. She smiled in acknowledgement at the ward staff, maintaining the façade so no one would follow her to make sure she was all right.

She closed the door behind her with a heaved breath and leaned against it with her eyes closed. When she opened them again, she noticed the DVD player that Kate had wired into her television set, the movie they had been talking about, and the unopened bag of popcorn on the bedside table.

"Shit." She didn't know if she could fix this. "Shit." Her leg finally gave way and she crumpled to the floor, welcoming the pain, pretending it was what made her sob so hard.

❖

Kate unlocked her back door, wondering how she had managed to drive home safely. It wasn't that she had been driving fast, it was just that she couldn't remember driving at all. She had been functioning entirely on autopilot, her thoughts tumbling over themselves. She hadn't reached any conclusions, hadn't made sense of anything, and the image of Sam and Cally—oblivious to everything around them as Cally kissed Sam's hand—seemed to be on a permanent instant replay in her head.

It was cold in the kitchen. An insidious drizzle had started at some point as she was driving, and mist hung low, shrouding the hills and turning the fields in front of her cottage eerie and grey. She shivered and pulled off her wet coat, hanging it over a chair to drip-dry. Switching all the lights on did nothing to banish the chill. Her face was damp and she wondered whether it was the rain or because she had been crying. She wiped a hand sharply across her cheeks, annoyed at herself for being weak, for being stupid, for not knowing what was going on and not having had the courage to ask Sam for clarity before this had happened.

A sudden clatter from the living room made her jump. She looked up quickly, her heart racing.

"Lotty?"

There was no answering meow, nothing but deathly silence. Then the clatter sounded again, and ceased just as abruptly.

"Shit."

Wielding a mallet from her tub of cooking utensils, she walked cautiously to the dividing door, took a deep breath, and pushed through into the living room. Light flooded the space as she flicked the overhead on, but there was no bogeyman waiting to jump on her, no horrors left on display for her to find, just a broken window and a large stone sitting in a mess of shattered glass. The window had been opened, and the frame, swinging free in the wind, was the source of the noise.

"Jesus." The curse escaped her in a rush; she didn't know whether someone was in the house, and fear prickled the back of her neck as she realised just how very isolated she was. With a shaking hand, she picked up her phone and dialled 999. She barely heard the reassuring instructions from the kindly voice on the other end of the line. Her hand gripped around the handle of the mallet, she huddled on her sofa and waited for the knock at the door.

❖

The police had arrived quickly. Having recognised Kate's address and linked it up to her recent history, it seemed they were seriously considering the possibility that someone might have been looking to settle a score. A female officer sat beside her on the sofa, scribbling notes detailing the anonymous phone calls and asking whether she had noticed anything else unusual.

"No, just the phone calls."

The police had found a further three on her answering machine, all silent hang ups. Following a thorough search, they had confirmed that the house was empty. They had found no other signs of disturbance, but Lotty was hiding under Kate's bed and refusing point-blank to venture out, even for food.

"Is it because of Steve?" Realistically, Kate suspected she knew the answer to that question, but the officer refused to commit.

"We don't know, Kate. The Garretts are quite a prolific family in terms of local crime, but the attempt on the jeweller's was bigger than anything they've ever been involved with. It's unlikely to be the parents. They're both elderly and in poor health, and Eric was refused bail."

"There was a cousin…The detective who interviewed me mentioned a cousin. I doubt he would have been too happy with a verdict of justifiable force."

The officer was nodding. "Tony. He went quiet once he realised that even the tabloid press wouldn't give him any credence. They gave him enough rope and just left him to hang himself. We'll pay him a visit though, make sure he's keeping his head down." She gave Kate a hopeful smile. "It might just be kids who've seen it all on the news."

Kate smiled too, not convinced. "I hope so."

"Do you want a unit to stick around for a while?"

With all the lights on and the house noisy with the chatter of police officers and their radios, Kate felt slightly braver and slightly foolish at having panicked. "No. No, I'll be fine. Thank you."

"Not a problem. Here's the log number for the crime and my work mobile number. Call if there's anything you're worried about, okay?"

"Okay. Thanks."

They left shortly after that, and the house fell silent again. Ten minutes later, Lotty emerged with her tail between her legs and sidled onto Kate's knee, tucking herself into a small, traumatised ball.

"I know the feeling, little miss."

Either side of the crank calls there had been messages from her mother. Kate picked the phone up. She had no real inclination to speak to her mother right at that moment, but she needed to speak to someone.

❖

An hour later, Kate was fervently wishing for silence again. Her mother, delighted that Kate had called, had taken it as implicit permission to recount all the news, wedding updates, and gossip that had been accrued since they had last managed to hold a prolonged conversation. Tired out and unable to get a word in edgeways, Kate had long since resorted to making polite listening noises at points she hoped were appropriate. She didn't know why she had phoned her mother. Kate couldn't talk to her mother about what had been happening to her at home, and she certainly couldn't talk to her about Sam. How could she ask her mother for advice or insight when hysteria would inevitably set in at the very suggestion that Kate might be gay?

"You really should come down here, sweetheart. It's the only sensible option."

Kate realised her mother was no longer reading her the news clippings that had been diligently saved to put in a souvenir album.

"What? Sorry. Pardon?"

"After everything you've been through, darling. You need time away from that hospital. You need your mother to look after you."

Despite her mother's flaws—the ill-timed phone calls, Conservative opinions, self-centred and irrelevant obsessions, and endless capacity for trivialising Kate's choice of occupation and living location—Kate felt her eyes prick with tears at the concern in her mother's voice. There was always that small part of her that was desperate for her mother's approval and always that part which needed her mother's comfort. Right at that moment, with her nerves still raw, she was grateful for comfort in any shape or form. She took a deep breath. "I might."

"You could stay in the guest room. Really, Kate, I think you should seriously consider it…Sorry, what did you say?"

Kate smiled, shaking her head in despair. "I said I might. No promises, Mum, but maybe getting away isn't a bad idea."

There was a short, delighted shriek on the other end of the phone. Kate winced, holding the handset farther away from her ear as her mother launched into a series of plans and began to tell her how good the new motorway toll road was. Kate, barely listening but soothed by the constant flow of noise, closed her eyes and let the words wash over her.

CHAPTER TWELVE

"S o have you given it any more thought?" Cally asked.

"Ow! Jesus!" Sam moved her good leg restlessly against the bed as the nurse peeled away the dressing covering the wound in her thigh. Cally squeezed her hand and then let out a squeak at the ferocity of Sam's grip.

"What? Have I given what any more thought?" Sam panted and struggled to isolate the conversation from the pain and the fact that Kate had always been there to do the dressing changes for her.

"Oh, yuck! And yet…" Cally bent lower, taking in the detail of the injury. "How very cool."

"Shit. Doesn't feel very cool. What've you poured onto it, acid?"

The agency nurse gave her a *don't be ridiculous* look and continued to clean the area with what smelled like an alcohol wipe. It was something Kate had never done, working on the basis that alcohol, added to raw skin, equalled an unnecessary amount of discomfort.

Cally's persistence cut through the haze. "Have you given any more thought about coming to stay at mine when they kick you out of here?"

Sam didn't answer. She looked past Cally, out the window where rain splattered against the glass and the hills had been swallowed up by an angry grey sky. The nurse swapped one wipe for another and started all over again.

Kate had been to see Sam twice in the past four days. Each time, an excuse to leave had been on her lips as soon as she had crossed the threshold. Nightmares had begun creeping back into what little sleep Sam was getting, and the days were passing by in a blur of exhaustion. It had all gone so wrong, and she just wanted to leave, to go home and wallow peacefully in her own misery. On his morning rounds, Tom had raised an eyebrow at her pallor and the dark shadows under her eyes, but he had finally nodded and agreed to her release for the next day. She bit her lip as the nurse's cold hands sealed a fresh dressing on her leg. She knew she wouldn't be able to manage on her own, and she finally nodded in answer to Cally's questioning expression.

"Yes. Yeah. If it's okay, I mean. Just while I get back on my feet?"

Cally gave a squeal and wrapped her arms around Sam, planting a wet kiss on her cheek.

The nurse screwed up her nose with disapproval, gathered the clinical waste, and left the room.

❖

"Well, you look like crap." Laura handed the bag of pastries to Kate and stepped into the kitchen when she moved aside. "I'll put the kettle on. You sit."

Laura busied herself making tea while Kate tried to get used to the idea of her unannounced visit. She didn't need Laura to tell her that she looked terrible. The grey sweats she was wearing had fit her comfortably a few weeks ago. They hung off her now and their washed-out colour did nothing to disguise how pale she was.

"You're not sleeping, then?"

Kate shook her head, not trusting her voice just yet. She took the cup she was offered and sipped it gratefully.

"Eat one of these. I'd have brought twice as many if I'd known you needed feeding up so badly."

"I'm fine."

"Yeah, and I'm the Queen of Sheba."

"I think it's just a bit of a bug. That's why I've not been around as much." Kate was getting better at lying on short notice.

Laura was having none of it. "Don't give me that crap, Kate. I'm your best friend. I know what's going on. Well, I sort of know. I'm guessing it has something to do with a certain paramedic who's been hanging around the hospital of late."

Kate toyed with a cinnamon swirl. "Well then, you *do* know everything." That was another lie; she hadn't told Laura about the break-in. The only person she had told was Mackenzie, who had taken it upon himself to look into the whereabouts of the cousin, and who had been sworn to secrecy. She had thought up a few creative and vicious threats to prevent him from telling Sam. If Sam was happy with Cally, then Kate would have to live with that. There was no way she was going to resort to emotional blackmail to try to turn things in her favour.

She realised her tone had been sharper than she had intended and put the pastry back onto her plate. "I'm sorry."

"Have you talked to Sam about Cally?"

"No. There's no need." She sat back in her chair, her hands clenched in her lap. "Laura, I saw them together, out in the grounds. They were so close, and Cally, she kissed Sam's hand."

"Oh." Laura bit her pastry. "So it wasn't full-on sex, then?"

The comment was so unexpected that Kate laughed, but she sobered quickly and shook her head. "It was enough."

"There might be an innocent explanation, Kate."

"I just…I don't think I want to know."

Kate watched as Laura shifted awkwardly in her chair and swallowed a mouthful of tea in a blatant delaying tactic. Wondering what else was to come, Kate braced herself as if to prepare for a physical blow.

"Tom's letting her go home tomorrow," Laura said at last. She took a deep breath. "Kate, I think she's moving in with Cally."

Kate nodded slowly. "Well, I guess there really isn't anything to talk about, then, is there?"

❖

Kate hadn't said much after that, but she had allowed Laura to sit with her on the sofa as she huddled under a throw and shivered. Laura had hovered for a little while before taking herself off to clean the kitchen. Pots and pans that Kate hadn't used in weeks clattered in the sink and the scent of pine disinfectant lingered heavily in the air. Without intending to, Kate dozed off to the sound of Laura's tuneless humming and the rhythmic tug of Lotty kneading her blanket.

The ringing of the phone shocked Kate awake. Having dashed in from the kitchen, Laura took one look at Kate and answered it instead, but she had barely said "hello" before she turned the handset around, a confused expression on her face. The dial tone sounded loud in the stillness.

"They hung up."

Kate nodded, trying not to react or let Laura know what had really been happening. "I've been getting them the last week or so. I answer, they hang up. Sometimes they leave it long enough that I can hear them breathing." That was as much detail as Kate was willing to give. There was no way she was telling Laura about the screaming down the line or that the man knew her name. "Probably some idiot been reading the newspapers, found my number from somewhere."

"Have you told the police?" Laura sounded alarmed, although Kate wasn't sure if it was due to the call or the fact that she didn't seem too interested in pursuing the matter.

"No. I don't think they'd be able to do anything about it. I'm sure the novelty will wear off eventually." She was logging the calls for the police. That had been the third one since the break-in, and the police were looking to trace the anonymous number through the telephone company.

"At least mention it to Mackenzie."

"Good idea. I will." Mackenzie had hopefully already paid Tony Garrett a house call.

"You'd better or I will." Kate nodded, barely awake enough to take in what Laura was saying. "Are you going back to sleep?"

Kate could feel her eyes drooping and she was struggling to hold her head up. She shook her head but didn't protest when Laura fluffed up a cushion and pushed her gently until she lay the length of the sofa.

"Sometimes they call in the night…"

Laura tucked the blanket closely around her and ran a hand through her hair. "It's okay. Don't worry about it. We'll get it sorted. I'll phone Ben, let him know I'll be late. Have a rest and I'll make something for tea."

"You might have to improvise a little."

"Okay then. You sleep. I'll go and buy some essentials and then make tea."

"Thank you."

"You're going to be fine, Kate. One way or another, it'll all work itself out."

Kate nodded, not convinced at all, but too tired to argue. She closed her eyes and fell asleep listening to the exasperated noises Laura was making as every cupboard opened revealed itself to be bare.

❖

Sam looked around the room one last time. The linen from the bed had already been removed and the side table was empty, stripped of all the personal possessions she had gradually amassed during her stay in the hospital.

"Right, you got everything?" Cally was breathless from carrying bags and boxes out to her car.

"Just this one left." Sam waved a crutch at a holdall. "I'll… you go. I'll catch you up. I want to say good-bye to the ward staff."

"No problem. I'll wait in the car. Take your time."

Sam waited until she had gone then sat on the edge of the bed. She had already said her good-byes to the staff, had already plied them with chocolates and flowers and her heartfelt gratitude. Now she was just holding on, delaying the inevitable in the hope that Kate would turn up to say good-bye. Earlier, Laura had muttered something about a nasty cold, a touch of the flu, maybe a chest infection, but she had blushed and struggled to meet Sam's eyes. Sam knew in her heart that Kate wasn't coming.

She pushed herself off the bed and found her balance on her crutches. Her progress was slow and deliberate, and she forced a smile onto her face as she waved at the staff and headed out into the corridor. Her stomach was churning, and she tried to convince herself it was just nerves, that she had been in the hospital for so long she had become institutionalised. That was true for a small part of it, but the act of leaving also meant the probability of never seeing Kate again, and that was tearing her apart.

When she reached the car, she refused to look back and kept the same smile she had used on the ward staff in play again for Cally, who fussed like a mother hen, guiding her into the passenger seat and helping her with her seatbelt before getting into the car herself. Sam closed her eyes as the engine started, then chanced a quick glance back to the main entrance. She thought she saw a familiar figure there; the right height, the right hair colour, but the figure had gone inside before Sam could be sure who it was.

Despite the rain, the countryside they were passing through was beautiful. Sam stared out the window, making non-committal noises as Cally chattered endlessly.

Kate had kept her promise. Sam *had* walked out of the hospital, but the fact that Kate hadn't been there to see it broke Sam's heart.

❖

Inside the main entrance, Kate stood with her back against the wall. When she had arrived at the ward, the nurse in charge had told her that Sam had already left. Kate had reached the entrance in time to see Sam make her way to Cally and smile as she was ushered into the car. She hadn't looked back, and Kate hadn't been able to do anything but stagger back inside. Feeling sick, she lurched toward the nearest public toilet. The first cubicle was empty and she locked the door and sat on the seat with her head low. Two girls, young and giggly, chatted by the sinks as she waited for the feeling to pass. A hand dryer blasted air out, then the main door swung closed and the voices faded. Kate stood gingerly and left her cubicle. Standing at the sinks, she studied her reflection in the fingerprint-smeared mirror.

"Coward." Her reflection offered no defence to the accusation. She had just let the best thing that had ever happened to her walk slowly out of her life, and she hadn't had the courage to do anything about it.

❖

Five years ago, after Kate had first shown her mother around her cottage, she had received a housewarming present in the post: a parcel containing security light timers and a set of bolts for her windows. Kate had phoned to thank her mother politely, pushed the box under her bed, and barely given it another thought.

Last week, however, the man who had repaired the smashed window in Kate's living room had fitted two of those bolts to lock it securely. When she pulled up in front of the cottage, the timers she had set ensured that light was blazing behind the curtains of every room.

It didn't make her any less reluctant to go inside, though, and the minutes passed as she sat in her Land Rover, gripping the steering wheel. Dusk gradually ate away at what little daylight the clouds had let through. She didn't want to be there, but there was no reason for her to be at the hospital any more.

Finally she pushed the Land Rover's door open. An icy breeze bit into her face and made something unseen bang behind her shed. She crossed the driveway at a jog, her key already in her hand.

She had a new routine now. Once inside, she methodically walked around the cottage, checking each room for signs of disturbance and making sure that everything she had locked that morning remained locked. It was only when she reached her bedroom that she took off her coat and boots and allowed herself to relax slightly. For the first time since the break-in, Lotty had been brave enough to venture back onto Kate's bed. Murmuring softly to her, Kate lay down beside her and pressed close to her warmth. As Lotty purred, Kate closed her eyes tightly and tried her best not to think about anything at all.

A sharp knock on the front door startled her from a light sleep and sent Lotty skittering beneath the bed. She heard a rustle and muttered swearing as her visitor attempted to push her letterbox open. It sounded like he had almost lost a finger in the process.

"Doc, you in? It's only me."

On recognising Mackenzie's voice, Kate swung her legs over the edge of the bed and ran a hand through her sleep-tangled hair. When she opened the door, Mackenzie nodded at her.

"Hey, Doc."

"Hey, yourself."

He smiled but it barely altered the serious set of his face.

Kate stepped aside to let him in. "I'm guessing you weren't just in the neighbourhood," she said.

"No, I wasn't."

She sighed. "I think I'd better put the kettle on, then."

With the stove warming the kitchen and the smell of hot, buttered toast making her stomach rumble, Kate could almost pretend she was entertaining a guest for the evening. But that guest had set an official case file on her kitchen table and there was a glossy photograph, deliberately placed facedown that he kept adjusting uneasily.

"You look…" Mackenzie sipped his tea, obviously fumbling for the right thing to say. In the end he settled on, "less bruised."

That made Kate laugh hollowly and he opened his hands in apology.

"Have you seen Sam?" she asked into the quiet that followed.

"No. I spoke to her earlier, though. She, uh, she gave me Cally's phone number." His hands opened again. "I think she's being daft, if it helps any, Doc. I was kind of hoping that you and she might…" He coughed once, as if afraid that he had overstepped the mark. "Well, anyway, she said she was feeling okay. Didn't say much else and didn't sound happy. I'll call round in a few days, see if I can talk some sense into her."

Mackenzie topped up Kate's mug from the teapot and waited as she added her own milk. She watched his fingers worry at the edge of the photograph and covered them with her own.

"You don't know where he is, do you?"

"No, we don't," he said and turned the photograph over. He slid it across the table until it rested in front of her. "This is Tony Garrett. It's a file photo, taken about eighteen months ago so he's probably not changed much."

Kate looked at the image and did her utmost not to recoil. Tony Garrett was a thickset man in his early thirties. He stared directly at the camera, a sneer twisting his lips, and he looked so much like Steve he made her feel sick.

"Sorry, Doc." Mackenzie took the photograph away from her and tucked it back into the file.

"No, it's okay. I need to know what he looks like if he's the one who's been phoning, and the one who broke in here. Jesus." She lowered her head into her hands.

"There was a new tenant at his last known address," Mackenzie said. "Tony's not been seen since Steve's funeral. Family and known acquaintances say he's just dropped off the grid."

"Is that something he would do?" Kate picked up the file and opened it. It contained a series of short statements that all concluded in the same manner: Tony hadn't been in contact and no one knew where he was.

"No," Mackenzie admitted. "He's barely been out of trouble for the last ten years. Whenever there was a decent brawl in the area, police were pretty much guaranteed to find he was the one who had instigated it. Either that, or he's been banged up inside. It's got the local police concerned enough that they're stepping up patrols around your area. But listen, Kate," he closed the file and waited until she made eye contact with him, "do you have anywhere else you could go?"

She folded her arms and shook her head in defiance. Despite her private misgivings about being alone in the cottage, she was suddenly determined not to be driven out of her own home.

"No, I'm not leaving," she said in a tone that dared him to contradict her.

"It wouldn't be a permanent move. Just until we find this idiot."

"This is my *home*," she whispered. She shook her head again, but then thought of the fortress she was gradually turning her home into, and the way that its creaks and groans, once familiar and comforting, now set her nerves on edge.

"I know, love. It's just a long way from help if anything were to happen." Mackenzie took a breath as if he had played the final card in his hand and knew that it was a game changer.

It was pleasantly warm in the kitchen, but Kate hugged her arms closer across her chest and tried to suppress a shiver. She was well aware how vulnerable she was at the cottage, but Mackenzie pinpointing that fact made it all the more daunting, and she didn't want him to see how frightened she was.

"My mum's been trying to persuade me to stay with her for a few days," she said with reluctance. "I suppose now would be as good a time as any."

Mackenzie nodded. "I really am sorry, Kate."

"I know. Thanks for everything, anyway."

She stood with him as he pushed his chair back and gathered his coat. "I think I'm still in your debt, Doc," he said. He kissed the top of her head and she smiled up at him. "You've got my number, right?" he said.

"I've got it."

"Phone any time."

"I will. Thanks, Mac." She laughed softly as he looked down at his boots. "Mac, you can go. I'll be fine, really."

"Yeah?"

"Yes."

"Promise me you'll think about staying with your mum."

"I promise."

"Okay." He seemed encouraged by that and shrugged into his coat. "Come and lock your door behind me," he said and led her into the hallway.

❖

The music was a song Sam knew but had never liked, and the voices were too numerous and too loud for her to be able to make any sense out of the conversations around her. Someone she vaguely recognised sat on the sofa beside her, the jarring impact against her leg making her dig her fingers into the leather of the armrest.

"You must've been really scared."

The woman was more than a little drunk, inhibitions dulled by the white wine Cally had bought in bulk. Sam made a polite, affirmative-sounding noise and didn't dignify the stupid comment with an answer. She looked around the room at Cally's idea of a "quiet evening in." There were at least twenty women scattered about the furniture or standing in small groups in the kitchen. Cally's circle of friends had always been extensive, but she had at least narrowed down the guest list to those who also knew Sam. It was only her second night out of the hospital, but she could feel herself being sucked inexorably back into the kind of life she and Cally had once shared. Cally was bending over backward to be helpful, thoughtful, and sweet, and Sam had let her. She was too tired and out of sorts to offer any resistance, and she didn't have the energy to consider that Cally might mistake that as an indication of a shared ideal.

"Can I get you a drink?" Another woman, one of Cally's colleagues and many exes.

Sam smiled politely and indicated the orange juice on the side table. "I'm on the wagon, thanks." She gestured at her leg. "Painkillers." She didn't mention she was pretty much teetotal at the best of times.

"Oh, of course. Sorry." The woman squeezed onto the sofa and offered her hand. "You probably don't remember me. It's Karen. I used to go out with Cally." She looked around the room and started to laugh. "As did pretty much everyone else here. Still, it's good to see the two of you back together…"

Sam's eyes widened, but before she could correct the misconception, Karen carried on. "Cally was in a real state when she found out you'd been hurt. They took her off her shift, you know. I gave her a lift home. Then within a week she dumped Jo, and here you both are playing happy families again."

Sam managed a thin smile, but a cold feeling was settling in the pit of her stomach. Cally had told her a different version of the break-up, blaming the split on Jo. At no point had she mentioned it had been her that had ended the relationship.

Karen sighed, oblivious to Sam's unease. "She always did want what she couldn't have, and she always found a way to bloody get it." She took a sip of her drink and leaned into Sam conspiratorially. "So tell me about this doctor of yours. Cal said she's quite the catch even if she's not sure which team she's playing for."

Sam blinked, stunned. Stunned that Kate was a topic of idle gossip in the room and sickened that the issue of her sexuality was being debated so casually. "I'm sorry." She struggled to her feet. "But that's no fucking business of yours." She moved through the room as quickly as she could, given the crowd and the crutches and the rush of adrenaline that was making her clumsy.

Cally must have noticed the look on her face, because they reached the back door at pretty much the same time. "Hey, Sam. You okay?"

Sam had stepped down into the backyard and was taking deep breaths of the freezing air. "I'm fine."

"What did Karen say to you?"

"Nothing. I'm fine." She looked at the sky, unable to see much besides light pollution. She closed her eyes, wishing she were at home.

"You don't look fine. Why are you pissed off?"

"It's nothing. She said something about Kate. I...I just don't think you should be talking about her when you don't know her and she's not here to defend herself."

Cally pulled the back door closed, shutting out the noise from the house. "Don't you think you're taking it all a bit seriously? For fuck's sake, Sam, you know what they're like. This is probably the best bit of tattle they've heard in months. As for Kate, *you* barely know her. She may've been a big hero, but she fucked you off pretty damn quickly as soon as things became a bit difficult."

Sam shook her head. "No. It wasn't like that."

"How do you know? You never even spoke to her about it. If you had such a good thing going, why did nothing happen?" Cally didn't wait for an answer. "I'll tell you why, because it was nice for a while for her to string you along, but when it came down to it, she decided it was safer staying in the closet."

Sam made no attempt to keep the anger from her voice. "Everything was working out fine until you showed up. Did you ever even think about that? Or did you just see something you wanted and decide to take it, and to hell with the consequences? As long as you're not suffering in the fallout, it really doesn't matter, does it?"

Cally looked stunned, her face pale. "I was trying to help."

"Yes, Cal, but you were trying to help *yourself*. That's the difference. Look," Sam opened the back door, "I'm going to bed. I'll get a cab home in the morning."

"Sam, come on. Don't be like this."

Sam ignored her, and made her way through the women in the kitchen who wouldn't meet her eyes and kept their voices hushed. As she got to the top of the stairs, she heard the conversation break out again, loud and animated. She shut the bedroom door, closing it all out.

❖

"And what time does that get into Euston? Five thirty? No, that should be fine." Kate scribbled the train times down on a pad of paper as the woman on the information line asked whether she would like to purchase an advance ticket for her journey.

"No. No thank you. I've not finalised my arrangements yet."

The woman concluded the call and disconnected. Kate set her phone down, still staring at the notes she had made. She had not given her mother a definite answer about going to stay with her, but after the conversation with Mackenzie, Kate knew she needed to do something. There had been no word from Sam. She had asked Laura and received a not-unexpected negative answer: Sam had left with Cally and had not been in touch with the hospital since.

Kate filled her kettle with water and dropped a tea bag into her mug. If she was going to phone her mother, she was definitely going to need tea.

❖

The soft jangle of cutlery against crockery woke Sam. The noise was coming from the kitchen, muted and careful. Cally was trying to be quiet. Sam eased herself onto her back and moved the alarm clock to check the time: 9:02 a.m. She had slept later than she had intended, largely a result of having been awake until four. She was about to get up to get dressed when there was a timid knock at the bedroom door.

"Sam? Sam, are you awake?"

Cally. She really, *really* did not want to see Cally this early, and she certainly did not want a repeat of the previous night's discussion. She just wanted to go home. Struggling to sit up, she noticed that the door handle was already turning; apparently Cally wasn't waiting for an answer.

"Hey, sleepyhead!" Cally was all smiles, bearing a tray laden with juice, tea, toast, and eggs. "Look, I cooked!"

Sam stared at her, lost for words, and genuinely surprised that she had managed to scramble an egg without burning the house down. "Cally, I don't—"

"Shh. Shh. I just wanted to say that I was sorry for last night. You were right about everything and I was wrong. About everything."

She sounded absolutely sincere, but Sam suspected she probably couldn't even remember what they had argued about.

"Eat your breakfast, and if you still want to head home, I'll give you a lift." She placed the tray on Sam's lap and gave her a quick kiss on the cheek. "Just watch out for shell in your egg. It all went to shit when I cracked it."

She was gone again as quickly as she had appeared, leaving Sam stunned and more than a little confused. She had expected a battle, possibly tears, recriminations, and sulking, but not this, not breakfast in bed and an admission of culpability. She sipped her tea and then gingerly experimented with a forkful of egg. Nothing crunched in her mouth, which she took to be a promising sign. She just wished the other signs Cally was giving her were so straightforward.

❖

"You don't have to leave, you know."

"Jesus!" Sam was zipping her holdall closed and hadn't heard Cally approach.

Cally sat on the bed, watching as Sam rested her hands on her bag and sighed quietly.

"I think I do, Cal. I really appreciate you helping me out, but I need to go home."

"I said I was sorry about last night, didn't I?" Cally seemed to be reaching deeply into her repertoire of persuasive tricks and was managing to be contrite and dewy-eyed simultaneously.

"Yes, you did. Do you actually remember what you were apologising for?"

"Yes! Someone said something bad about Kate, and, um…I'd had quite a lot of cheap white wine."

Sam smiled and shook her head. "Yeah, it was something along those lines." She heaved the bag onto the floor and sat on the bed beside Cally. "Cal, did you tell everyone last night that we were back together?"

"No! No, not at all." She grinned at Sam. "Hey, I can't help it if lots of them jumped to a perfectly logical but erroneous conclusion." She put her hand up and twisted a strand of Sam's hair in her fingers. "We fit together, me and you. I think that's what they saw. You must see it too, Sam. This last week, it's been just like old times."

Sam moved her head away from Cally's touch, but Cally persisted, cupping her cheek and then kissing her gently on the lips.

"Cally, don't." Sam shook her head and rose unsteadily. "I have to go." She reached the door just before Cally, who put both arms around her and pushed the door closed.

"Tell me you really don't want this and I'll stop." Her voice was low and honeyed, and Sam might have found the sultry lesbian cliché amusing if she hadn't been pinned quite so effectively.

"I *really* don't want this." Sam's tone left no room for misinterpretation.

Cally took a step back, genuinely bemused. "*Seriously?*"

"Seriously."

"Shit. Now I feel fairly stupid."

Sam laughed, unable to help herself, and was relieved when Cally joined in.

"You really do love that bloody doctor, don't you?"

Sam nodded, her heart lifting in her chest. "Yes. I really do."

"Oh fuck. Just don't…Don't let her break your heart."

"I'll try not to." Sam smiled at her. "Can you call me a cab?"

"I can drive you home, Sam."

"Not with your hangover. Call me a cab."

Cally shrugged, picked up two of Sam's bags and headed downstairs. "C'mon, hopalong. Let's get you safely back in the arms of your good doctor."

Shaking her head, Sam had a feeling it wouldn't be quite that simple.

CHAPTER THIRTEEN

Kate dropped a bottle of shampoo into her wash bag and zipped it closed. She had never been able to stand her mother's brand of toiletries. Checking her watch, she allowed herself another couple of hours before she would need to call a taxi. That was plenty of time to finish packing and then steel her nerves in preparation for her trip down to the capital.

"Oh, Lotty."

She sat beside the case that lay open on her bed and stroked the head of her cat, who was curled up fast asleep on her folded clothes.

"I know you've only just got me back, but it'll only be for a week or so, and Mrs. Ryan and Laura are going to feed you. Yes, *that* Laura, the one who gives you tuna and thinks I don't know."

Lotty blinked at her, looking nonplussed but extremely comfortable.

"It'll only be for a week," Kate repeated, uncertain whether she was trying to persuade herself or the cat. "Then I'll be home and everything will be back to normal."

❖

The taxi driver had dropped her bags inside the front door, wished her well, and left with an expression on his face that suggested he was trying to remember why Sam looked so familiar. He hadn't asked and she hadn't offered any details, just thanked him and closed her front door, relishing the absolute silence. A silence which lasted approximately ten seconds before a black and white tornado launched himself downstairs at her and, emitting a series of happy cries, attempted to wind himself around her feet with every awkward step she took.

"Mitts, let me…Just hold on…Let me sit down." She collapsed onto her sofa and was instantly sat on and kneaded intently.

"Missed you too, little man."

She looked around her living room. Nothing had changed aside from the thin layer of dust that had gathered on her surfaces. The television guide was still open to the day before she had been shot. She shook her head and thumbed it closed. That day seemed like several lifetimes ago.

Now she was home, she realised that she had no idea what to do next. She wanted to see Kate, that was indisputable, but she had no idea where Kate lived or what her phone number was. There was an obvious way to get that information, however, and she toyed nervously with the phone's handset for a moment before pulling the outpatients' appointment leaflet from her bag and dialling the number for the hospital's main switchboard. In the weeks she had been a patient there, she had memorised the shift pattern for most of the nurses, and she knew that Laura would be on duty. When the call was placed through to the ward, it took only two rings before Laura's familiar voice answered.

"Laura? Hi, it's Sam."

There was a pause, during which she could hear Laura pulling out a chair and sitting down.

"Hi yourself, what's the problem?"

Sam caught the edge in her voice and didn't blame her for starting off on the defensive. "I…um. Shit. There's no problem. Not really. Well, not medically."

Somewhere in the midst of her stammering and stuttering, Laura must have taken pity on her. "Kate's not here, Sam."

"I know. Well, I would have guessed that." Sam pulled in a deep breath, trying to steady her voice. "I need to speak to her,

Laura. I can't…even if nothing's ever going to happen between us, I can't leave it all like this."

"So it's true then?" The edge was back and sharper than before. "You are back with the paramedic?"

"What? Cally? Oh God, no!" Sam realised, too late, how her last statement must have sounded. "No. That's what I need to explain. Nothing ever happened and it all just went so wrong and I didn't know how to stop it."

She heard Laura sigh, pick something up, click it three times, and put it down again. "You and Kate want your bloody heads banging together."

Sam was so surprised she let out a short laugh. "Yeah, I think you might be right."

"You got a pen?"

Some kind of affirmative noise squeaked from Sam's throat. She took down Kate's address as Laura reeled it off. "I really appreciate it, Laura."

"You hurt her and I'll come round to yours and kick your arse." Laura only half-sounded like she was joking. "Don't forget you can't run very fast on those crutches."

"I'm not going to hurt her, I promise."

"One other thing, Sam. I don't know when she was planning it, but she was going to London for a while, to stay with her mum and have a break. Get away from those phone calls."

"What?" Sam's mouth felt dry as she heard Laura swear quietly on the other end of the phone. "Laura, what phone calls?"

"Bugger." A deep sigh. "I forgot she hadn't told you. It's probably nothing, but some idiot's been phoning her and hanging up. She's a bit freaked out."

"Jesus." Sam felt sick. She had arrogantly assumed that her playing house with Cally had been the sole source of Kate's misery. The fact that something else might have been going on to compound the situation had never occurred to her. "Is she okay?"

"She's okay, but you might want to go round there sooner rather than later."

"Shit." Sam reached for the telephone directory, thumbing through to *Taxi Firms*. "Thanks, Laura, for everything."

"Just don't fuck it up. If you're letting her down, do it gently. She loves you, you know."

The phone clicked off and Sam was left stunned, listening to the dial tone. She hadn't known. Not for sure. She hadn't dared even to hope for that. Her hand trembled as she dialled the taxi number.

The receptionist confirmed her address and told her ten minutes. Sam thanked the lady, barely listening, and tried not to think what she would do if she was too late.

❖

"This is it, love. Well, it's where the sat nav reckons it is. You ask me, it looks like the middle of bloody nowhere."

From her vantage point in the backseat, Sam could see *Kinder Lea* on the gate and knew they were in the right place. "Thanks, mate. What's the damage?"

"Twenty-four quid. You sure you're okay on those crutches? It's pissing down."

"I'll be fine." She handed thirty pounds over. "Keep it. Thanks for coming out so quickly."

Flushed with his tip, the driver ventured out into the rain and held the car door open for her. "Have a nice one."

"Yeah, thanks. I hope so."

He watched her find her balance on the crutches, then returned to the driver's seat and started the engine, obviously thinking she was quite mad.

Dusk had brought with it a steady rain that had become progressively more torrential the further into the countryside they had travelled. The lights of the taxi rounded a bend and disappeared from view. Sam stood at the gate, wind whipping her face, her coat and jeans already soaked. Apprehension momentarily stilled her hand on the cast-iron gate, but she drew in a long breath and pushed it open, struggling to balance on the uneven path she encountered.

"Oh, bloody hell."

The path ran through a small field, parallel to a second, wider track that provided vehicular access to the cottage. The cottage itself was only just visible in the distance, a yellow light in its front window flickering dimly through the sheets of rain. With a feeling of futility, she pulled her mobile phone out, to be greeted by a flat line indicating she was in an area with no reception.

"Terrific." She pocketed the phone and began to make slow, determined steps up the driveway. Choosing to look on the bright side, she realised that at least the unexpected effort was taking her mind off her shredded nerves.

❖

The ability to look on the bright side lasted for approximately ten minutes. With a harsh gasp, Sam stopped. She sagged forward on the crutches, her fingers and wrists cramping and her leg aching furiously. The light didn't seem to be any closer and she was shivering so hard it was becoming difficult for her to stay on her feet. She wiped a hand across her face, trying to dry it a little and clear her vision, but a fresh belt of rain blasted across the field, forcing her to concede defeat and begin moving again. Rocks and gravel gave way to soaked grass and she lost control of her left crutch, her weakened wrist unable to maintain its grip as the support slipped. She twisted, trying to avoid an impact on her right leg, and crashed instead onto her left knee, swearing viciously as something sharp cut its way into her jeans.

She was still on her hands and knees when she heard the car approaching. She raised her head quickly, smiling with relief at the unexpected development. It was difficult for her to stop her crutches sliding on the wet ground and she struggled for a foothold, desperate to stand, flag the car down, and beg the driver for a ride to the cottage. The possibility that it was Kate occurred to her, quickly followed by the more likely possibility that it was a taxi coming to take Kate off to London. Her efforts became a little more frantic. The car was already beyond her and, balancing precariously on one crutch and one leg, she was about to start waving her other crutch when the car slowed to a crawl and extinguished its lights.

"What the hell?"

She squinted through the rain, recognising the familiar shape of a Subaru Imprezza—fast, expensive, and definitely not the car of choice for a taxi firm—continuing its gradual, almost undetectable progress toward the cottage.

"Shit."

Her instincts were screaming a warning at her. There was nothing about this that felt right, and she thought of the crank phone calls Laura had told her about. Without a plan, and without giving herself the opportunity to change her mind, Sam set off again, fear for Kate masking every discomfort as she watched the car pull in and stop at the side of the cottage.

❖

The knock was earlier than Kate had expected, but she knew that meant Ernie was probably going to blag a cup of coffee out of her before he ran her to the station. Shaking her head, she dropped the bin bag by the kitchen door, scooped up her keys, and walked through to the hallway. When she unlatched the front door, the slightly sarcastic comment she had all fired up and ready to launch died instantly on her lips.

"You should be more careful who you're opening your door to."

The man smiled at her without humour, his teeth bared, the Garrett family resemblance striking. Kate took a step back. Her hands moved instinctively to try to push the door closed, but Tony's foot was already inside and he shook his head at her.

"No, you don't. I think it's time you and me had a little chat, Kate."

His right hand was suddenly around her throat, forcing her back as he slammed the door shut with his left. He tightened his grip, grinning when she gasped for air and clawed at his fingers to try to pry them loose.

"Actually, fuck that. I'm not really in the mood for talking."

❖

Sam was barely fifty metres away when she saw the man knock at the door.

"Don't open it, don't open it." She didn't stop, barely conscious of having spoken, as Kate appeared in the doorway. Sam was close enough to see the look of shock on her face, close enough to see the terror in her eyes as the man gripped her. The door had closed then, the bang swallowed up by the rain and wind.

"Oh God…" With forty metres still to go and no idea what to do when she got there, Sam bent her head low and focused everything on moving forward.

❖

Dark spots danced across Kate's vision as her head swam and she felt herself beginning to lose consciousness. It was almost a relief to succumb to it; her limbs were too heavy to struggle anymore, and the desperate fear was fading. She hit the floor with a clatter when Tony released his hold, awareness rushing back in, leaving her choking and terrified at his feet.

She couldn't speak, her throat too bruised to allow much sound to escape, and she looked around frantically for anything she could use as a weapon. His booted foot kicked her squarely in the abdomen and she moaned quietly, trying to curl herself into a ball to give him less to aim at. A metre away from her, a traditional coal bucket sat at the side of her fireplace, with a cast-iron poker balanced across its rim. She reached out and touched the cold metal but she failed to find purchase before he wrenched her back to her feet.

"You fucking bitch."

The same voice, the same tone from that first phone call, and she found herself waiting for his big monologue, the one where he taunted her and blamed her for his cousin's death and justified his reasons for seeking retribution. But there was no speech, and when his fist connected with her cheekbone she realised that he was just a thug, that his reasoning was based only on a need to lash out in revenge, and that this was the way his life and Steve's had always functioned. There would be nothing deep or meaningful about this—he backhanded her and blood began to trickle from her nose—he was only there to make her hurt.

❖

Stooping low, the crutches the only support between her and a face full of dirt, Sam fought for her breath and tried to formulate some kind of plan. The front door of the cottage was shut, the security catch making it impossible for her to open it from the outside. The windows were only single panes of glass, but climbing through one in a hurry wasn't an option. She could hear the sounds of a struggle in the front room, and, making a quick decision, she began to hobble around the side of the house intending to try the back door, or at least to smash something and draw the man's attention away from Kate.

The back door opened when she tried the handle. She pushed it gently and paused, drawing in a deep breath as her hand shook and her legs suddenly felt like jelly. A small cry of pain from the front room made her shut everything else out. She abandoned one crutch in favour of a cast-iron frying pan, and then threw two plates from the draining board onto the stone tiles of the kitchen floor. The plates smashed and splintered, the noise covering up the sound of Sam moving into place behind the adjoining door. The muffled thuds from the next room ended abruptly.

"What the fuck?" A man's voice, hard and demanding. There was a pause, and Sam's stomach turned over as she waited for Kate to speak, to say anything to indicate that she was still alive.

"I don't know." Kate sounded exhausted but defiant and genuinely puzzled.

Tears sprang into Sam's eyes and she wiped them away, her fingers slick with sweat around the handle of the frying pan.

"I have a cat."

Another thud, followed by a low moan. Sam resisted the urge to rush in there; she needed to catch the man off guard and she wanted him away from Kate.

"Wasn't a fucking cat."

He was quicker than Sam had expected, caution thrown to the wind by an ego fuelled with violence and his own sense of invulnerability. The door she was hiding behind was thrown open, almost catching her in the face before she managed to block it with her foot. As the man strode fully into the kitchen, she stepped out of the shadows and swung the pan at him with as much force as she could muster. It caught him across the back of his head and shoulders and he let out a yell of pain, staggering forward and slamming bodily into the porcelain edge of the Belfast sink. The momentum of the blow had also brought Sam forward, as the weight of the pan carried it to the floor and bounced it back off the tiles. It sent a jolt through her arms, but she barely felt it, already readying herself for another attack. Her second blow struck lower across his back as the strength in her arms waned. He didn't fall, and she was about to turn and attempt to blockade the door against him when he spun around and his fist caught her in the face. Blood filled her mouth with heat and salt. She spat it onto the tiles and watched it spatter in crimson roses as she stood her ground. Kate had done this for her, had stood between her and another man and taken a beating to try to save her life. To Sam it had seemed like pure idiocy at the time; now it seemed like a reasonable strategy.

The man came at her again, swinging wildly, his own pain making him uncoordinated and reckless, but enough of his attempts were connecting. Sam staggered and gripped the pan with increasing futility as he gave her no opportunity to defend herself. He could see he was gaining ground and he smiled at her, taking a moment to stand back and admire his handiwork, as she struggled for breath. "You're the copper." Not a question, and he seemed pleased by the turn of events. "That's just too fucking perfect."

His hand came up then, toward the collar of her coat. She shrank away as he reached for her, but his movement was stopped when something black slammed across his arm. He let out a shrill howl of pain as bones shattered under the impact, and he dropped his guard as instinct forced him to cradle his broken wrist.

Seizing the opportunity, Sam slammed the pan across his face. A large gash opened up on his forehead. He fell to the floor without uttering a sound, twitched once, and lay still. Unable to stay on her feet, Sam dropped to her knees with a gasp and edged away from him, back toward the safety of the shadow in the corner. Arms wrapped around her, halting her retreat, and she stiffened, a whimper escaping her before she heard Kate's familiar voice—dropped low into a whisper—and she buried herself into the embrace.

"Shh, it's okay. We're okay."

Sam wasn't sure who was talking, who was reassuring whom as they knelt together, shuddering and aching and watching the man as he breathed through bubbles of blood and showed no signs of getting up again.

❖

"Kate, come on, sweetheart. Keep your eyes open and stand up with me. Good, that's good."

Less than a minute had passed before Sam had felt Kate begin to sag into her arms, and she forced herself to snap out of the stupor she had been languishing in and start thinking about what she needed to do. Although Kate managed to get to her feet, she was barely able to stay there, and she leaned heavily against Sam, as a combination of sheer determination and residual adrenaline allowed them to stagger slowly into the living room.

"Easy, sit down. You're safe now. Just sit down."

Sam tried not to panic when Kate offered no resistance, sitting on the sofa and resting her head back with a grimace. Her face was a mess, bruises beginning to blossom on both cheeks as her nose bled steadily. She was breathing shallowly, her eyes screwed shut with pain. Sam, remembering the dull, thudding sounds, wondered how many ribs the man had broken by kicking her. There was a blanket over the back of the sofa; Sam draped it over her then took her hand.

"Kate?"

Kate opened her eyes slowly and tried to focus on what Sam was saying.

"I need to go into the kitchen for a minute. I'll be as quick as I can, okay?"

Kate shook her head. "No. I'll…I'll come too." Her voice was thick, but she was already trying to push herself up.

Sam put her hands on her shoulders, barely needing to touch her to put a halt to her efforts. "Don't be an idiot. What're you going to do, slump on him?" To Sam's relief, Kate shrugged and gave her a small smile. "Look, if he was up, then he'd be in here. So I'm guessing he's where we left him, and I'll be fine. Just sit tight."

Not giving Kate any further opportunity to move, Sam pressed a soft kiss to the top of her head, and then limped cautiously into the kitchen. She had been right. The man still lay where he had fallen, deeply unconscious with a small pool of blood gathering beneath his head. Sam dropped down at his side, and ran her hands methodically over him, falling back on her police training to search him thoroughly. By the time she had finished, she held a loaded handgun, a flick knife, and a roll of duct tape. She had barely managed to wrap a length of the tape around his wrists before she turned away and vomited, her stomach clenching again and again as she realised how many random twists of fate had been necessary to produce this outcome where Kate lived, and the man who had come to her house with his jacket full of weapons lay insensible on her kitchen floor.

When there was nothing left inside Sam and the dry retching had stopped, she ran a hand across her face, wiping away cold sweat and blood, and then crawled back to the man to check his bindings. After adding another few layers of tape, she was finally satisfied he was secure. She pulled herself back to her feet and filled a bowl with warm water. There were tea towels folded neatly on a shelf and she bundled one of them around the weapons, before gathering the rest up. She didn't spare the man another glance as she closed the door firmly and made her way back into the living room.

"Kate?" Sam placed the towels beside the sofa and laid her hand gently on Kate's cheek. The tightness in her chest eased a little when she felt the pressure of her touch returned. "Kate, where's your phone?"

"Side of..." Kate caught her breath, licking blood from her lips. "Side of the chair. I called already."

"You called the police?" Sam scrambled over to the chair.

"Called nine nine nine. No time to talk." She smiled faintly. "Had to help."

"You certainly helped, Kate." The phone now in her hands, Sam could hear the slightly frantic voice of the emergency operator still trying to raise the person who had placed the call. Sam identified herself as a police officer, gave her collar number, and requested police assistance and two ambulances. The operator assured her that several police units and an ambulance were already en route—the sound of a violent struggle had played out clearly on the open line—and Sam thanked the woman profusely before she ended the call and returned to Kate's side.

"They'll be here soon. Let me have a look at you."

Kate felt the sofa dip as Sam sat next to her. Using a warm cloth, Sam began to ease the blood from her face and Kate saw her wince in sympathy at the injuries she was revealing. Too exhausted to resist, Kate allowed Sam to fold the blanket down to her waist. Her hands were clasped together in her lap. Sam gently disentangled her fingers and then placed her hands on the sofa.

"He kicked you?"

Kate nodded, unable to elaborate. She had lost count after he had knocked her to the floor for the second time, but every breath she took raced needles of fire through her abdomen and chest.

"God, Kate."

Sam had opened Kate's shirt, revealing the damage to her torso. Kate looked down to see the red and purple blotches covering her skin, and wondered dully whether this would be the last time she would have to bear the imprint of a man's boot across her chest. Catching the stricken expression on Sam's face, she managed a smile.

"It's not too bad."

"It looks awful," Sam countered without hesitation. "God." She seemed completely at a loss. "Is there anything I can do to help?"

Kate shook her head. "It's okay. I'm fine. They'll be here soon." Sam's hand was still tracing the injuries on her chest and she could feel the slight tremor in her fingers as Sam fought to stay calm. Kate wrapped them in her own and decided to change the subject. "You walked all the way down, didn't you?"

"Yeah."

"Laura didn't tell you that I lived in the middle of a field?"

"No. She forgot to mention that."

Kate laughed softly. "I'll bloody kill her." She felt Sam laugh then shiver, and pulled her closer, realising for the first time that she was soaking wet. "Jesus." Arranging the blanket over both of them, Kate rested her head against Sam's shoulder as they huddled together. "Thank you," she whispered. She felt Sam nod against her throat, then begin to cry. Tightening her hold, Kate murmured quietly to her as she heard the first vehicle scream to a halt at the front of the cottage.

❖

Tom arrived with the paramedics. His soaked coat dripped water all over the carpet as he stared at Kate and Sam.

"I was chatting with the crew in the ambulance bay. When they got the call, I recognised your address," he said before Kate had even drawn a breath to ask. "I can't turn my back on you two for a minute, can I?"

He didn't seem surprised to see Sam, but just shook his head and dropped to one knee beside the sofa.

"Christ, Kate." It wasn't often that Tom allowed his professionalism to slip, but she heard the quaver in his voice. It was like the worst case of déjà vu; he made exactly the same gesture he had made in the ITU, cupping her chin and turning her head into the light to allow him to examine her injuries. Beside her, Sam sat pale and still, clutching her hand.

"You didn't have to come all the way out here, Tom," Kate said in an undertone, sucking in a breath when he pressed his fingers against a particularly tender area.

"Sorry." He dropped his hand away and then smiled at her. "You know I'm a sucker for tagging along in ambulances. It's the blue lights, they make me all giddy."

It was true, and it made her laugh, her arms coming to rest across her chest as the movement jarred her ribs.

Tom's eyes narrowed as he watched her. "Dare I ask what other injuries you're hiding?"

Sam answered for her. "Her chest is a mess."

"Is it now?" Tom said, looking directly at her.

Kate opened her mouth, fully intending to downplay Sam's damning assessment, but she was cut off by a paramedic appearing in the living room doorway, his gloves stained with blood.

"Doc?" The paramedic waited until Tom looked up in acknowledgement. "We're going to move this one first. He's talking...well, he's swearing, actually, but he was unconscious when the police got in here and he's still bleeding."

"Do you need me to take a look at him?" Tom was beginning to stand, but the paramedic waved him down.

"We've already got him on a long board. We're getting a police escort. He's lively enough to make me think he'll make a full recovery."

"Terrific." Tom's tone implied he was thinking just the opposite.

The paramedic looked at Kate and Sam, obviously uncomfortable when he spoke again. "Will you be okay until the other ambulance gets here? They gave an ETA of twenty-five minutes."

With a sigh, Tom nodded and the paramedic left the room. Kate knew they were right to take the most seriously injured first and that Tom was being careful not to show his frustration with their decision. There were police officers all over the living room, documenting the scene, bagging up evidence and affording them no privacy.

"Think you can manage the stairs?" Tom said, as an officer pointed to a splatter of blood and a camera flashed twice in quick succession. "I want to take a proper look at you both."

Sam nodded and looked to Kate, who said nothing but started to push herself up off the sofa.

Tom caught one of Kate's arms, Sam took her other and between the two of them, she managed to stand.

"I'm okay," she said, daring them to contradict her.

"I bloody hope so." Tom was smiling. "There's no way I'm carrying your arse if you faint halfway up."

❖

Kate didn't faint. She sat on her bed, held a wad of gauze to her bleeding nose, and allowed Tom to open her shirt.

"Take a deep breath for me."

The stethoscope was cold against her chest, but she ignored it, concentrating instead on doing as she was asked. Something low on the left side of her ribcage ground painfully as she breathed. She could tell there were fractures there.

Tom probed the same area carefully. "Probably a couple of fractures," he said, pulling her shirt closed again. "Looking at the bruising, I expected worse."

"I know." Kate nodded. "Guess we got lucky."

A stifled sob came from the corner of the room where Sam, reluctant to sit on the bed with her clothes soaked, had sat on a wooden chair instead. Kate looked up sharply. She splinted her ribs with her hand and walked over to kneel beside the chair. Sam's hand was ice cold when Kate touched it, and she was shivering uncontrollably.

"Shit," Kate said softly. "You're freezing." She turned back to Tom. "Second drawer down, there should be sweatpants and sweaters. Socks and underwear in the smaller drawer."

He moved with alacrity, and Kate heard him curse himself for neglecting to consider Sam's condition. After searching hurriedly through the drawers, he handed a pile of clothing to Kate.

"Thanks." Kate glanced back at Sam. "Can you give us a minute, Tom?"

"Sure. I'll update the police. Shout if you need me, okay?"

Kate waited until the bedroom door had closed behind him. "I need to get you undressed, Sam. Get you out of those wet clothes."

Sam made a murmured noise of assent and sat quietly as Kate took her boots off and unzipped her jacket. She lifted her arms when she was asked and accepted the towel she was given in lieu of her sweater. Kate watched Sam struggle to perform the simple tasks and her brow furrowed with concern. "You're hypothermic, Sam." She took the towel from Sam's loose grip and rubbed Sam's chest and arms briskly, trying to warm them. "I can't believe you walked all the way down here."

Sam hugged her arms together as Kate moved the towel to her back. "It wasn't that far."

"It's a quarter of a mile."

"Mmm?"

"In the pouring rain."

"Yes."

"On crutches."

"Yes. They were a bit of a pain, really."

"In the dark." Kate sighed as Sam just shrugged and smiled blearily at her. "Can you lift your bottom up?"

Sam's jeans went the same way as everything else. She winced as they scraped against the jagged tear in her knee.

"What happened here?" Kate was rubbing the towel down Sam's legs, but she patted carefully around the laceration.

"I slipped." Sam's bottom lip began to tremble as tears filled her eyes. "I slipped, and I tried to flag him down, Kate. I was so close." Tears spilled as her eyes closed. "It was so fucking close."

"Shh." Kate barely articulated the sound. Without giving herself the chance to second guess or overanalyse, she took Sam's face in her hands and gently kissed where the tears fell. Salt and fresh rainwater were cool on her lips, and she heard a low moan as she tentatively changed direction and pressed her lips to Sam's. It wasn't much of a kiss, just a slight pressure, the faint taste of strawberry lip balm and a flick of tongue against teeth, but it was enough to make them both smile. When they broke apart, Sam's face had a sudden flush of colour in it.

"Oh." She was holding on to the chair, as if afraid she would keel over onto the floor.

"Sorry about that."

"Oh no. No. It was fine. Don't apologise."

"It seemed like the thing to do."

Sam nodded. "Well, it worked for me. I'm a bit warmer now."

The stunned understatement made Kate laugh and she pulled a sweater over Sam's head and waited while Sam pushed her arms into it.

"That knee needs stitches," Kate said, threading Sam's feet into the sweatpants.

"So does this." Sam's fingers brushed against Kate's forehead, where she could feel a deep split still bleeding persistently down her cheek.

"Nothing that painkillers and a cup of tea won't fix." Kate tried hard for levity, but she choked on the words and her hands began to shake.

Sam pulled the sweatpants the rest of the way up, and then carefully lowered herself to the floor and gathered Kate into her arms. They held each other silently, and it was ten minutes later, when a tentative knock sounded on the door, before either of them moved again.

CHAPTER FOURTEEN

The hospital grapevine was efficient and lively. By the time Kate and Sam had finally arrived, Laura had been pacing the ambulance bay. She had burst into tears, hugged them both, then wiped her face dry and directed them into a side room with two beds. For two hours there had been plenty to do: X-rays, sutures, wound assessment, and dressing. The police photographer had been courteous and as unobtrusive as possible as he documented their injuries. Brief statements had been taken, before Tom had told the police politely but firmly that his patients were in no condition to undergo prolonged questioning. The officers had left without complaint, taking up seats outside the room, protecting its occupants rather than preventing them from fleeing.

The room was quiet now. The main overhead lights had been extinguished in favour of the bedside lamps' dim glow. Laura had left to raid the kitchen and make cups of tea, while Tom was busy writing up orders for pain relief.

Kate touched the swollen area surrounding the stitches in her forehead. She sucked in a sharp breath and then hissed when the pain in her ribs cut through her.

"Kate? You okay?" There was a rustling in the next bed as Sam turned slowly to face her.

"I'm fine. Go back to sleep."

"Mm. Wasn't sleeping." For someone claiming to be awake, Sam sounded incredibly drowsy. "Did you get one of these warm air things? They're really cosy."

To counteract the hypothermia, Sam was mostly hidden under thick blankets and a blow-up sheet that circulated heated air over her. Laura had even found a woollen hat for her to wear, which made her look like a hibernating pixie.

"I can tell you're cosy." Kate smiled. "You were snoring."

"Oh! I was not. I heard everything Tom said to you—five stitches, two fractured ribs, and you need to breathe deeply and cough." Sam shifted slightly and grimaced. "I would sleep, but both my bloody legs ache now and my head's killing me."

"Yeah, mine too." Kate closed her eyes; even the dim light seemed too bright.

"We make a right pair, don't we?" Sam said softly.

Kate opened her eyes at that. "Well, you never know. Given the chance, we might."

Sam's eyes widened in surprise as Kate laughed helplessly and shook her head.

"You know, most couples start with dinner and a movie." Sam was laughing now, the bobble on her hat wobbling back and forth.

Kate stopped laughing as she considered what Sam had said. "Actually, that sounds nice."

"It certainly sounds safe." Sam nodded in agreement.

"Okay, then. It's a date."

Sam leaned back against the pillows. "It's a date."

❖

The scream forced Kate from a nightmare of her own. She scrabbled for the light switch, her hand slick and clammy. The abrupt movement made pain twist in her chest, but she ignored it. In the next bed, Sam was still screaming, the sound harsh and frantic and terrified. The floor was cold against Kate's bare feet as she crossed the short distance between the beds; she shivered, goose pimples immediately prickling on her bare arms.

"Sam?" Kate's voice cut the volume on the screaming, making it drop to a series of low whimpers. "Sam, wake up, honey. Wake up."

Sam slowly blinked against the light, her eyes filled with confusion.

"Shit." Her hand came up to wipe her face, the last remnants of the nightmare finally releasing their grip on her. "Sorry," she whispered. "I didn't mean to wake you."

"It's okay." Kate handed her a tissue and then a glass of water. She waited as Sam took careful sips before putting the glass back down for her.

"I didn't get there in time." Despite the water, Sam's voice was barely audible. "I tried, but I couldn't move fast enough."

"I know." Kate's dreams had been a variation on the same theme. She shivered again, but this time it had nothing to do with the coolness of the air.

Sam looked at her for a long moment and then moved over in the bed. She turned back the sheets and blankets.

"Come up here."

Kate didn't argue, a small sigh escaping her as she nestled down in the bed.

Sam wrapped an arm around her. "Better?" Kate nodded. "Going to take some time, isn't it?" she said, her breath warm against Kate's cheek. Another nod, and Sam dropped a soft kiss into Kate's hair. "Good thing we're not in a rush then…"

❖

Sunlight was creeping beneath the curtains when a metallic clang from the corridor jerked Sam awake. Kate was still curled beside her, warm and soft and watching her with a smile edging onto her lips.

"Morning." Kate's voice was low, the bruising encircling her throat making her hoarse.

"Morning." Sam winced as she traced the deep purple contusions on Kate's cheek. Then her eyes widened as a thought occurred to her. "Oh shit. You should get back to your own bed before someone sees us!"

Kate's smile brightened and she shook her head. "I wouldn't worry, hon. Grace Longford saw us an hour ago. The entire hospital and probably most of the village will know by now."

Sam pulled back a little, studying Kate's face carefully. "That doesn't bother you?"

"No," Kate answered without hesitation, and there wasn't a hint of doubt in the word. "I thought it would, but it really doesn't. Besides, Grace tucked you in and called you a sweetie."

"She never did."

"She did." Kate laughed. "She's obviously got good instincts."

Sam ran a tangle of Kate's hair through her fingers before leaning in and kissing her. The kiss was languid and gentle, but they were breathless when they pulled apart.

"So what do we do now?"

Kate raised an eyebrow in lieu of an answer, her eyes full of mischief.

Sam laughed out loud. "Yeah, like we're in any shape for that."

Kate sighed dramatically, but after a second her face turned serious. "I don't want to go home alone," she admitted quietly.

"Do you want to go to your mum's?"

"No." She reached for Sam's hand, entwining their fingers together. "Could you stay…just for a while? I don't want to rush you into anything," she added hastily. "I just…I can't…"

"I know." Sam pressed a kiss against Kate's fingertips. "I know."

❖

The police had taken statements, the forensic team had completed their work at Kate's house, and Tom couldn't think of any legitimate reason to keep them in the hospital for another night.

"I'll come over and have a look at you both tomorrow," he said, his voice laced with concern, his face grave. At no point had he questioned their relationship; he just seemed relieved that neither of them would be alone.

There had been no shortage of people offering them a lift home. Some of those offers were undoubtedly rooted in curiosity, many were genuine, but Laura had turned up on her day off and settled the issue immediately. She gathered up medications and fresh dressings and handed Kate a bag of clean clothes.

"You're both about the same size, so I picked out a set for Sam as well, seeing as she has a nasty habit of losing her trousers in hospitals," she said with a grin.

Kate chuckled at Sam's look of indignation. "I don't know why you're so upset. They were my bloody trousers that they cut off you this time."

Sam thought about that for a second or two, vaguely remembering Kate stripping her off and giving her dry clothes, and she blushed as she also remembered what had happened next. "Oh," she stammered, her face warm. "Yeah, sorry about that."

Laura was watching the two of them. She narrowed her eyes suspiciously, evidently catching an undercurrent of something she was missing out on.

That made Kate laugh even harder and then wince as her ribs flared with sharp pain. She handed Sam a share of the clothing. "Let's get out of here."

Sam took a deep breath, nerves and a thrill of happiness twisting her stomach into knots. She nodded, meeting Kate's eyes with a shy smile.

"That sounds like a really good idea."

❖

There was no blood on the kitchen floor when they walked in through the back door. The shattered plates had been swept up and disposed of. A fire burned brightly in the living room hearth, and furniture that had been upended was restored to its original position, hiding the evidence that less than twenty-four hours ago two people had been fighting for their lives there.

Wrapping her arms around Laura, Kate pulled her into as tight a hug as she could bear.

"Thank you."

"You're welcome." Tears choked Laura's voice and she kissed Kate gently on her forehead. "You know where I am if you need me." She looked across at Sam. "Both of you."

She didn't wait for them to reply, but just touched her hand to Kate's cheek briefly and left them alone. The back door clicked shut, and they heard the grinding of her car's tyres on the gravel as she drove away.

The fire crackled and popped in the silence that followed. Sam glanced at Kate; her face was pale, her arms folded across her chest to support her ribs.

Sam put her arm around Kate and guided her to the sofa. "Sit. No arguments. You look as if you're about to drop."

To Sam's relief, Kate didn't seem to have the energy or the inclination to argue, and she leaned against the cushions with a sigh.

"Kate?" Sam sat beside her and arranged a blanket over her knees. "There's just one thing that I need to know."

"What?" Kate opened her eyes, her brow furrowed with concern.

Sam smiled. "Where do you keep your teabags?"

The anxiety left Kate's face and she laughed easily. "Middle cupboard, top shelf. Milk, no sugar."

"Right, don't go anywhere." Sam was already limping toward the kitchen. She glanced back as she reached the door. Kate had closed her eyes again. She didn't look like she was going anywhere for a good while.

❖

Taking a deep breath, Sam quietly pushed open the door to Kate's bedroom. She could see the pinkish light of a bedside lamp, but that didn't necessarily mean Kate was awake. Feeling foolish, she used her T-shirt to dry the sweat on her face and was about to head back to her own room when she heard Kate's voice.

"It's okay. I'm not asleep, Sam."

"Oh." Sam stepped into the room, running her hand through her hair and stopping short of the bed. "Sorry."

"Couldn't sleep either? Or…" Kate studied Sam's face carefully. "Bad dreams?"

"Dreams," Sam confirmed with a small shudder. She felt more exhausted than she had before falling asleep.

Kate turned back the quilt and edged over in the bed, unintentionally echoing Sam's gesture to her in their hospital room. "She won't mind," Kate said, nodding toward the tabby cat curled up at her feet. "Not after spending all night on your knee."

Sam smiled and then shivered. The room was cold, the fire in the hearth burned down to embers.

"You going to stand there till you get pneumonia?"

"No." The double bed looked warm and inviting, but it was Kate's bed and that was somehow different from their night in the hospital.

Sensing Sam's unease, Kate held her hand out. "Sam, I want you to."

"Yeah?" Sam met her eyes, suddenly shy.

"Yes."

Sam took the final four steps and climbed onto the bed. She eased herself gratefully beneath the covers. The light went out with a soft click and she felt Kate turn over so they were facing each other. In the silence, Kate's fingers were gentle as they touched her cheek, followed the line of her lips, and then cupped her chin. She closed her eyes as Kate leaned closer and kissed her.

"The spare room was a stupid idea anyway," Kate whispered, her lips still so close to Sam's that Sam felt the heat of her words.

Swallowing hard, Sam nodded in agreement. "I think so." She laid her head onto Kate's chest and allowed the steady beating of Kate's heart to lull her to sleep.

❖

"You sure this will work?" Sam's face was the picture of scepticism as she watched Kate daub tuna oil on her cat's head.

"I read it in a book. Hell, it's worth a try. She's done nothing but beat him up since you brought him here."

Mitten gave Sam a mournful look, which turned more curious when he smelt the fish on his own fur.

"Poor little guy. You'd rather that be in your dish than on your head, huh?" Sam bent low and scooped the cat into her arms. "Right, where's your nemesis, then?"

"Where she usually is." Kate led the way into her bedroom and perched on the bed as Sam cautiously set Mitten down close to the sleeping tabby. The more sociable of the two, Mitten had spent the last week trying his best to make friends, and had been violently rebuffed every time.

Kate watched Lotty turn an interested face toward Mitten and make no attempt to murder him as he closed the distance between them. "I think she loves tuna more than she loves me."

"Well, I'll be damned." Sam's mouth dropped open and then curled into a smile. Lotty was not only tolerating the presence of the other cat, she was licking his head and purring as he cuddled into her.

"So," Kate said, her voice dropped low, the gentle stroking of her fingers on Sam's arm making Sam shiver. "You want to maybe stay here too?"

Sam looked up at Kate, and when she smiled, the light danced in her eyes. "I would love to."

❖

The movie had been predictable, with a negligible budget and a bland cast, but the cinema had been almost empty, and Kate had held Sam's hand as they laughed along with all the terrible jokes.

"There you go." The waitress smiled and set down the tall glass crammed with fruit, ice cream, and meringue. "And two spoons."

"Thanks, Toni." Kate blushed as she unwrapped her spoon from the napkin.

Sam already had her mouth crammed with the dessert. She gestured after the waitress with her spoon. "I suppose you know everyone in the village."

"It's a very small village, Sam. Hence the one-screen cinema."

By mutual consent, they had decided that their first *date* be a local one, and so far no one had attempted to run them out of the restaurant at the business end of a pitchfork.

Sam nodded and dropped her voice conspiratorially. "Did you know that the waitress plays for our team?"

It took Kate a second or two to decipher Sam's meaning, and when she did she almost choked on an errant berry. "Toni? She never does!"

"Oh, she does. Trust me." Sam licked the back of her spoon and winked.

"It's not like there's a secret bloody sign," Kate protested, and then hesitated, unsure of herself. "Um…is there?"

Sam was laughing almost too hard to reply. Her shoulders shook silently, her spoon dropping ice cream with abandon. "No. There's no secret handshake, no code or password." She paused thoughtfully. "Although, that would make it all a hell of a lot easier."

"Then how?"

"You just get to know these things." Sam grinned and wiped cream off Kate's cheek, then licked her finger and made Kate blush all over again. "She has a…quality." She swallowed another spoonful before nonchalantly adding, "Plus, it kind of gave the game away when she checked your arse out all the way to the table."

❖

"That's Orion, isn't it?" Sam traced the well-known con-stellation with her gloved finger, the cold air making her nose and cheeks glow pink.

"That's it," Kate confirmed. She craned her head back. "So many they're making me dizzy."

The sky was crystal clear and the stars were almost over-whelmingly bright.

Kate shivered and moved to stand behind Sam, who leaned back into her embrace. She kissed the side of Sam's cheek and felt the involuntary, sharp intake of breath. "Let's go back inside."

It was difficult to run upstairs and shed clothes at the same time, but they managed it without breaking anything or tripping over the cats, who had appeared to see what all the fuss was about.

The fire in the bedroom hearth cast fingers of heat and a sunset glow of light as Sam cupped Kate's face in her hands and they kissed. Sam heard herself moan at the first tentative flick of Kate's tongue against hers and she met no resistance when she unbuttoned Kate's shirt and dropped it to the floor.

They stumbled to the bed, more clothing falling in their wake, until, finally naked, they lay back together.

"So beautiful," Sam said quietly, her finger tracing the curve of Kate's throat, her mouth following its path downward. Taking her cue from the rough cadence of Kate's breathing, she circled her tongue around Kate's breast and smiled when Kate swore incoherently. "So beautiful." Sam's hand stroked lower. "But such a very filthy mouth."

"Mmhm." Kate wasn't going to argue. Not when Sam was gently parting her thighs. And certainly not when Sam's fingers slipped inside her. "Oh God." Her head thudded back against the pillow as Sam began to move, achingly slowly, within her. Her own hands reached out to pull Sam closer, to try to share the sensations she was feeling.

"Shh, easy." The hand that wasn't stroking deep between her legs cupped her chin and it was enough to still her frantic movements. "Just let me."

Her eyes wide, her breath coming in gasps, Kate nodded in acquiescence.

"I love you." The softest of whispers before Sam lowered her mouth to Kate's again, the rhythm of her hand never faltering.

Closing her eyes, Kate bit her lip hard as the intense surge of pleasure began to overwhelm her.

❖

When Sam finally opened her eyes, she was greeted by sunlight streaming in through the bedroom window. The bedside clock told her she had slept in far later than usual, but then it had been the early hours of the morning before they had finally gone to sleep. With a lazy smile, she turned over to find two very cosy cats curled up where Kate should have been. She stroked Mitten lightly, watching as Lotty nestled even closer to him, purring loudly.

"Hey, little one." Lotty pricked up her ears and blinked at Sam's voice. "Where's your mother?"

Wrapped warmly in a bathrobe, Sam followed the smell of frying downstairs. In the kitchen, Kate stood by the stove, flipping rashers of bacon with a spatula and humming quietly.

"Hey."

Spatula still in hand, Kate turned and smiled when she saw Sam leaning up against the door jamb. "Good morning."

Sam crossed the kitchen and wrapped her arms around Kate. "Smells fabulous."

"Good." Kate grinned. "Thought we might've burned off enough calories last night to have earned it." She moaned low in her throat as Sam kissed the side of her neck. "Stop," she whispered hoarsely. "We get distracted and, knowing our luck, we'll accidentally burn the bloody house down." She felt Sam laugh behind her, which sparked the odd fluttering in her stomach that had nothing to do with being hungry. A thought occurred to her and she tipped her head back to rest it on Sam's shoulder. "I almost forgot. I bought you a present."

"A present?"

"Yep. Because, apparently, my memory is better than yours."

The box was beautifully wrapped and sitting at Sam's place on the table. She set her plate down, then picked up the box and shook it carefully.

"Pretty heavy."

"It is."

"And it's not ticking. That's a good sign."

Kate grinned and slid a mug of tea over to her. "No, it's not ticking. Be quick. Your breakfast's going cold."

It was all the encouragement Sam needed. She tore the paper off, her actions slowing as she revealed the illustration on the box.

"New boots." Her voice was distant because she *did* remember now, and at the time Kate had made her the promise she had never expected to live to see it fulfilled. "Thank you."

"You're welcome." Kate lifted Sam's hand and kissed the back of her knuckles. "I thought you might need decent walking boots, seeing as you moved your cat in and everything."

Sam nodded in agreement, and then laughed when she pulled out a new pair of socks. "Didn't forget a thing, did you?"

"Hey, a promise is a promise. Eat," Kate said, gesturing with her fork. "Then we can go and break them in a little."

"Okay." Sam ate quietly for a minute before setting her fork down and looking up at Kate. "Can we go up Kinder Scout?"

"Sure," Kate answered without thinking, then did a double-take as she realised what Sam meant. "What, *today*?" At just over two thousand feet high, the circular routes on Kinder Scout were all strenuous hikes. "Oh, Sam, I don't know."

They had been out walking over the past few weeks, but mainly on flat terrain or gentle slopes. Sam was certainly stronger than she had been—they both were—but Kate was not convinced she was ready for a ten-mile slog up and along what passed for a path on Kinder.

"I just want to try," Sam said reasonably. "I'll stop if I'm knackered. I promise."

Kate considered that and then laughed softly. "Well, you did manage to walk for a quarter of a mile in a storm on a pair of crutches."

Crunching bacon, Sam nodded proudly, making Kate laugh even harder.

"You're an idiot."

"Yeah." Sam grinned at her. "But I'm *your* idiot."

❖

Kate reached the top of Jacob's Ladder and bent low, her hands on her hips as she struggled to catch her breath. A seventeenth-century packhorse trail, the ladder was an uneven and torturously steep arrangement of rock steps that curved around to provide an approach to the southern edge of Kinder Scout.

"You okay?" She looked across as Sam, panting harshly, adopted a position similar to her own.

"Yeah." Sam wiped sweat from her forehead. "I'm fine. I'm good." She stood up straight and grimaced. "Oh God, I'm lying! Remind me again why I thought this would be a good idea."

Kate laughed. "Because you like a challenge." She turned serious. "You know we're not at the top yet, don't you?"

"Yes. Yes. I'd noticed that the rest of the hill is right there."

To their right, the plateau of Kinder Scout loomed, its ancient stone formations dark and forbidding against the brilliance of the cloudless sky.

"So…" Kate offered a water bottle to Sam and waited while she drank deeply. "You want to carry on? Or call it a day?"

Sam was already picking her hiking sticks up, and she pointed up the hill with them. "No way I'm giving up now. Lead the way."

❖

"Leave your bag and give me your hand, c'mon."

Sam did as she was told. After finding a firm foothold, she boosted herself up as Kate pulled. She clambered onto the massive gritstone boulder and swayed slightly before Kate steadied her.

"Oh, *wow*."

The summit of Kinder Scout was deeply frozen. Icicles clung to the undersides of rocks and sparkled at the edges of the tiny bog-fed streams. The peat glistened with a thick covering of frost, its cotton grass brittle and eerily still despite the brisk breeze. Below them, the valley dropped away sharply, but the peaks filled the horizon, bleak and beautiful in the thin winter sunlight.

Still holding Sam's hand, Kate helped her to sit on the rock. She was shivering as the exertion of the climb wore off and the cold began to seep in.

"Come here." Kate wrapped her arms tightly around Sam and smiled when Sam sighed happily and burrowed deeper into her hold. "Warmer?"

"Much."

"Glad you came?"

"Very." Sam lifted her hand and cupped Kate's cheek before kissing her softly.

Kate smiled, her lips still touching Sam's. "Your nose is cold."

"I can't feel my face." Sam started to laugh. "Or my toes…or my bum…"

"When we get home, I think a hot bath might be in order."

"Right." Sam was already pushing herself to her feet, her eyes dancing with mischief. "What are we waiting for?"

They clambered down onto the path, their boots biting into the frozen peat. Sam caught Kate's sleeve as she straightened.

"Have I told you today that I love you?"

Swallowing hard, Kate shook her head. "Not today." She looked at Sam shyly. "You really do?"

"I really do."

She let her breath out in a rush. "I love you too."

Sam laughed, the sound echoing back from the rocks and filling the air. She took Kate's hand in hers.

"Let's go home."

The End

About the Author

Cari Hunter lives in the Northwest of England with her partner, two cats, and a pond full of frogs. She works full-time as a paramedic and dreams up stories in her spare time. Cari enjoys long, wind-swept, muddy walks in her beloved Peak District and forces herself to go jogging regularly. In the summer she can usually be found sitting in the garden with her feet up, scribbling in her writing pad. She also loves hiking in the Swiss Alps and hanging out in various television fandoms. Although she doesn't like to boast, she will admit that she makes a very fine Bakewell Tart.

Snowbound is her first novel.

Books Available From Bold Strokes Books

High Impact by Kim Baldwin. Thrill seeker Emery Lawson and Adventure Outfitter Pasha Dunn learn you can never truly appreciate what's important and what you're capable of until faced with a sudden and stark reminder of your own mortality. (978-1-60282-580-2)

Snowbound by Cari Hunter. "The policewoman got shot and she's bleeding everywhere. Get someone here in one hour or I'm going to put her out of her misery." It's an ultimatum that will forever change the lives of police officer Sam Lucas and Dr. Kate Myles. (978-1-60282-581-9)

Rescue Me by Julie Cannon. Tyler Logan reluctantly agrees to pose as the girlfriend of her in-the-closet gay BFF at his company's annual retreat, but she didn't count on falling for Kristin, the boss's wife. (978-1-60282-582-6)

Murder in the Irish Channel by Greg Herren. Chanse MacLeod investigates the disappearance of a female activist fighting the Archdiocese of New Orleans and a powerful real estate syndicate. (978-1-60282-584-0)

Franky Gets Real by Mel Bossa. A four day getaway. Five childhood friends. Five shattering confessions…and a forgotten love unearthed. (978-1-60282-585-7)

Riding the Rails: Locomotive Lust and Carnal Cabooses edited by Jerry Wheeler. Some of the hottest writers of gay erotica spin tales of Riding the Rails. (978-1-60282-586-4)

Sheltering Dunes by Radclyffe. The seventh in the award-winning Provincetown Tales. The pasts, presents, and futures of three women collide in a single moment that will alter all their lives forever. (978-1-60282-573-4)

Holy Rollers by Rob Byrnes. Partners in life and crime, Grant Lambert and Chase LaMarca assemble a team of gay and lesbian criminals to steal millions from a right-wing mega-church, but the gang's plans are complicated by an "ex-gay" conference, the FBI, and a corrupt reverend with his own plans for the cash. (978-1-60282-578-9)

History's Passion: Stories of Sex Before Stonewall, edited by Richard Labonté. Four acclaimed erotic authors re-imagine the past...Welcome to the hidden queer history of men loving men not so very long—and centuries—ago. (978-1-60282-576-5)

Lucky Loser by Yolanda Wallace. Top tennis pros Sinjin Smythe and Laure Fortescue reach Wimbledon desperate to claim tennis's crown jewel, but will their feelings for each other get in the way? (978-1-60282-575-8)

Mystery of The Tempest: A Fisher Key Adventure by Sam Cameron. Twin brothers Denny and Steven Anderson love helping people and fighting crime alongside their sheriff dad on sun-drenched Fisher Key, Florida, but Denny doesn't dare tell anyone he's gay, and Steven has secrets of his own to keep. (978-1-60282-579-6)

Better Off Red: Vampire Sorority Sisters Book 1 by Rebekah Weatherspoon. Every sorority has its secrets, and college freshman Ginger Carmichael soon discovers that her pledge is more than a bond of sisterhood—it's a lifelong pact to serve six bloodthirsty demons with a lot more than nutritional needs. (978-1-60282-574-1)

Detours by Jeffrey Ricker. Joel Patterson is heading to Maine for his mother's funeral, and his high school friend Lincoln has invited himself along on the ride—and into Joel's bed—but when the ghost of Joel's mother joins the trip, the route is likely to be anything but straight. (978-1-60282-577-2)

Three Days by L.T. Marie. In a town like Vegas where anything can happen, Shawn and Dakota find that the stakes are love at all costs, and it's a gamble neither can afford to lose. (978-1-60282-569-7)

Swimming to Chicago by David-Matthew Barnes. As the lives of the adults around them unravel, high school students Alex and Robby form an unbreakable bond, vowing to do anything to stay together—even if it means leaving everything behind. (978-1-60282-572-7)

Hostage Moon by AJ Quinn. Hunter Roswell thought she had left her past behind, until a serial killer begins stalking her. Can FBI profiler Sara Wilder help her find her connection to the killer before he strikes on blood moon? (978-1-60282-568-0)

Erotica Exotica: Tales of Sex, Magic, and the Supernatural, edited by Richard Labonté. Today's top gay erotica authors offer sexual thrills and perverse arousal, spooky chills, and magical orgasms in these stories exploring arcane mystery, supernatural seduction, and sex that haunts in a manner both weird and wondrous. (978-1-60282-570-3)

Blue by Russ Gregory. Matt and Thatcher find themselves in the crosshairs of a psychotic killer stalking gay men in the streets of Austin, and only a 103-year-old nursing home resident holds the key to solving the murders—but can she give up her secrets in time to save them? (978-1-60282-571-0)

Balance of Forces: Toujours Ici by Ali Vali. Immortal Kendal Richoux's life began during the reign of Egypt's only female pharaoh, and history has taught her the dangers of getting too close to anyone who hasn't harnessed the power of time, but as she prepares for the most important battle of her long life, can she resist her attraction to Piper Marmande? (978-1-60282-567-3)

Wings: Subversive Gay Angel Erotica, edited by Todd Gregory. A collection of powerfully written tales of passion and desire centered on the aching beauty of angels. (978-1-60282-565-9)

Contemporary Gay Romances by Felice Picano. These works of short fiction from legendary novelist and memoirist Felice Picano are as different from any standard "romances" as you can get, but they will linger in the mind and memory. (978-1-60282-639-7)

Pirate's Fortune: Supreme Constellations Book Four by Gun Brooke. Set against the backdrop of war, captured mercenary Weiss Kyakh is persuaded to work undercover with bio-android Madisyn Pimm, which foils her plans to escape, but kindles unexpected love. (978-1-60282-563-5)

Sex and Skateboards by Ashley Bartlett. Sex and skateboards and surfing on the California coast. What more could anyone want? Alden McKenna thinks that's all she needs, until she meets Weston Duvall. (978-1-60282-562-8)

Waiting in the Wings by Melissa Brayden. Jenna has spent her whole life training for the stage, but the one thing she didn't prepare for was Adrienne. Is she ready to sacrifice what she's worked so hard for in exchange for a shot at something much deeper? (978-1-60282-561-1)

Suite Nineteen by Mel Bossa. Psychic Ben Lebeau moves into Shilts Manor, where he meets seductive Lennox Van Kemp and his clan of Métis—guardians of a spiritual conspiracy dating back to Christ. But are Ben's psychic abilities strong enough to save him? (978-1-60282-564-2)

Speaking Out: LGBTQ Youth Stand Up, edited by Steve Berman. Inspiring stories written for and about LGBTQ teens of overcoming adversity (against intolerance and homophobia) and experiencing life after "coming out." (978-1-60282-566-6)

Forbidden Passions by MJ Williamz. Passion burns hotter when it's forbidden, and the fire between Katie Prentiss and Corrine Staples in antebellum Louisiana is raging out of control. (978-1-60282-641-0)

Harmony by Karis Walsh. When Brook Stanton meets a beautiful musician who threatens the security of her conventional, predetermined future, will she take a chance on finding the harmony only love creates? (978-1-60282-237-5)

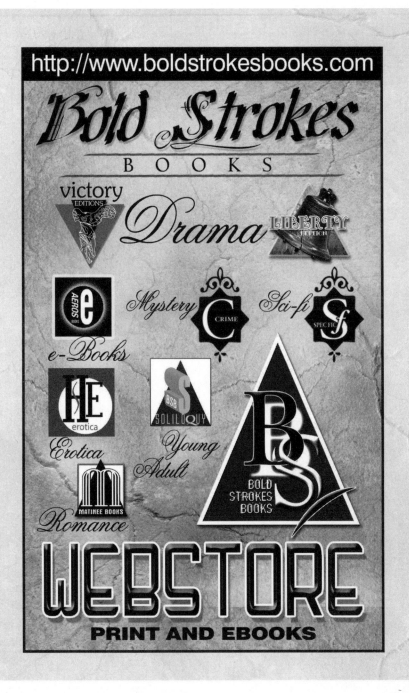